BAKERSFIELD
BOYS CLUB

A NOVEL

ANNE DA VIGO

Published by Quill Driver Press, PO Box 5272, Saramento, CA 95817

ISBN 978-0-9745722-2-2

Printed in USA

Cover design by Karen Phillips
Interior design by Vanessa Perez

Author Photo by Beth Baugher

FOR TONY

1

▬

JANUARY 1978

In the yard the neighborhood cat cries. Suzanne leans against the kitchen sink and squeezes her eyes shut. She'd swallowed a Valium last night to sleep, and now the animal's yowling feels like a needle in her brain.

She calls up the back stairs. "Danny, have you been feeding that cat?" There's no answer. Maybe he's jogging with his friend Kristen.

The wailing begins again, this time right up against the back door. When she opens it, cold air surges in, damp and stinking of oil vapor expelled from the refineries. The cat trots inside, pale gray hair standing on end. It's Narcissus, her neighbor Reggie's Siamese.

"Out. Shoo." Electricity from the animal's fur tickles her ankle. She uses her bare foot to nudge it toward the open door. That's when she notices the prints on the linoleum. Four toes and a broad, fleshy pad.

Dark red.

Her stomach lurches, imagining a dead rat or gutted squirrel lying on the porch. She creeps outside, slipping on the fog-wet concrete. There's no body. Instead, a trail extends, paw by paw, down the porch steps and across the patio to a hole in the fence.

Narcissus rubs a flank against Suzanne's robe as if urging her on, but she can't move.

Cold penetrates the soles of her feet and chills the tip of her nose. She hitches up her robe and climbs onto the porch's retaining wall. Over the fence in Reggie's backyard, the kidney-shaped swimming pool is covered in gray plastic. The terrace is bare of furniture.

It's easy to see the paw prints. They trail across the flagstones to the landing at the top of his steps. Fed by a trickle from the house, a bloody pool has formed by the door. It glistens in the fog.

Please, not again.

Her involuntary step back dangles in midair. She tumbles off the wall, lands on her ankle. Putting weight on it sends pain flashing up her leg. "Danny, please come help me!"

He doesn't respond. Her eyes fill with tears, and she scrubs at them with her sleeve.

Maybe Reggie cut himself or has a scalp wound. Those bleed a lot. He might not be . . .

She limps through the house and out of the front, taking halting steps across the coarse, oily grass of the yard. Reggie's Mercedes is missing from the driveway. She uses the wrought iron railing to haul herself up his steps.

He doesn't answer the bell. The door is firmly shut, but the latch yields when she presses it.

"Reggie? It's Suzanne."

Her foot hovers at the threshold. If she steps inside, it will be impossible to ignore the truth of Reggie's alternative life. She shivers at the possibility of repercussions for her. For Danny.

Still, Reggie saved them financially after Carlo died. Without him, she would have lost the house. Straightening her spine, she moves into the entry.

"Reggie?" There are no voices. No television, no dripping faucets, or creaking floorboards. She edges down the hall, the cat trotting beside her. The house smells of soft cheese, oozing because it's too warm. A shiver of revulsion sweeps over her, and she feels her heartbeat. In the dining room the black-enameled table is crowded with a platter of dried-out ham, turkey, and the brie. Meatballs sit in a chafing dish surrounded by congealed sauce.

The kitchen is littered with empty bottles. A bucket of melted ice sweats on the tile counter. Beside it is a key ring, cold and a little greasy to the touch. Sweat dampens her pajamas, worse than during the blazing summers in Taft. Her legs wobble. She ducks her head and braces herself against the shelf.

When she looks up, she sees Reggie, lying on the service porch floor. He's naked, half-sitting against a storage cabinet, his hairless stomach drooping over his cock. His body is covered with stab wounds and the side of his skull sunken with blunt-force blows.

A fat, black fly darts around his head.

She screams and swats at the dirty, vile thing that's infesting Reggie, who was always fastidiously dressed and smelling of expensive cologne, Reggie, who was her friend after Carlo died, Reggie reduced to bloody, broken flesh. Broken like Carlo had been in the accident.

Like her father.

Her pulse pounds again—not in her chest but her injured ankle—hammering as though it would split the skin. Blood has trickled down Reggie's right arm, across the floor, and through the half-open back door.

Oh, Reggie. She's not sure if she's said it aloud or the words have ballooned in her head. She snatches the key ring from the shelf, shoves it into her bathrobe pocket and limps to the phone in his home office.

2

—

"I'm Detective Alex Barton." He hands her his card. *Sergeant, Bakersfield Police Department.* "You were a good friend of Mr. Roman?"

His voice raps like a hammer. She huddles in the corner of Reggie's couch and props her throbbing foot on the coffee table. They're in the garden room, windows overlooking the pool. That's what Reggie had called it, *garden room,* with a rich-bitch purse of his lips.

Rec room, she shot back, and he'd laughed.

She hunches her shoulders, shielding herself from grief like she did when she was a kid after her father died. Her eyes sting like hell.

"We live next door." Her voice cracks.

"We?"

She slides her hand into her bathrobe pocket, touching the key ring with a forefinger. "My son and I."

He frowns. "No husband?"

"Widow."

His eyes do a slow scan from her wild, uncombed hair to her dirty feet. "You often visit Mr. Roman early in the morning?"

Barton's bulk compresses the cushion of Reggie's favorite chair. One of his size fourteen lace-up shoes looks as though it could crush her bare foot. The last time she saw Reggie, he was lounging in that same silk-upholstered chair, legs crossed, sandal dangling elegantly from one toe.

"It was Narcissus."

Barton raises his eyebrows.

"Reggie's cat. She came over, her footprints . . . she'd walked through his blood."

The crime scene techs have finished with the room, and now the police photographer kneels on the rug beside the coffee table.

"Your foot." The photog frowns at Suzanne who repositions her ankle on a couch pillow. The clicking shutter seems to be counting the five stubbed-out marijuana roaches in an ashtray, the razor blade and mirror, pack of Virginia Slims, four wine goblets, and two highball glasses.

Suzanne's heart beats against her ribs. Are Danny's fingerprints on the blade? The mirror?

"You saw bloody cat prints and blood coming from Mr. Roman's house, but you didn't call police?" Barton leans forward, hands clasped between his widespread knees. The acid smell of coffee taints his breath.

"I thought I should hurry."

"You had a key to the house?" He gaze is sharp, probing for a weak spot in her story.

"The door was unlocked."

"What did you do when you first entered?

"I walked through the house to the kitchen."

"Did you notice anything unusual? Hear anything?"

She hears the investigators' voices from the kitchen, calm enough that they could be ordering breakfast. Thoughts of the photographer's flash illuminating Reggie's nakedness make her cringe.

"There was a fly buzzing around his head." She twists her bathrobe sash around her wrist and winds it tight.

Barton utters a small cough. "Did you touch anything?"

"No."

"Move anything?"

"The front door latch and the telephone in his office. . . " Reggie's left arm had crossed his chest, twisted like a broken toy. She'd reached out to straighten his poor, fucking arm but pulled back.

"Did Mr. Roman have any enemies?"

"None that I know of."

"What about his social life? Any girlfriends?"

She shrugs.

"Boyfriends?" His cheeks flatten when he says this, as if tasting something sour.

He knows. Suzanne has heard it, the deep-throated male laughter through the open window during parties at Reggie's after the Bakersfield bars close.

"He was a good neighbor, kind to Danny and me after my husband died, but we weren't party buddies." Her pulse throbs against the bathrobe cord.

"How about last night? Did you see anything? Anyone arriving or departing?"

"I went to bed early. About nine."

"And your son?"

"He stayed up, reading." A shaft of sun from the window catches the razor blade on the coffee table.

"I'll need to question him."

"He's only fourteen. He doesn't know anything."

"We're interviewing everyone in the neighborhood, Mrs. Ricci, your son included."

"Sergeant?" A motorcycle cop in knee-high leather boots appears in the doorway, his face ruddy from the cold. His helmet dangles from his fingers. He'd been first to arrive, a few minutes after she'd called 911.

Barton hefts his bulk from Reggie's easy chair and crosses the room. With his back to her, he tips his head to listen.

Her lips tremble.

"No," Barton says to the officer. "Until I give the word, keep Filbert and Vallejo closed to all vehicles except residents' personal cars."

Inside her bathrobe pocket, her fist clenches the key ring. She doesn't need to look at it to know it's fake gold, with a small lacquered replica of a Mercedes logo dangling from the chain. The metal is sweaty from her hot palm. A year ago Christmas, she'd given it to Danny in his stocking as a joke. He'd teased her that when he turned sixteen, he expected a Mercedes, which was ludicrous because she could barely keep her VW van in tires.

Now, though, the ring she gave Danny has a Mercedes ignition key attached.

3

Suzanne crosses the lawn. The street is clogged with police vehicles, and the coroner's van is poised at the curb with its rear doors open. Neighbors huddle in clumps on the far sidewalk, their breath hovering close to their faces. Along the traffic barrier at the end of the street, two television vans and a car bearing a radio station logo wait with engines running. Exhaust swirls in the damp air. Reporters wave and yell questions, but she ignores them.

A man in one of those terrible polyester leisure suits, probably a detective, is knocking on the doors. She enters her house, closes the door and locks it. The smell of coffee in the percolator, usually so welcoming, makes her eyes water and nose burn. She calls Danny, but hears only voices from outside.

His bedroom is locked; she hammers on the door panel.

No answer. She snatches a small screwdriver from her dresser and uses it to pop the lock. His room is empty, but the window is open. Cold snakes up the legs of her pajamas, down the back of her neck. She slams the window shut and breathes onto her fingers. The key ring had been a few feet from the body. Did Danny witness Reggie's death? Is the murderer after him?

The doorbell rings. Her ankle throbs on her way downstairs. On the porch, the detective in the bad suit flips open his leather badge case. "I'd like to speak to your son now, Ma'am."

"He's jogging. With a friend. I'll call you as soon as he gets back." The detective leaves his card. It goes into her pocket along with Barton's card and the key ring. Last night, did Danny tell her where he was going? The sleeping pill has left her with a slippery memory.

In Danny's closet, she paws through the rows of tennis shoes, boots, and slippers, ignoring the sweaty-foot smell. Beneath the pile, a pair of Nikes lie side-by-side. Her hand slips inside one of them. Cold and dry.

Using the phone beside Danny's bed, she dials Kristen's mother. "Joyce, it's Suzanne Ricci."

"Nice to hear your voice, Suzanne. How's Danny?"

"Didn't he and Kristen go jogging this morning?"

"Kristen is at band camp this weekend." A pause. "I haven't seen Danny for six months. Maybe longer."

"But you drove the two of them to the ninth grade dance in November."

Joyce's voice is puzzled. "Suzanne, Kristen went to the dance with Matt Bourne."

"I'm obviously mixed up this morning, Joyce. Sorry to bother you." She hangs up. Her throat burns all the way down, as if she's swallowed acid. She studies the shelves over Danny's bed—soccer trophies from grade school, Dodgers's baseball cap, photo of him and Carlo beside a wellhead at the Elk Hills oil reserve. Manly memorabilia.

A search through his drawing paper, pen-and-ink sketches, even the wastebasket, reveals nothing. When she fans the pages of his algebra text, she discovers five half-completed homework assignments he'd assured her were handed in. Nothing in his backpack, other than a five-dollar bill and two partially-crushed Butterfingers.

His eight-track tapes fly as she rips through the shelf, but she finds only his known favorites: Bob Seger and the Silver Bullet Band, Elton John, Rod Stewart, Queen.

She lowers herself onto the bed and rubs her ankle. In the photo, Carlo and Danny look something alike, although Danny is taller now at fourteen than Carlo was as a grown man. She realizes that during the last few months, his eyes have started to slide away from hers like Carlo's used to. A small shift of focus, a blur that over time builds into an impenetrable barrier.

Light from the window suddenly seems unbearable. She stifles the urge to cry; instead she presses her fingertips against her closed eyes. They twitch, as if to avoid secrets and dark places.

She tackles the laundry hamper. His pockets yield lint, wadded papers, and a ticket stub with a telephone number jotted on the back. No one answers when she dials. The stub goes into her pocket along with the cards and key ring.

She sniffs a T-shirt. The odor clinging to it isn't his usual Right Guard; rather it's a forest odor suitable for either a man or woman. Something like Reggie's pricey cologne, which she remembers from her latest visit to his interior design shop in La Verne Square.

The day of Carlo's car accident returns like an unwelcome guest—the call from the police, Carlo dead of a crushed chest, his slut girlfriend in Emergency with a gash on her forehead. The woman had been crying, her bloody hands lying in her lap. Suzanne recognized her, a waitress at the Basque restaurant. It was the woman's faint, familiar perfume that had triggered Suzanne's own tears: the same smell had risen from Carlo's shirts when she tossed them in the machine. Later, people she had thought were friends told her they knew about the affair, but concluded it was none of their business.

She repeats the ritual of mistrust learned four years ago. Danny's nightstand drawer squeaks; she pulls it completely off its track and turns it over. He's not very creative: an envelope is taped to the unpainted, splintery wood. Inside is a stack of Polaroids.

In one, Danny sits behind the wheel of Reggie's red Mercedes two-seater. He assumes a vampy pose, wrist propped on the wheel, hand dangling. In another, he leans against the car's hood, his legs white below the ragged threads of his cutoff jeans. Reggie is beside him, and the fucker's hand rests on Danny's thigh, about to slip his index finger under the fringe.

4

Danny tosses his skateboard from the bedroom window, climbs out onto the porch roof. He sees Mrs. Hedges peering from her window and waves to her. The old lady nods and puts a finger to her lips.

He scrambles down the magnolia tree to avoid being spotted by police in the street in front of Reggie's. As the board bumps along the sidewalk, his soles register each seam and crack. He pumps hard, splashing through the mud puddles, riding the back wheels to jump the curb. After a few blocks, his body warms, and he unzips his hoodie.

How could he have been so stupid, not going home last night after he smoked weed and ate the Sara Lee cheesecake from Reggie's refrigerator? Instead, he'd fallen asleep in Reggie's bedroom. He'd crept home a couple of hours before dawn, his skin icy cold.

Hot, stinging spray from a shower hadn't warmed him or scoured away the image of Reggie's body. He'd been too frightened to go back to sleep, but tiptoed several times to the window in the upstairs hall to peer out at the street. Eventually, dishes rattling told him his mother was awake. When she yelled up at him, he huddled under the blanket, barely breathing. He'd heard the door close as she left. In a few minutes, a siren had broken the Saturday silence.

He kicks up the board's speed, and in ten he's at Bakersfield Rancho. Lights framing the motel's arched sign switch off as he passes. A few breakfast customers have parked in the front lot near the restaurant. He skirts the driveway and ducks into the alley on the west side of the complex, dismounting from the board to squeeze past the dumpsters filled with trash and rotten food.

In the areas hidden from customers, the owners have let the complex go. The stucco is cracked and stained from leaking rain gutters. A dandruff of peeled paint lies on the ground along the foundation.

The motel is like Reggie and his friends, all prettied up with nice haircuts, fine clothes, and sports cars up front, but dirty and disgusting under the skin.

He counts seven bathroom windows along the back of the motel. With his board tucked under his arm, he hops up onto a milk crate pushed against the wall. His knuckles tap twice on the glass, first lightly, then again, harder.

"Reno. It's me." Danny whispers hoarsely through the half-open window.

From inside, he hears Reno's mother cursing, her voice phlegmy from too many cigarettes.

"Come on, Reno, we're in a shitload of trouble."

There's a crash; then Reno's head and torso appear, high enough that Danny figures he's standing on the closed lid of the toilet. Reno's lower lip is swollen.

"Jesus, what happened?"

Reno shrugs. "Same-o, same-o."

He's thirteen, a year younger. Sometimes Danny has the strange thought that if he tried to draw Reno's face, half would be young and half, a burned-out old man.

"Reggie's dead." Pain darts up from Danny's temples. His mouth is dry. "Somebody knifed and beat him. Police are at the house."

Reno pokes his bruised lip. "Let's go over to the store. Pick up a few items before the cops get there."

"Did you see it?" Danny's voice rises to a squeak.

"No, but I heard." Reno leans his forearm on the sill.

"How?"

"I have ways." He scrambles out the window and drops onto the muddy, unpaved alley.

They set off, past the restaurant, where a waitress watches them from the window, her mouth hard and tight. She knows Theresa Goulet—everyone at the motel does—the woman who rents one of the dark, smelly rooms in the back and turns out her son Reno as a prostitute.

Danny tells himself he's not like Reno. He's not doing anything for money. Besides, he and Reno look nothing alike: Reno is pale, his body smooth and slight, lips faintly pink, while Danny looms over him, feet nearly twice as big, hair dark and curly compared to Reno's, which is bleached by his mother every three weeks.

Reno never says his mother beats him when he doesn't come home with enough money, but he doesn't have to—he grimaces in pain sometimes. Danny has stuffed bills in Reno's hand when his friend comes up short. He wonders why Reno doesn't threaten Theresa Goulet with the knife strapped to his ankle under the cuff of his jeans. Danny has seen him use it to slash tires or pry the lock off a store window to steal an eight-track tape player, but never against a person.

This morning, Danny wanted to tell his own mom everything. His life is careening down an unmapped route, about to smash into something. His impulse to spill the story had lasted only a second before he'd pulled the blanket over his head.

Danny rides his board. Reno trots beside him, not stopping to commit his usual malicious pranks: throwing stones at a snarling German shepherd or tipping over a Harley-Davidson parked in a dirt yard.

When they're a half block from La Verne Square, Reno diverts their course down an alley behind Reggie's shop, Roman Designs. The building's L-shaped extension on the north side hides the loading dock from the street. Normally, Reggie's sofas and chairs and rugs are delivered there, but today the roll-up door is closed. Next to the dock sits Reggie's Mercedes 450 SL.

Danny touches the front pocket of his jeans, where he usually keeps his key ring, threaded with the duplicate key Reggie had given him. It's not there.

Reno grabs his arm and hauls him behind a dumpster. "Wait. The cops might be watching the place."

Crouching in the confined space with his thighs against his chest, Danny smells his own morning breath. He's surrounded by ugliness: the dents and scratched paint, the smell of mold and garbage. After a minute or two, Reno taps the metal with his knuckle, and they crawl out. Reno pulls a cluster of keys from his pocket, ones Danny saw last night on the dresser in Reggie's bedroom. Reno opens the back door, and they slip inside. Danny closes it quickly.

They cross the storage area to the showroom where gray light creeps between the blinds. Reggie didn't usually open them until noon to keep the sun from fading fabrics on the upholstered chairs and sofas. Color chips and swatches are stacked on the desk; the tables, lamps, and chairs are arranged in groups. It's quiet, like a house where the owner's asleep.

Reno rummages through the small refrigerator in Reggie's office and finds a bottle of champagne. He untwists the wires and laughs as the cork pops, sloshing frothy liquid on the floor. He tips the bottle into his mouth. Danny snatches a handful of paper towels from above the sink. He swirls the towels with his foot until every drop is gone.

Reno lounges in a leather armchair with his feet on a matching hassock. The wet bottle rests on a teak lamp table. From his shirt pocket he pulls two half-flattened joints. "Get the lighter. It's in the desk drawer."

"We shouldn't."

"Come on, Danny boy." Between his teeth, Reno jiggles an unlit joint.

"Did you do it? He had—there was blood everywhere." Danny's voice cracks.

"No, I didn't do it! I told you. I left before . . ."

"Come on, Reno. Who did? Don't you care?"

"Reggie never cared. Would he have cared if one of us croaked?"

"He was our friend." Danny remembers the azure water of Reggie's pool on a Bakersfield summer day. When he was ten, nothing was as cool and pure as the first splash on his skin.

"Friends don't make you do blow jobs." Reno fetches the lighter and settles again.

He looks lonely, a thin figure in the oversized armchair, gazing at the slanted light from the window through a gray haze of smoke. Danny hefts the lighter, the engraved silver heavy in his palm. He lights the other joint. They toke for awhile. Danny blots out thoughts of last night, focusing on a sketch he'll do in pen and ink of a supernatural being, half-deer and half-man. He imagines the sharp contrast of black and white, but the picture keeps slipping. Instead, he sees flashes of crimson.

5

Phone calls have turned up no sign of Danny. His friends—boys Suzanne remembers as his friends—haven't seen him for months. His lies weigh so heavily she can't pull herself out of her chair. Where did he go, those times when he told her he was meeting Seth or Josh, when she dropped him off at the basketball game or bowling alley?

She's at the dining room next to the phone, not bothering to move the mess on the table: typewriter ribbons, newspaper clippings, boxes of magazines, and stacks of notebooks. A half-finished page sits in the typewriter platen where she left off last night. She's missed the deadline for this week's *Bakersfield News-Daily* column, and will have to beg her editor for another twenty-four hours. The mortgage is due Tuesday, and without her column, there won't be enough money to cover the check.

The doorbell rings. Detective Barton's heavy body seems to block the light. "Son home yet?" His eyes rove past her shoulder, exploring the entry and staircase.

"Not yet. I'll call you when he comes in."

Barton's jaw twitches. "You do that."

After his unmarked car pulls away, she slips into jeans and layers a cardigan over her pajama top. Any other time, she'd wear a skirt and her one pair of not-so-runover shoes, her attempt to fit into this upscale neighborhood. Today, she's in a hurry. She's backed her green VW van halfway down the driveway when a police black-and-white blocks her exit to the street. A lump rises in her throat making it difficult to breathe.

A knuckle raps on the window, but she doesn't turn her head.

The van door opens. "Suzie, it's best to check the rear-view before backing up." Officer Liza Theuss reaches across her lap to turn the key and kill the engine.

"Thanks for the tip." Suzanne's voice is unsteady.

Liza's a solid woman, her navy blue uniform stretched over broad hips. A black leather duty belt is cinched around an ample waist. Her blonde hair is tightly plaited in a French braid.

She and Suzanne had met the night Carlo died. The doorbell rang two short bursts, and Liza stood on the porch, her departmental cap in her hand. Behind her were the haloes of the streetlights, distorted by sharp, slanting rain. Her police-issue winter jacket bulked up her shoulders and contrasted with her small head. In a low, calm voice, she told Suzanne that Carlo had died of a crushed chest on the way to the hospital after his pickup crashed.

Liza had been kind that night. Parked in the police department's Dodge outside the emergency room, she warned Suzanne that Carlo had had a female companion with him. That's how she'd said it: *female companion.*

At the time, she and Liza seemed to have little in common—Suzanne, a widow coping with a grieving son and Liza, Bakersfield's first female patrol officer. Yet when they compared their common roots growing up in the oil fields—Suzanne in the rough-and-tumble city of Taft, and Liza farther north in Coalinga—they'd become friends, refugees who told themselves they had gone on to better things in Bakersfield.

Today, Suzanne wants Liza gone. She imagines Danny witnessing the blows to Reggie's skull, listening to the sound of a knife entering flesh. Danny hiding from the murderer.

"Take a deep breath. Not every Saturday morning you discover a stiff," Liza says.

"You heard?"

"I've been listening to radio traffic all morning."

"Any suspects?" It's strange to think that a few high frequency radio blips are transmitting the terrible details of Reggie's beaten and stabbed body.

"Investigators, unfortunately, don't share information with patrol lackeys. Hopefully that will change once I make detective." She pats Suzanne on the shoulder. "Anyway, I'm due for break. Let's go inside and have a cuppa instant."

"Can't. I'm going out."

"Wearing your pajamas?"

"I'm a little upset, but I'll be fine." Suzanne restarts the engine.

"Go in the house, Hon, and take a pill. Sleep for awhile."

"I don't need a pill. Move your car, and stop calling me Hon." An angry buzz fills Suzanne's ears.

"I've got a couple Valium, if you don't have any." Liza steps away for an instant.

Suzanne slams the van door and starts the engine. She cranks the wheel with the flat of her hand, sending Liza scrambling. The van makes a U-turn on the lawn, twin tracks ripped into the sod.

She putts along, the VW's engine endowed with the power of a lawnmower, north on Filbert, past homes framed by careful flower beds and barbered shrubs, away from the last of the police and coroner's vehicles clustered in front of Reggie's. By the time the van turns east on Delta, the flashing red light atop Liza's car appears in Suzanne's rear view mirror.

The black-and-white is a car length behind, snapping at her heels like a surly mongrel. Suzanne drives twenty-seven miles an hour, just under the speed limit. In a few blocks the nice houses with silky lawns slide away, and the town's gray bedrock emerges. Just to the north are the Kern River Field and Oildale, the town where Carlo's brother, Vince, paraded down Chester Avenue in the early 1960s at the head of a KKK rally.

The van sputters east into the barrio. These houses, once painted blue and pink and lime green, are faded from the relentless sun, like washing left too long on the line. Trees with a few remaining dead leaves struggle behind chain-link fences in the dirt-packed yards. Suzanne squeezes the wheel, wishing it were Liza's neck.

At Flower Street, Liza switches on her siren. A mother pushing a baby in a stroller pivots to watch their slow-motion chase. The black-and-white is so close that the bursts of sound jolt Suzanne like cattle prods. She finally gives in and bumps over the curb into the parking lot of a liquor store pretending to be a market. The single fuel pump is hung with a sign, No Gas Today. Liza wheels her car around so their drivers' doors nearly touch. She switches off the siren and props her arm on the open window.

Suzanne listens to the engine sounds: the deep, throaty rumble of Liza's Dodge and the VW's tinny soprano. Slowly, she rotates the window handle.

"Your car needs a tune-up," Liza says. "Lots of tailpipe emissions."

"So, write me a ticket."

"Does this have anything to do with Danny?" Liza says.

"Zip."

"Come on, Suzie."

"Shut up, you nosy Nellie." Even as Suzanne says it, Liza's sympathy undoes her. A rain of tears and snot drips down her cheeks and upper lip. She gropes in her purse for a tissue.

Liza doesn't blink. "Tell me."

A tricked-out Impala struts by with a flash of chrome rims and a thump of music from its open windows.

"He's somehow mixed up with Reggie."

"You mean, with the murder?"

"No, no, of course not." As she says it, Suzanne hears a quiet click in her head: don't even think about it.

"Then what?"

"Danny had formed an . . . attachment to Reggie." The admission rocks her, like the extraction of a stubborn tooth.

Liza pounds the steering wheel with her fist. "That fucking man causes me more heartburn. Twice this month, I've chased him away from the bathrooms in Wilson Park."

"Doing it with boys?"

"Sometimes," Liza says.

"You didn't arrest him?"

"The elite wives of Bakersfield buy their fruitwood furniture at his shop. I tell him to behave and then stand by until he leaves. If I do anything else, I'll get a week off without pay."

"But that doesn't have anything to do with Danny. He isn't sexual, not like that."

"Then why was he hanging out with Reggie?"

"Danny earned money helping him out at the store, moving furniture and sweeping up." While she's saying this, she thinks about the Polaroid, and Reggie's creeping finger.

"Reggie Roman didn't need any help at the store. He was thinking of his pecker."

"That's disgusting."

A dusty pickup rattles alongside the gas pump, three men crowded into the cab and two others sitting in the bed. When they see the black-and-white, their laughter stops, and the truck drives away.

"Boys that age often have crushes on older men." Suzanne has no idea if it's true. Certainly, Danny missed Carlo, even though he wasn't a great father.

Liza frowns. She tilts her head to listen to the police radio. "There's a BOL on Reggie's Mercedes. It's missing from his garage."

"I've got to find Danny," Suzanne says softly.

"Leave the van. We'll go together."

———

The skateboard park is crowded with weekend customers despite the cold mist.

Liza leans over to retrieve a stack of files from the back seat. "Uniforms make people nervous. I'll wait in the car and knock off a couple of reports. Button your sweater. Your pajamas are showing."

Suzanne pays the two-dollar spectator's fee at the entry shack and walks inside the chain-link fence. Saturday dads are perched on concrete benches separating the spectators' area from the course. All the boarders are boys, from teenagers with thick, muscled calves down to six-year-olds whose heads wobble under the weight of their bowl-shaped helmets. Riders crouch on the boards, their legs bend and flex, the boards' resin wheels creak and scrape.

Danny isn't here. She sinks onto one of the benches and bites at her thumbnail, already down to the quick. An instant of silence falls on the crowd as a red-haired boarder goes airborne, his body tilted against the sky; the board doesn't fall, but seems to cling to his feet.

A man with two long-haired Chihuahuas straining on leashes lowers himself on the bench beside her. "Where's Danny today?"

Given his firm voice, his appearance is oddly unkempt. He's in his sixties, his cheeks flushed with rosacea or drink. Tufts of gray hair bristle under his chin where his razor missed. Chino pants are cinched high on his waist like her grandfather, as if the belt somehow keeps him from falling apart.

"Should I know you?" She looks at him over her shoulder.

"Maybe. I'm Galen Franzen."

To hide her surprise, she watches the course, where the boy's red hair flies like feathery wings. This man is police commissioner, a member of the power structure that oversees the BPD. In a *News-Daily* picture three months ago, his hand was raised as he swore in the new police chief. He looked vastly different in the photo, dressed in a vested suit and striped tie. His hair was neatly trimmed.

"Too bad about Reggie Roman." One of the dogs claws at his pants leg. As he rubs his thumb against the leather leash, she hears the rasp of dry, rough skin.

"Very sad." She thinks about Danny's swimming lessons at the pool, his boyish flesh rosy with exercise, dark curls plastered against his head. Reggie's eyes had never wavered from Danny; his hands had rested on bare thighs below his swim suit without the twitch of a finger. At the time, she hadn't found Reggie strange.

She supposes she'd been too wrapped up in her fury and loss over Carlo's death.

"Most of the usual Saturday morning crowd has shown up today," Franzen says. "It's a good place for kids to hang out. Exercise. No low-lifes or trash."

Suzanne holds out a hand to one of the dogs, who snaps at her fingers.

"The Police Association co-sponsors this place, along with the city rec department." Franzen nods toward Liza's car as though he personally assigned her to patrol the premises.

The red-haired boarder has just finished his run, and Franzen gives him a thumbs-up.

"Danny's good on the board, but not one of the standouts. Too cautious. Afraid he's going to break something."

"Caution is good, don't you think? Keeps people out of trouble." Under Suzanne's stare, he looks away.

Danny's skateboard wasn't in his room when she searched. She tries to recall when she saw it last. It's decorated with his design of a unicorn in purple and yellow that he'd painted onto the wood before he laminated it. He'd spent days working on it.

She clears her throat. "I haven't been by here for a while. Didn't realize the park was so popular."

"Lots of kids, candy, Cokes, music. What's not to like? Hey, Kevin."

"'Lo." The red-haired boy approaches them, slouching and round-shouldered, his posture like Danny's when he's trying to look disinterested.

"Where's your helmet and pads?" Franzen says.

Kevin shrugs.

"Bring them next time, or you're out." He hands Kevin a five, who tucks it in his jeans as he heads for the snack bar, his boy-odor trailing behind him. She remembers it from summers when she was a kid. She and her four brothers hopped on their bicycles for day-long rides, the sun beating on their necks; when they stopped they loosened their shoelaces and ate Spam sandwiches in the shade.

"Has Danny been here this morning?" she asks Franzen. "He took off before I could remind him of an appointment."

"It's been, what, a couple of weeks. Maybe a month." He signals Kevin, who's returning with candy bars stuffed in his back pockets and a Coke in a red-and-white cup. "Seen Ricci?"

Kevin sucks on the straw for a long moment. "Nah."

Franzen tips his head toward Suzanne. "His mother's looking for him." There's caution in his voice.

Kevin smirks. "If I see him, I'll let him know."

She wants to slap the condescending smile off his face. When she climbs back in the car, Liza stacks the reports in back.

"I see you met Franzen."

"Says Danny hasn't been around." She looks back and catches a glimpse of Franzen near the snack bar talking to Kevin. The old man's head is bent as though pouring words directly into the boy's ear.

Liza follows her gaze. "Galen's okay. At the police academy, he was my weapons instructor. He's a little lost since his wife died."

Liza props her wrist on the wheel. "Got another idea?"

6
—

Liza backs the car into a parking space in front of Sampson Brothers Art Emporium ready to roll in the event of an emergency call. Suzanne hurries inside.

Skylights throw the kind of even, clear light that artists adore. Since she was here a year ago, it hasn't changed, still smelling of paint, linseed oil, and the raw wood used in the canvas stretchers.

"Hey, stranger." Will Bosch, the manager, teeters on a ladder as he threads a selection of frames onto a pair of metal wall brackets.

Suzanne steadies the ladder. "Don't you know better than to stand on the top step?"

Will clambers down, the wooden treads groaning under his weight. He absently pats down a straw-blond cowlick. When she first met Will, she thought he was a rube from a valley potato farm. After several visits to the store, she'd discovered he was an accomplished water colorist who exhibited often in Carmel and Palm Springs.

"We've got a great sale on mongoose-hair brushes." His eyes are teasing behind rimless glasses.

"I'm trying to visualize harvesting hairs from a mongoose," she says.

He laughs. "Very quickly."

From the first moment Danny stepped inside Sampson Brothers when he was eight, he was transfixed. He wanted the tubes of cadmium yellow, burnt sienna, and viridian green with the same intensity as his earlier fixations on Matchbox cars and GI Joe action figures. His hand brushed the pen holders and nibs; he'd rubbed chalk between his fingers and sniffed the large pink rubber erasers. Thick creamy papers, blank canvases, easels, drawing boards, and pencils lit him up like she'd never seen. After that first visit, Suzanne enrolled him in Will's Saturday art classes in the studio at the rear of the store.

Chatter drifting from the studio lifts her mood. He's probably here. "I just stopped by to catch up with Danny."

Will shuffles his feet. "Kids are cleaning brushes and putting things away, but Danny's not here."

"He was here earlier, right?" Even as she speaks, she knows it's wishful thinking.

"For class? Not in a year, maybe," Will says.

"A year? What are you talking about? I wrote checks for classes."

"I haven't seen Danny or any checks." His voice is tight.

Danny told her months ago she didn't need to drive him to class; he'd leave his supplies in a locker at the store and ride his bike. He'd folded the yellow Wells Fargo checks she gave him and tucked them in the pocket of his jeans. "Thanks, Mom," he always said.

She remembers during Carlo's affair, how the lies, the small falsehoods, piled up in her chest like pebbles. It wasn't until they were so heavy she couldn't breathe, that she became aware of them.

"I'm sorry Danny dropped out," Will says. "He has talent up to his eyeballs. His pen and ink drawings are especially good."

"Has he been in to buy supplies?"

"Now that I think about it, he was in last Saturday for a few minutes. He needed some extra-fine nibs."

"Did you talk?"

"Nope. He chatted with Grace Stannard—she's in the teen oil painting class."

The class is breaking up, and she hears laughter. A boy, twelve or so, comes out, walking sideways, and hoots at someone out of sight. He carries a large brown portfolio, like the one she saw this morning in Danny's closet.

"See you next week, Kyle," Will says.

Two more boys shamble out with the arrhythmic walk of youths whose muscles aren't quite under control. Then the girl. She's pale: blonde hair, milk skin, eyes the blue of shaded snow drifts.

"Grace," Will says. "Did you enter the county fair contest?"

"I don't want to."

"You should submit the acrylic series of pork chops and steaks. You caught the bloody quality. Makes meat seem disgusting, and I'm a carnivore."

"They're no good. No one likes them."

Suzanne feels Grace's resistance, like tough silk thread, beneath her delicate face.

"That's just Bakersfield," Will says. "Everyone here wants wildflowers and old barns. How about *Student Art* magazine?"

"Even my Dad thinks the series is weird."

"He's a great guy, but what does he know about art?"

"Everything, to hear him tell it." Her mouth twists.

Will frowns. "If you don't enter them somewhere, I'll be very, very upset."

"I'm so scared."

He laughs. "I'm taking a group to Lake Isabella for a sketch day next Saturday. Want to come?"

She tilts her head, considering. "I can't. My friends are having a party."

"Have you seen Danny? This is his mom; she's looking for him."

The air seems brighter, suddenly. "You're a friend of his?" Suzanne asks.

"Sort of."

"I missed him when he went out this morning, and there's been a family emergency."

"Sorry." The girl's glance flicks to Suzanne's baggy sweater over her pajama top.

"Please, if you see him, call me." Suzanne snatches a scrap of paper from her purse and scribbles her telephone number on it.

"Sure." Without a glance, Grace stuffs it into the hip pocket of her jeans.

Will watches as she zips her coat, leaves the shop, and runs across the blacktop to the bus stop. "She's got such talent. Should be developing it more, instead of hanging out with your son."

"Danny's never mentioned her," Suzanne tries to absorb this new facet of his unrevealed life.

"She talks about him a lot—Danny this, Danny that."

"She's Danny's girlfriend?"

"His *friend*."

"I see."

"No, Suzanne, I don't think you do."

"What? Tell me." She grasps his wrist, hairs coarse against her fingers.

"Boys like Danny often get adopted by a small cluster of girls. He's like one of them. They gossip, talk about hair, look at guys."

She takes a deep breath; sweat pops out on her forehead. Danny. Reggie. She feels as though she's driving on a dark road along a cliff edge.

"Will, do you know Reggie Roman?"

He hesitates. "Slightly."

"Reggie lives next door to us. He was murdered last night."

Will scans the aisles, but there are no customers, only his assistant at the cash register. He hustles Suzanne into the storeroom, where boxes are stacked cheek high, cutting the light from a dirty window. "Do they know who did it?"

"Not yet, but Danny . . . he might have seen something."

"He was one of Reggie's boys?"

"You knew about Reggie?"

He twitches, shifts from foot to foot, picks at a scab on his arm. "I'm gay. People tell me things."

She backs away from him, into the ladder, which tips and clatters against some boxes. "You go to Reggie's parties?"

"I never, ever have been at his parties. Reggie's associated with dangerous people. I warned Danny to stay away from him."

"You didn't tell me Danny was seeing these people. Why not?" she cries.

"Danny said sure, sure, but instead, he dropped out of class."

Will peers out the storeroom door, then closes it again. "Bakersfield is a red-neck, homophobic place for people like us, but even for here, Reggie's gang is over the edge."

"Gang?"

"Powerful people. Let me tell you something, Suzanne. Not long after I warned Danny, I stopped at a convenience store to get gas. A group of five or six guys jumped on me, pulled me down, and kicked me in the face. I've been attacked before—it could simply have been a gang of queer bashers."

She counts to ten, slowly, heart beating faster and faster.

"Or, it could have been about Danny. A message to me that Danny is high on someone's wish list." Will twists his head aside. When he turns back, a set of upper dentures squats on his palm. The teeth are wet and shiny with saliva. "That night, they kicked my teeth out."

7

Back in Liza's car, Suzanne hunches her shoulders. Danny's adult teeth have come in white and even. She imagines him kicked and beaten, crouching in the willows along the river or hiding in an alley.

"Where to next?" Liza revs the engine.

"Take me back to the van."

"Good God, what happened?"

"Will hasn't seen him."

"There are other bushes to beat. How about Hart Park and the soccer field?"

"Not now." Suzanne sees puzzlement on Liza's face, and something else, a quick widening of her eyes.

In the convenience store lot, Suzanne says goodbye and climbs into the van, which, miraculously, hasn't been stripped of its tires and hubcaps. When Liza's out of sight, she drives to Reggie's shop. Blinds are lowered in the show windows, but through the glass front door, past the Closed sign, she spots figures moving around. She guides the van along the street on the north side, and slows almost to an idle, peering at the rear of the store. A dumpster overflows with flattened furniture boxes, and a detective's gray car is parked near the delivery door, propped open with a cast iron garden urn. She accelerates before anybody spots her.

On Filbert Street, the black-and-whites are gone. Yellow crime scene tape is strung across Reggie's porch steps; the plastic snaps in the wind.

The furnace in her house hasn't been on all day, and she shivers when she steps inside. "Danny," she calls, "Danny, are you here?" Floor boards creak under her feet, and the kitchen faucet drips slow, maddening drops. She lowers herself into a chair at the dining room table. Her head aches, and her leg throbs from this morning's injury.

The room seems smaller, her wirebound notebooks and piles of carbon copies and slick-paper annual reports from oil companies sucking up the space. Everything on the table is within arm's length of the typewriter, which reigns over the side closest to the window. Weak winter sun struggles over the seven-foot fence between their place and Reggie's.

He'd just opened the shop when they moved to town ten years ago. He was slender then. She saw him occasionally in white shorts and court shoes carrying his racquetball bag to the house from his Volkswagen bug. His legs were tanned and muscles taut. Then the shop had began to thrive. *He bought a Mercedes. This morning, despite her shock at his terrible injuries, she'd noticed his abdomen sagged, and graying chest hair was tangled in his gold chain.*

Her forehead wrinkles as she tries to remember when Danny began to spend so much time with Reggie. She's been too busy juggling her freelance assignments and keeping Danny in jeans and shoes to pay attention. Last spring, when Danny's feet were growing what seemed like an inch a month, Reggie bought him a pair of Adidas, leather soft as squirrel pelts. It was an odd gift, she realizes now. Too personal.

She trudges up the stairs and plucks the Adidas off Danny's closet floor. *The soles are scuffed and the heels a little worn on one side. He must have worn them many more times than she remembers. Her eyes blur with tears.* The real Danny is nothing like the son she thought she knew. He isn't going to be elected high school class president or dance at the prom with some cute blonde girl with straight teeth. He's not going to fall in love with a woman like the daughter she always wanted, have a church wedding, give her grandchildren.

Suzanne's dad had wanted things for her: go to secretarial school, learn shorthand, and land a cushy office job where she could wear pretty dresses and high heels. Not slave in a commercial laundry like her mother.

Never mind that at eleven, Suzanne had no idea what shorthand was and already had shot up taller than any kid in the fifth grade. His face got all dreamy when he talked about his plans for her, as if he were describing some other girl. He died in the explosion before reality dawned on him that she, Suzanne, wouldn't do any of it.

Holding the damned shoes, she rubs tears from her cheek with the back of her hand. She can smell Danny on the leather. She dumps them in the garbage can outside the back door. Narcissus slips past her into the kitchen, meowing loudly. Suzanne piles some chicken scraps on a plate.

Emptiness settles in her chest, as if everything she knew about Danny has been scooped out. Their lives seem dark, distorted. Lies have skewed conversations with Danny that she thought were clear. How will she know this stranger?

In her bedroom, she searches for the robe she wore this morning, pulling it off the rumpled bedcovers. A fusty scent clings to it, the same odor as her pajama top, which itches her skin. She fumbles in the pocket. The key is there and the ticket stub with the number she called earlier.

This time a man with a strong, confident voice answers.

"This is Suzanne Ricci. Is Danny there?"

Silence, then a click and a hum.

She redials and lets it ring, but no one answers. Her heart beats quickly. She disconnects and calls the PD, but the dispatcher says Officer Theuss is busy responding to an incident.

Next, she tries Carl Hedges, her editor at the *News-Daily*. He's the son of her neighbor, Maude.

"Where's your column?" Carl asks. "We're past deadline."

"I've got a family emergency." Without a column this week, she won't get a freelance check. She'll have to get a loan from her brother, Lucky, to cover the house payment.

"I'll let it go this once," Hedges says.

"I've got a favor to ask."

"You don't have much in the way of credit right now, Suzanne."

"I'm really sorry, but this involves my son. Is there any way I can find out who has a certain telephone number?"

"Not unless you have a source at Pacific Bell. The reverse directory *should* carry that kind of info, but it doesn't. Maybe someday."

"Okay, Carl. Thanks."

As soon as she hangs up, Narcissus begins rubbing against her ankle. She's about to pick her up when the phone rings. Carl calling her back?

"Mrs. Ricci, it's Detective Sergeant Barton from the BPD. We have your son in custody."

"He . . . what?"

"A patrol officer apprehended him."

"He's not hurt? He's all right?"

"No injuries, Mrs. Ricci, but we've got a situation here."

Her legs fold under her, and she sinks down onto the rug. Narcissus jumps into her lap. "Where is he? When can I see him?"

"If you come to juvenile hall, you can visit for a short time before he's processed."

"Juvenile hall?" She gathers Narcissus against her chest. The fur between the cat's toes is still matted with dried blood. The animal's heart thumps against her palm.

"He was caught along with another juvenile driving a stolen Mercedes registered to Reginald Roman."

8

On Thanksgiving, six weeks before Danny was arrested, he had a run-in with his cousins. He and his mother always drove to Taft for holiday dinner with her family, the Marlowes. She pretended to be eager to see them, but never seemed to enjoy it.

The van was loaded with three kinds of salad, a couple of pecan pies, and a cake with coffee and cocoa in it. She never cooked or baked like this other times of the year; it was like she was trying to make up for something.

That day, they left Bakersfield about noon. He propped his feet on the van's dashboard, but she told him sharply to get them down, as if the van were some fancy ride. He imagined himself racing down this road in Reggie's Mercedes, headed for the coast. Although he'd only been at the wheel of the Mercedes once, and that was in the parking area behind the store, he was sure he could handle it. The nearer they got to Taft, the thicker the fog that settled in the low spots between the sage-covered hills. His stomach began to hurt.

At Uncle Red and Aunt Dora's, a black cloud rose from the back yard, where, just as in past years, a turkey was incinerating on the barbeque. Pickup trucks lined the curb: a Suburban, a GMC, and a Chevy Luv. No sign of Ham and Arnie, Red's sons, who were sixteen and seventeen, or the boys' 1949 Ford truck.

Danny's pain eased a little.

Inside the house, the air was thick with cigarette smoke and noise from two televised football games. Red, Stan and Bernie, or The Three Stooges, as Danny called his mother's oldest brothers, clustered around one TV drinking beers. The fourth, Lucky, slouched in a sagging chair before a second screen in a dark corner of the living room with a 7UP in his fist. Lucky was a recovering lush.

Actually, Danny liked Lucky, who had a sly sense of humor that occasionally took a poke at his brothers' obsession with sports and hunting rifles. Lucky cocked an eyebrow at him and raised his aluminum can. "Hey, Dan-boy. How's school?"

"Terrific. Just wonderful."

Lucky grinned.

The Stooges barely moved their lips to greet him. They were heavy, but not tall like his mom, lazing like grizzlies in their cages. Lucky was different: six-foot two, lean and gray. He had a scar that ran from the corner of his mouth to his ear that drew Danny, as if the unsightly flesh were an offer of friendship.

Danny slid the large trays holding the pies and cake onto the kitchen counter and kissed Grandma's cheek. She smelled of booze and dry, flaky skin.

"Sweetie, get me another, will you?" Grandma swirled the half-melted ice cubes in her bourbon glass.

"I'll get it, Mama." Suzanne closed the refrigerator on the salads and snatched the glass as if she didn't want anyone to beat her to it.

At the stove, Aunt Dora sprinkled brown sugar and marshmallows on a pan of canned yams. She shouted at Danny over the noise. "Ham and Arnie are shooting baskets at the school. Go see them."

"OK. Soon."

Aunt Dora tucked a strand of her straight brown hair behind her ear. She was thin, as if any blips of residual fat had been rubbed off by the self-centered Red and her two demanding sons.

"The girls are down the hall. They've come out every ten minutes to ask if you've got here yet," Dora said. The girls were

Mandy and Randy, Bernie's twin daughters by an ex-wife. He saw them one Saturday a month and Thanksgiving. Danny didn't blame the departed wife. He didn't like Bernie much either.

In the master bedroom, Mandy and Randy had a suitcase full of Barbie dolls and outfits spread across the carpet.

"Danny, Danny, Danny!" they screamed, and wrapped themselves around his legs. Randy, the heavier of the two girls, hung on until Danny's leg muscle cramped and he shook her off.

"Look at Barbie's new dresses, Danny," Mandy said. "Which one do you like better?" From the pile she plucked two satin and net outfits scattered with sequins.

"Nice, especially this one." Danny peered over his shoulder, worried his uncles might be watching. "Um, you girls keep playing. See you later."

Back in front of the TV, he hunkered down in one corner of the couch, his arms folded across his chest, watching the Stooges watch the game. Their hands had half moons of dark oil under the nails.

"You going out for basketball, son?" Stan asked, eyes glued to the TV.

"No." Danny raised his shoulders around his ears to deflect their disapproval.

"Too bad; you got the height," Stan said.

"I'm not doing too good in school, and Mom says I've got to bring my grades up." It was a lie he told frequently to cut off the people who asked him about playing basketball.

"Suzie always was big on grades, not that it did her any good." Stan turned to Red. "Are you going to take that bird off the fire sometime before it turns to ashes?"

"In a minute."

Dora emptied three cans of chicken gravy into a saucepan. "Red, the turkey. And where are the boys?"

"Dan, run down to the school and tell the kids dinner is ready." Red backed toward the patio door while watching a Rams' kickoff return.

Danny sank lower into the couch, but Suzanne pushed him on the shoulder and set him in motion. Outside, the fog had lifted slightly. Weak sun filtering through the mist lit up dirty water in the potholes and sodden bits of newspaper clinging to the bushes. He kicked a rusty soda can in front of him as he walked. Down the block, piles of dog poop on somebody's lawn had grown a moldy fuzz.

He heard their shouts and the thump of the dribbling basketball before he turned the corner. At the court, the cousins pretended not to see him. Ham, smaller but more solid, took a shot, missed, and elbowed his brother to snatch the rebound. Arnie spewed a string of curses and stomped on Ham's foot.

"Your mom says dinner's ready," Danny shouted.

"It's Danneee." Arnie wiped sweat off his cheekbone with the hem of his T-shirt.

Ham flapped a limp wrist. "Hey, Danneee."

Danny breathed quickly. A hot spurt of stomach acid burned his throat. He hunched over against the pain and started back toward the house. Before he'd walked a block, his cousins caught up with him, one on each side. He felt their weight: their heavy muscles and solid bones, the burden of their hatred. Shoulders bumped his. He stumbled.

"Don't be a faggot, Danneee," Arnie said.

He walked faster, trying to outdistance them, but they trotted alongside, punching him lightly, as if they were taking practice dribbles before a game. They drew closer; an elbow dug into his side, a hand twisted his bicep.

"Stand up, pussy boy. Come on. Fight me, hit me." Ham landed a hard blow on his back that made Danny's eyes sting.

He broke into a run, but he was so frightened his feet didn't obey; instead he slid on the wet sidewalk.

"Danneee's a little pansy who's gonna to pay for his dirty little life." Arnie's hard fingers squeezed his arms. Between the two of them, they dragged Danny onto the lawn covered in dog shit and shoved him down. He kicked at them, bucking and heaving, but they were relentless, digging their feet into the lawn and putting their backs into it as they pushed his face into the stinking mess.

An old woman appeared behind the screen door. "Arnie Marlowe, get off my grass. Go on, take yourselves home, you nasty boys."

Shaking himself free, Danny raced past the last few houses. From the Marlowe's front window, Lucky was watching, the soft drink still in his hand. Danny turned on the hose, scrubbing his face with chilly, alkaline water until his skin was raw and his cheekbones ached. He wanted to scrape his skin away, rid himself of this person who was so tainted, so flawed. No matter how much he scratched with his nails, the stink didn't go away. He'd reek of shit forever, he thought; this was his future.

The boys sauntered to the front walk, their chins thrust forward at Danny in mock aggression. Wet and shivering, Danny jumped into his mother's van and locked it. His eyes stared straight ahead at the garage door. Lucky strolled out onto the porch, where he paused to strike a flame from a paper matchbook and cup his palm to light a cigarette.

When Ham set his foot on the step, Lucky blocked the front door. "How was the game?"

"Okay." Ham tilted his head in feigned inquiry.

"You play good?" Lucky's voice was soft, and they glanced at him uneasily.

Arnie gave the ball a single bounce. "It wasn't a game. We were just fooling around."

"That kind of thing can get you hurt."

"Wait a minute. Did that faggot say something?" Arnie's face reddened.

"He didn't say nothing, but you listen real good to what *I'm* telling you." Lucky spit a shred of tobacco on Arnie's shoe. The boy rubbed it on his pant leg.

"Some people just can't take a joke," Ham whined.

"This here's no joke," Lucky said. "You ever fool around like that again, I'm going to squeeze your balls like lemons for lemonade. Understand?"

Slowly and carefully, the boys slid past him. Lucky crossed the lawn and knocked on the van window. Danny refused to turn his head. His humiliation was complete. He would've kept the dog shit incident a secret. It was his fault he was different. Some cruel force created him dirty and despicable, instilled in him twisted urges that infected his blood, bone, and brain.

How could he face Lucky, the one person in his family who seemed to like him?

"Let's get out of here." Lucky didn't look at him; instead, he studied a rust spot on the rain gutters.

"Go away."

"Come on. I hate turkey, especially Red's turkey. Like chewing old shoes."

The corner of Danny's mouth quirked up. After a minute or two, he lifted the door lock and climbed out. Dusk had left the street gray and shadowy, an alternate world where it was difficult to see clearly, and everything had blurred edges. They crossed the street to Lucky's Chevy pickup.

It was old, but immaculate inside: the floor mats clean, the dashboard free of dust, the seats reupholstered with clean fabric that felt warm under Danny's hands. Lucky fished a towel from behind the seat and handed it to Danny, who dried his wet hair. With the engine running, Lucky propped his forearms on the wheel.

"I've heard McDonald's has an outstanding holiday menu."

9

The probation officer unlocks the door of Danny's room. "You've got a visitor." He motions Danny into the hallway. In the other bed, his sleeping cellmate closes his mouth and rolls over.

"Hands in pockets." The officer's buzz cut reveals his pink scalp. He secures the door and lets the heavy key ring clink against his thigh.

Danny stuffs his fists into the pockets of his tan jail-issue pants. In the three days he's been at juvie, he's learned that wards are allowed to walk the halls only if their hands are hampered from punching or stabbing. His cloth shoes whisper on the concrete floor: no laces, no steel shank in the instep.

The probation officer walks four steps behind. As they pass other rooms, wards lean against their wire-reinforced windows, grimacing and making obscene gestures. Danny doesn't turn his head. He pretends his ears are clogged with wax, because if he listens, his skin will split with terror.

Reno warned him to be cool. "They know that you and me, we're buds," he whispered to Danny the first day. "They won't whup or ream you."

Danny was astonished Reno didn't seem scared, that is, until Reno showed him the knife, made from a sharpened toothbrush handle.

"Got it from a guy who owes me," Reno looks different in juvie, like fluffy snow turned to ice.

Stories abound of beatings and rapes of gay kids, but Reno, rather than hiding out, seems calm and focused, using money from some secret source to buy the knife, plus contraband cigarettes and weed. On his second day here, Reno negotiates an easy job for himself working in the facility's school library after classes, which allows him to sneak a few unsupervised minutes on the phone.

A black female officer unlocks the sally port, and Danny steps into a narrow, concrete hall. When the door shuts behind him, he's contained between the grasping, hungry world of the lockup and the visitors' room. Which is real? In this cold cocoon, he's not sure. At the far end, another officer opens the door.

When Danny emerges, he's greeted by an uneven rhythm of dozens of voices. Tables are lined up in rows, each section long enough to accommodate two families. Fathers and mothers sit on benches across from the wards, shoulders bent as if this drawing-in of their bodies can screen their failures from outsiders.

He spots his mother immediately. Her spine is straight, and her eyes follow him unblinkingly. This is the first time he's seen her since their brief visit after his arrest. New creases bracket either side of her mouth. Her hair is tangled in a messy cloud around her head.

Longing plucks at his heart. He wants to burrow his face in the curve of her neck. It was always she, not his father, who was his safe place, a nest where he wasn't afraid. But his old way of knowing her has been shattered. He feels an immense sadness he knows will return with greater force late tonight, when a single bulb illuminates his cell, and his eyes are wide and dry.

He throws his leg across the metal bench. Before meeting his mother's eyes, he flicks a cautious glance at the others in this row: a Hispanic father with a farm laborer's straw hat, a mother with silver crosses circling her neck and hanging from her ears. The ward is a fifteen-year-old with teardrop tattoos cascading from the corners of his eyes down his cheeks. Danny's seen the boy in the dining hall, a *La Emé Hombre*, one of the fledgling Mexican Mafia gang members. Don't look at them, Reno told Danny, or one might cut your eye out.

Danny's mother inhales, as though she's about to jump off the high dive. "I've hired an attorney. The probation department has filed a petition alleging you're out of control and guilty of auto theft. The hearing is scheduled for Thursday, next week."

"I hate it here. How long before I can get out on bail?"

"The lawyer says there's no bail for juveniles."

His voice falters, going up an octave and sounding squeaky. "The food is garbage, I can't sleep, and there's no fucking TV in the cells."

She leans in, inches from his face. Heat radiates from her skin. "Don't you dare use that language. What's this stinking mess you've gotten into? Tell me every single detail."

He does a mental scan. What's the least he can say?

"My friend Reno got the key from Reggie to the 450SL, like, to take it to the car wash and stuff. Sometimes I rode shotgun while Reno drove around the unloading area to practice his driving. But the morning Reggie died, he went further—school, the parking lot at Bakersfield Rancho, the bluffs. I finally got him to give me the wheel, because he'd smoked weed and was weaving and stuff. Right after, that's when the cop stopped us."

She grips his arm, and the contact feels good, even if she is really pissed.

Knuckles rap the table. "No contact." An officer hooks his thumbs in his belt, and she pulls her hand back.

"That's a lie. I know that Reggie gave *you* a key." Her voice is so twisted with disbelief he scarcely recognizes it. "Tell me."

Danny jiggles his leg to relieve tension.

The mother next to them berates her son in a molten flow of Spanish, silver crosses swinging across her heavy breasts. Her son squints, the tattooed tears looking like they're running down his cheeks.

"Okay, okay. I'd been hanging out with Reggie for awhile. Helping him out at the shop, running errands, stuff like that. He'd give me money, or let me drive sometimes when he picked me up from school."

His mother's jaw moves as if she's chewing something tough. "I found the photo of you and Reggie. He's got his hand on your leg."

"He was showing off, like."

"Who snapped the picture?"

"Reno. That's how we met. Reggie paid him to do other stuff—personal stuff." He blinks so he won't reveal any of the things he's seen Reggie and Reno do in the office and at house parties.

"Liza told me he's been picked up several times by juvenile authorities. As a prostitute." Spit flies from her mouth.

"Don't talk about him like that! He's a friend."

"A friend? A trashy thirteen-year-old who sells himself to men for money?"

"Shut up. Do you want someone to hear?" Danny whispers. He angles his shoulder to shield them from the tough kid's view. "Listen, Reno's not trash. He knows a lot of people, big-time dudes who look out for him because his mother's an alkie."

"People like Reggie? That's where the two of you were the night he died, isn't it?"

"I don't know anything about who killed him, honest. I only know Reggie invited some friends over. Said there'd be plenty of weed and coke."

"You used cocaine?"

She's so shocked, he bites his lip to restrain his laughter. She's the child, and he's the grownup.

"No, Mom." Reggie and the others had licked it off their fingers or put it up their noses. Danny wanted to, but he'd wimped out. It would have been nice to do it and forget the shame. It's as if he has a club foot or cleft palate, except being gay is worse, because it's so deep inside.

"Who was there, besides you, Reggie, and Reno?"

"An old fat guy, a hairy bear, and a college dude from out of town, somebody Reggie picked up at the Rancho."

"Names?"

"I dunno. "

"What else can you tell me?"

He jiggles his leg, faster this time. He doesn't tell her about the "thank you" suck job. Reggie'd been nice to him over the last year, picking him up from school so Danny didn't have to walk a mile out of his way to avoid bullies. They'd go to the shop, and Reggie paid him to break down cardboard boxes, run the vacuum around the showroom, sweep sidewalks outside. For those simple chores, Danny had pocketed a little green stuff each week.

The night of the party, he'd done it to Reggie in his private bathroom. That part was strange. The white marble floor was cold under his knees; Reggie's pubic hair prickled his face. His groin smelled of herbal soap and something else, a complex odor that was both disgusting and alluring.

When he awoke, alone in Reggie's bed, he could hear a drip in the bathroom sink. He was hot under the duvet. Light from the bedside lamps filtered over him like runny egg yolk, and after a second or two, nausea overtook him. He pushed himself onto his elbows, stumbled to Reggie's bathroom, and vomited most of the cheesecake he'd eaten earlier.

"You didn't see who killed him?"

At the end of the table, the tough boy's mother begins loud, dramatic weeping accompanied by facial contortions. The boy leans back in his chair with folded arms and looks over at Danny and Suzanne.

Danny whispers close to his mother's ear. "When I woke up, I didn't see Reggie or anybody upstairs, so I washed my face and went down." He remembers how relieved he felt to rinse his mouth and rinse the smell of sex out of his hair.

"Someone had opened the silver chest in the dining room and stolen the really old stuff Reggie bought in England. I thought Reggie might blame me, so I went looking for him to say I didn't do it."

In death, Reggie seemed small. He was naked, half sitting against the storage cabinet, one arm bent strangely. The wound on

Reggie's head was a terrible violation of his round, symmetrical skull and thin face. There was so much blood, Danny couldn't believe there was room for it in a body that also contained flesh and bone. He looked down and saw that someone had stepped in a small, red pool.

Danny had cried out in terror. Whoever did it might still be hiding somewhere in the house. He backed slowly into the kitchen, then wheeled and ran down the hall to the front door. The street was empty, and he raced across the lawn, took the stairs two at a time.

After he tells her this, his mother squeezes her eyes closed. Blue veins crisscross her eyelids, and a yellow residue is crusted in her lashes.

"Why didn't you tell me?"

"I was too scared. One of them might have come after me. Might still try to kill me." He moistens his finger with his tongue and rubs at a dirt spot on the tabletop.

"No. I mean all of it."

"I tried to, at Thanksgiving when we went to Taft, but I couldn't."

"I'm listening now."

"Another time," Danny says. From the corner of his eye, he sees the tough boy pick his lip and study them closely. Other juvie wards are crowded at tables behind them. Even the probation officer standing close by could circulate stories. Despite Danny's earlier warning, Suzanne is blind to the threat of the dozen pairs of ears around them. After only three days, he knows confidences are a luxury from a past life.

10

Suzanne sits on a varnished wooden bench near the juvenile courtroom, waiting for Danny's lawyer. The hallway is lined with hearing rooms, each with a bench outside, where families and their attorneys talk, heads close. There is a lively commerce in failure here, and her funereal black dress and heels seem to reinforce her status as a Bad Mom.

The bench's edge digs into the soft spot behind her knee. Beside her is a tubular metal ashtray where a lipstick-smeared stub still smokes slightly. She rubs her eyes. "If onlys" crowd in: if only Carlo hadn't died without insurance; if only she hadn't been near bankruptcy and had to earn a living; if only she'd been more alert to Danny's problems.

Last night, she didn't sleep but huddled miserably in front of the television. When Lucky had called after his night shift to wish them good luck, she blubbered in his ear.

At the end of the hall, she sees Dutch Haag's short, stocky figure scurry toward her. "You're late," she says.

"Peña hasn't called the case, has he?" Haag's eyelids are swollen, as if he also hasn't slept.

"He's running behind."

Haag sighs. "Juvie always runs behind."

After she visited Danny in juvenile hall, she called Lucky and spilled everything. He didn't seem shocked, perhaps because he knew life's dingy side from years as a drunk. When she asked for a loan to pay the mortgage and a lawyer, he not only agreed but referred her to Haag, who once had gotten him off on a drunken driving charge. Lucky's $5,000 check arrived in the mail accompanied by a note, scribbled on a scrap of paper: "Tell Dutch to give you the Marlowe rate."

Suzanne double-checked Haag's reputation with Liza, who thought he was scum. An endorsement, coming from police. It means his clients beat the charges. "Drives an orange Corvette macho-mobile," Liza said. "Years ago, I had to write him a citation. He was drunk on his ass, but got off."

"How do things look?" she asks.

"I talked to Osterman in the DA's office a couple of days ago. He was willing to reduce the auto theft to a misdemeanor and go for home supervision."

Her breath rushes out of her lungs. "Wonderful!"

"Maybe. Something else is brewing. "

"Like what?"

"The BPD's made an arrest in the Roman murder."

"Who…who is it?" A vibration plucks at her stomach. In her purse are the Mercedes key and key ring she picked up at Reggie's house.

Haag motions her down the hall, out of earshot of the families and lawyers milling around the hearing room door. "Some guy from a wealthy San Diego family. A student who registered at the Bakersfield Rancho as an Agro-Chem salesman."

He props a scuffed shoe on a wooden bench. "They're not saying much, but I've got a pipeline. The police think Danny and the other boy became acquainted with the San Diego man at the motel. Together, they hatched the plan to kill Roman."

"Danny, in league with that boy whore? Don't be ridiculous!"

Haag backs up a few steps. "The DA's got somebody on tap, probably the other kid, Goulet. Same name as that terrible singer. Anyway, Goulet's been arrested a couple of times, theft and prostitution. He knows the ropes. Might've offered to tell everything, and pin it on the Agro-Chem guy and Danny in exchange for a dismissal or misdemeanor."

"So, what about Danny?"

Haag looks grim. "If the court determines he was an accessory, he could be made a ward of the court. That means time in a juvenile facility. Even CYA."

Suzanne collapses onto the bench. California Youth Authority, equivalent of state prison for adults, is where the baddest of the bad kids go, gang members and murderers.

Down the hall the door of their hearing room opens. The Hispanic boy with the disfiguring teardrop tattoos, whom she remembers from juvenile hall, struts out as if he just scored a winning touchdown. His smiling parents trail after him.

A woman in a navy blue suit carrying a heavy briefcase stops to talk to Haag. "Illegal search," she murmurs.

The bailiff calls *People vs. Ricci*. Dutch adjusts the knot on his tie. Suzanne's legs are shaky, and her mouth is dry as she enters the courtroom. There are no spectator seating or jury box; in the closed session of juvenile court, the outcome depends solely on the judge. The smooth surfaces of the prosecution and defense tables gleam, the bailiff's keys clink, and the air conditioner puffs a cool breath.

Court is in recess. Osterman hasn't arrived yet, but a woman with a stack of manila folders sits at the prosecution's table. Haag strolls over to talk, but as he listens, his forehead creases in a frown.

After a moment, he slides into the seat next to Suzanne. "They've switched probation officers. That gal is Sarah Granger. She's on Danny's case now."

"Is that good or bad?"

"She's the prosecution's go-to girl." He's opened his mouth to add something when the side door opens and the bailiff ushers Danny in, hands cuffed in front of him. His elbows are sharp, and his skin a dull, flat white. An orange T-shirt and tan pants hang on his bony frame.

As soon as he spots her, he mouths, "Hi, Mom." The bailiff

uses a key from his belt to remove the cuffs. Danny takes his seat on the other side of Haag. She leans over to touch his arm, but Haag gives her a warning shake of his head.

"Court is now in session," the bailiff says.

Judge Kevin Peña is a short man, the top of his bald head just visible as he mounts the steps of the raised dais. Once he's settled in his chair behind the bench, his clerk stands on her tiptoes to place a foot-high stack of manila case files at his elbow. Suzanne read a story recently in the *News-Daily* implying Peña is a token Hispanic appointed by the young governor, Jerry Brown, to stifle protests about discrimination in judicial selections.

She feels Haag tense. Someone opens the gate and seats himself at the prosecution table. The latecomer is a fat man. Despite his silver gray hair, his face is unlined. A carefully tailored suit minimizes his bulk, and a starched shirt cuff slips back to display a heavy gold watch. Although his face is calm, his ear lobes are flushed an intimate pink.

Peña raises his eyebrows. "Mr. Vinson, you're on this case?"

"Mr. Osterman has a conflict, your honor. I'm stepping in."

The judge directs his gaze at Haag. "Do you have a problem with the state's substitution of counsel?"

"No, your honor, as long as the agreement we negotiated with Mr. Osterman still stands."

She clasps her hands tightly, feeling her joints crack. Vinson is second in command at the prosecutor's office, just below the elected DA. She glances at Danny, who is usually fidgeting or chewing a fingernail. Not an eyelash quivers.

"Actually," Vinson says, "in the light of new information obtained from law enforcement, we have withdrawn our offer of probation and parental supervision."

She grasps Haag's arm, but he shakes her off. "We haven't received any such information from Mr. Osterman, your honor. He assured us we had a deal."

Vinson stacks his hands on the tabletop. "We have witnesses

who have implicated this juvenile, Daniel Marlowe Ricci, as an accessory to a homicide."

"This is very serious, Mr. Haag," Peña says.

Danny tugs Haag's sleeve. When the attorney leans over, Danny cups his hand carefully over his mouth. It's a small motion, but tells her, more than Danny's cropped hair or orange jail T-shirt, that secrets and distrust are now a fact of his life.

"Defense requests this matter be put over, your honor. And we ask the court to remonstrate most strongly with Mr. Vinson about his lack of timely disclosure."

Vinson ignores Haag. "No petition has been filed regarding this defendant. The homicide investigation is not yet complete."

"In that case," Haag says, "the deal worked out with Mr. Osterman should remain in place. Danny Ricci has an involved parent. His best interests will be served if he's in home supervision."

Peña riffles through the pages of Danny's file. "Probation? What do you have to say?"

Sarah Granger pulls a handkerchief from the sleeve of her dress, blows her nose, and slips it back under her cuff. "Sorry, your honor, it's allergies."

Suzanne remembers that Grandma Marlowe did this, stuffing damp, mucous-soaked tissue in her sleeve as if it were a secret treasure.

Granger slides on her glasses. "The young man admitted he was complicit in the auto theft, although to a lesser degree than Mr. Goulet, the co-defendant in this case. If this were the only instance of Mr. Ricci's illegal activity, probation would agree with Mr. Haag's proposal for home supervision."

Danny is staring at his tightly clasped hands. Suzanne holds her breath to stop whatever's coming.

"It was brought to our attention this morning, however, that a number of checks, written by the juvenile's mother to Sampson Brothers Art Emporium, bore forged endorsements and were subsequently cashed by the murder victim, Reginald Roman."

"A moment, your honor." Haag turns to Danny, his shoulder

blocking their whispered conversation. Suzanne refuses to be shut out. She slides her chair over and pushes between them.

"What?" She makes a supreme effort to keep from yelling.

"I didn't keep the money. I gave it to Reno."

"The boy prostitute?" she asks.

"For his mother. She hits him if he doesn't bring home enough."

With the three of them huddled together, she catches Haag's stale liquor odor and a whiff of juvie's antiseptic soap. There's no smell for outrage, but she's unable to say whether she's angrier at Danny or Reno's sicko mother.

Haag sighs. "We're not going to win on home supervision. Let's stipulate to a short time in a group facility."

"No, no," Danny moans.

"Will he be safe?" Suzanne, ignoring the admonition about touching, leans over to rub the soft hairs on Danny's arm. His skin is very cold.

"Safe as any place," Haag says. "We'll talk more about the murder, but not here."

11

After court, handcuffs are snapped on again, and Danny is led away. Suzanne and Haag stand on the sidewalk outside the Kern Youth Facility.

"What just happened?" The dizzying drop from elation to despair has left her hollow.

Haag scans the parents and lawyers clustered near the entrance. A couple of police officers smoking cigarettes at the curb. Granger, the probation officer, wheeling a wire cart stacked with files across the street to her office. "Let's take a walk. Fewer big ears," he says.

They cross against the traffic light. Haag's briefcase thumps against his thigh. January sun struggles through the late morning fog. The temperature is probably in the high forties, but the chilly dampness creeps up her pant legs and down the back of her neck.

Danny didn't look at her when he left. Instead, he was mouthing something to another boy being brought in. The newcomer was smaller than Danny, his peroxide-blond hair dark at the roots. This must have been Reno, the kid who did most of the driving of the stolen car, according to Danny. They're nothing alike, she tells herself, desperate to believe it.

After walking a block, she jostles Haag's shoulder. "So?"

"I was asleep at the switch." He doesn't meet her eyes.

"You mean about the checks? I should've told you, but so many things have happened so fast, I forgot." Suzanne's so scared and upset, Haag has to thrust out an arm to keep her from stepping in front of a truck, ending up as roadkill.

"It would have helped if I'd known about them," he says, "but in addition, I missed some signals."

"Like what?"

"The fact that Osterman didn't call me back yesterday, and Sarah was tied up in a meeting."

"They think *Danny* killed him?" Her fingers ache with cold. She balls them into fists and blows on them.

"Not necessarily, but they'd love to have him testify against whoever did. The trouble is, Danny says he doesn't know, and it's probably true. He's told me virtually everything, but I think there are one or two details he's holding back."

Suzanne remembers Danny's reticence during her visit to juvie. What has he told Haag that he hasn't told her? Does she want to know?

"Virtually all of it would be, what?"

Haag ticks off events as if reciting from one of his yellow legal pads. "That he was there all night, beginning about nine. That there were six people there, four men and the two boys. That quantities of various drugs were consumed. That the younger boy performed oral sex on three men. That Danny did the same to Mr. Roman, then fell asleep and didn't awake until nearly dawn, when he found the host dead in the kitchen."

"Reggie forced Danny to . . ." She can't stop the clear images of Reggie's bare flesh, Danny's mouth, the thrusting and sucking. Her skin is clammy, as though she's about to heave.

"No, but he undoubtedly coerced him. Subtly, of course." Haag's voice is gentle.

She takes a deep breath. "So Danny's innocent. He was asleep when it happened."

"We can certainly contend that, if Danny's charged as an accessory to murder."

"But these men are victimizing boys! Why aren't they in jail?"

"Well, one is in jail, and one's dead."

"I mean the two other men, they're just like that filthy Reggie. My friend at the police, she's caught him doing things to boys in the Wilson Park bathrooms, but he never faced charges."

"Alarm bells should have gone off in my head when you first told me it was Roman's car they stole," he says, red-faced.

"Who are the other two men? Why don't we know?"

"The suspect is from out of town. I assume Danny hadn't met the two local men before, although he may know their names. Reno certainly knows who they are. In any case, both boys are too frightened to say."

"We've got to get these guys."

"Back off, Suzanne. Danny will be out of the group home in a few months, and this will go away."

Taller than Haag, she looks down at him, specks of dandruff on his shoulders, hair thinning on top, shoes damp and muddy. The sidewalk is gritty under their feet. Fog has trapped the emissions from the refineries. Oily smut touches her face.

"So we ignore the fact they're molesting boys?"

"Lower your voice," Haag says urgently. "I've heard for years about a group of men calling themselves The Club. They're among the most powerful and well-connected people in the county. There's nothing you can do to fight them."

"I can't believe this."

As Danny left the courtroom in handcuffs, she noticed the metal cut into his wrists. The shackles on his ankles clinked with every step. The soft-soled jail shoes were too small for his big feet, so his bare heels trod on the fabric. She feels battered, like his ill-fitting shoes and raw skin.

"Listen to me, Suzanne. It's no coincidence that Gregory Powell, the Onion Field killer, kidnapped those two Los Angeles cops and brought them up here. Powell thought it was as far away from LA as he could get. He gunned one down and tried to shoot the other."

"It's not as if we're only accessible by wagon train."

"Two hard hours' drive over a steep mountain road that sometimes closes in winter. And on this side, we're surrounded by grapevines, cotton fields, and sagebrush for a hundred miles. Bakersfield's an island. Nobody in the rest of California gives a damn about what goes on here."

"So you lie down and let them screw you? You should be ashamed."

"I am, from time to time." He digs a breath mint from his suit pocket and slips it in his mouth.

"If there's nothing you can do, how can you represent Danny?"

"I do my very best, Suzanne. You won't find anyone in the county more willing to stick his neck out than me. But my advice is, let it go. Play it safe for the sake of your boy."

12

The High Endeavor group home is not as advertised. Dutch Haag assured Danny there would be school. Activities. Decent meals. A little freedom to walk to the park, say, or buy a burger at Wendy's.

Not so. School is a half day of classes held at the group home's scarred dining room table. Danny and the seven other wards are taught by a retired high school teacher with bristling chin hairs. The boys spend school hours dozing over their books, sticking ballpoint pens into their arms and faces to create homemade tattoos, or shooting each other with darts made from straight pins.

The five-bedroom group home was once a fine residence: wainscoting and curved moldings, glass-paned doors between the living room and dining room, and golden oak floors inlaid with strips of mahogany. But years of misuse by teenage felons has degraded the house to the status of an old man who's lost his teeth and now shows bare gums. The glass doors have been carted away, moldings stripped, floors gouged.

Six weeks after he arrived, Danny wakes up, as usual, to the resident counselor's shout. "Up, you slugs. Inspection in thirty." Danny hates that meaty fist of a voice. It punches them out of bed, him and his roommate, Diego Luhan, a kid who sold a bindle of heroin to an undercover cop.

Diego stirs. He's twelve, his face and arms smooth and hairless, like a newborn puppy. His mother died a couple of years ago when the two of them were sneaking across the border from Mexico. Diego lived with his uncle, but now the guy, a member of *La Eme,* is in Soledad Prison.

"Anybody that's late gets ten demerits," bellows the resident, and he's off down the hall, pounding the wall. Danny and Diego wait outside the bathroom for an older boy, Jesus Aragon, who's supposed to be showering and shaving, but instead stands naked at the sink, examining his teeth in the mirror. The group home allows no closed doors except to the director's office—not the bedrooms, not even the toilet.

"What you looking at?" Jesus wheels to stare at them.

"Nothin'." Danny averts his eyes.

Jesus punches him in the side. Danny leans against the wall for a few minutes while he recovers his breath. He shows no frustration or rage. If he gets angry, the other boys will double down. He's learned a lesson at High Endeavor that isn't algebra or American history from the senile old teacher. It's the rock-bottom basic skill for survival in prison—never reveal feelings.

Awhile back, he created a series of pen-and-ink panels, a horror story about a man buried alive, so closely encased he can't get out. It's like that here. Pity, anger, joy, and sexual longings are suffocated. He's in a coffin, and he wonders if he's ever going to *feel* things again.

The resident rings the breakfast bell. Danny takes a pee but skips a shower, hoping to avoid being written up for lateness. He tumbles downstairs with his Nikes in hand.

"Ricci. Five demerits."

Reno's already there, having finagled a spot at the head of the bathroom line. He arrived at High Endeavor three weeks after Danny. The DA agreed to dismiss a larceny charge involving thefts from Reggie's shop but sentenced him on the auto theft. The San Diego college student accused of Reggie's murder was held for trial after a preliminary hearing, and the deputy public defender has listed Reno and Danny as potential witnesses.

Boys crowd the kitchen, which smells of disinfectant. After breakfast, whichever kid is assigned to kitchen detail will pour Lysol into mop water and spread it over the cracked linoleum.

It's a hallmark of the group home's culture that no one sits with feet on the floor squarely facing the table. They straddle chairs or reverse them, leaning over the backs to get to their plates. Danny takes the most inconvenient seat, against the wall between Reno and Diego. No one squats, even for a second, in someone else's place.

Reno and Danny, mostly due to Reno's mysterious influence, aren't harassed or beaten. Danny hears the whispered words—fag, pussy, queer—the same ones hurled at him by Arnie and Ham and kids at high school, but here murmurs are stifled, like swear words in church.

Led by the resident, the boys pray before the meal, and his stern gaze prevents any titters or eye rolling. The cook, a tall woman so thin Danny wonders if a morsel ever passes her lips, slaps platters of runny eggs and dripping bacon on the table. Danny misses his mother's breakfasts, ham slices and golden fried potatoes with plenty of pepper. The bright spot in his week is Wednesday night, when she visits, with a batch of snickerdoodle cookies in a box lined with waxed paper. Sometimes the cookies are still warm, and the scent of cinnamon makes him want to cry.

The day drags like a club foot. During the morning, they study; then, to show how completely fucked up things are, the teacher and resident advisor load up the Chevy van for an "out event." By that time, the temp is in the 90s. Heat rising from the concrete at the skateboard park penetrates their shoes.

Before dinner this particular day, he gets a call on the house telephone from Grace Stannard. He hasn't seen or talked to her since they took the bus to Bakersfield College in December to see an exhibition of psychedelic posters at the college gallery. Her low voice, threaded with complex textures, triggers his longing. He wants to be like her, soft and beautiful, with skin that seems to have been created from the smooth inner lining of a seashell. Grace can trace the lines in his pen-and-ink drawings with her fingertips and tell him the meaning of the image before Danny's aware of what he's created.

"Hey, D.R.," she says.

"Gracie, how did you find me?" Danny glances quickly over his shoulder. Nobody is loitering nearby waiting to use the phone. He slumps on the oak bench in the entrance hallway, a location purposely chosen for its lack of privacy to discourage the wards from hatching escapes.

"Through Mr. Franzen."

"You hanging out with him?" He feels a surge of unease. Word is, the police commissioner provides heavy-duty drugs to boys and the occasional girl who attend his parties.

She laughs. "I don't have a cock, at least not last time I looked, so he's not interested. Anyway, how are you, sweetie?"

"Fine." Horrified to hear his voice tremble, he clears his throat.

"You getting hurt?"

"No, not like that. It's just so, so…"

"I know," she says. "So dead."

He nods as if she can see him.

"You doing any work?" he asks, remembering the classes at Sampson Brothers.

"Not right now."

"You haven't given up your series on food, have you?"

"It wasn't all that great."

"Yes, it was. The best stuff from any of Mr. Bosch's classes. Good enough to get in *Young Art*."

Her exhalation creates a small tornado in the receiver. "Art is for kids."

"You don't sound so good yourself, Gracie. What's wrong?"

"She took off, D.R"

"Jesus. To Nashville?"

"Merle had an opening for a backup singer on his new tour. I came home from school, all her stuff was gone. She left a note. A goddamned note."

Grace's mother, Janet, is a bar singer who performed a couple nights a week at Trout's on North Chester. Grace said her mom talked about her music all the time, like she'd given up some megastar career to get married and have a kid.

"Screw that old lady. You don't need her."

Grace begins to cry.

"Or maybe she'll stink, and Merle will dump her for someone with more talent, and she'll come home," Danny says.

"She's good, Danny. I know it. She's good, and she'll go to the top and never come back."

—

Late that night, a hand jiggles Danny's shoulder.

"All quiet. The guy's asleep." Reno's whisper crackles in his ear.

Danny's already dressed in Levis and a muscle shirt. The luminous dial on his watch reads 10:30. He punches up his pillow and shoves it under the blanket.

The night resident had snapped out the bedroom lights and double locked the outside doors at ten. Once he's settled into his chair in front of the rec room television, he'll sleep for hours. The wards, however, are still restless. Muffled laughter comes from the bathroom, where Jesus and two older boys play poker and sniff glue in the shower stall.

Danny and Reno carry their shoes, stepping carefully to avoid squeaky floor boards on the back stairs to the kitchen. The *Fantasy Island* theme song plays on TV.

Reno eases open the cellar door. When no shout comes from the night resident, they tiptoe down the steps and cross to a small hinged window. In seconds, they've hoisted themselves up, wriggled outside, and stepped into their shoes. A thin crust of moon hangs in the southeast, and the night bubbles around Danny like champagne.

He's been so guarded during these last weeks, so careful to pretend indifference to jeers and provocations from the other wards, that the darkness reeks of freedom. They walk two blocks, peer from a distance through front windows where Friday night boxing flickers on television. Car tires squeal on a nearby street. He hears a man laugh and imagines it coming from a handsome mouth.

"There it is." Reno grabs his arm.

Pulled up at the curb in front of a row of small, three-bedroom houses is a black Cadillac limo. Danny holds his breath while he memorizes the look of it: the crouch of the fenders and gleam of its waxed black surface. The engine purrs. Tinted windows screen the occupants from view.

The rear door swings open, and Reno slides across the smooth leather seat. Danny hesitates on the sidewalk. His Nikes make a scuffing noise on the uneven concrete, and he rubs the goosebumps on his arms although the night is hot. The limo's interior is an envelope of secrets.

Reno leans out. "Come on!" Illuminated by the street lamp, his peroxided hair is startlingly white.

Danny ducks his head and scoots inside. The door closes with a heavy thump. Through the glass barrier, the driver scratches his sideburn with a heavily tattooed hand and shifts into gear. The interior light flashes on. Reno sits in the middle of the wide seat; beside the far window is Galen Franzen. His legs are spread wide, and pants are belted high on his waist to show off his package. Facing him in one of the two jump seats is a red-haired boy about sixteen. Danny has seen him at the skateboard park. The boy studies him a second or two, then looks away.

"Hey, Danny. Good to see you. This is Kevin." The old man leans forward to stroke Kevin's thigh.

The limo slides through the traffic, which parts to let them pass, as if the Caddy were the lead car in a motorcade. People gawk, trying to catch a glimpse of the passengers behind the smoky glass.

"How are you cats? Cool?" Galen snaps his fingers and taps his palm with a closed fist as if he were some '50s hipster.

Reno stifles a laugh. "We're great, Mr. Franzen."

The Friday night crowd is on the move. At a red light, a Chevy

Impala pumps up and down on hydraulics. Fast-back Mustangs sail by, and pickup trucks with enormous tires. Bakersfield hums with electricity; people released from jobs, schools, and jails are free to kick the evening's ass. Danny inhales the perfume of male sweat in the car, the harsh acid scent that lubricates his fantasies and stirs his blood. After weeks of boredom, he wants adventure. Excitement.

Franzen leans over to kiss Reno on the mouth, but Reno turns his head. Kevin gives Reno a surreptitious kick. Reno retaliates by stomping on his foot.

"Cut it out, you guys." Franzen opens a refrigerator installed between the two jump seats and unscrews the cap on a whiskey bottle. They share, and when Danny drinks, he can taste the residue of other lips. The whiskey burn in his throat makes him dizzy. He looks up to see the limo driver studying him in the rear view mirror.

Galen rubs Reno's leg. "Good week for a party. It'll take your mind off the courthouse."

Sweat springs to Danny's forehead. He's heard from Dutch Haag that Wade Thurston, the college student arrested for Reggie's murder, is about to go on trial.

"Will we have to testify?" Danny asks.

"Thurston's big-shot defense lawyer wants you to. He might insist you appear and take the Fifth. That would plant doubts in the jurors' minds," Franzen says.

"So we're in his sights." Reno's hand drifts down to the knife strapped to his ankle under his bell-bottom jeans.

"Looks that way."

Danny remembers a Western he watched on TV. A cattle drive, in which trail drivers herded the longhorns through a series of narrowing chutes until they were squeezed one by one into rail cars headed for the slaughterhouses. He takes another gulp from the bottle.

The limo turns left on Aster Street. The car slows as it passes mansions screened by magnolia trees and shaggy-trunked eucalyptus, oleander bushes and privet hedges. Two blocks pass; the limo glides right into a driveway blocked by a wrought iron gate. When the driver flashes the headlights, the gate swings open.

13

⎯

The limo's headlights brush the mansion's portico and front entry decorated with slim columns in perfect proportion to the facade. The car skims along a driveway to a wide garage, where it parks beside two other limos. Suspended from the ceiling is a black carriage, poised as if it were about to be lowered to the floor and attached to a pair of sleek horses. The tattooed driver cuts the engine and opens the door for Franzen, As the passengers pile out, Kevin sticks out a foot to trip Danny. Danny shoves him.

They cross the dark driveway, and enter the grounds through a bougainvillea-covered archway. Flashes of azure light from the swimming pool dance on the green curtain of oleander and privet, which hides the party from neighbors.

Naked men cluster in groups, relaxing on cushioned lounges, playing catch in the water with a rubber duckie, or whispering to each other on the pool steps. This is not like the showers after gym class or juvenile hall, where almost everyone is young and slim. Many of these men are older, jowls thickening, guts protruding, body hair gone gray.

A couple is having sex in the pool's shallows, unconcerned that others watch. During the limo ride, Danny's head was filled to splitting with fears about Reggie's murder trial, yet now he's alive with energy, fascinated by the freedom of these men.

Someone steps onto the veranda from the house. "Galen, we've been expecting you. And your friends." He's tall, with thin, elegant bones, long face, and chin as sharp as a wedge. Danny wants to touch his open-necked silk shirt and soft linen slacks.

"Whitman, you know Reno. These two are Kevin and Danny," Franzen says.

Danny stares. Harris Whitman, half owner, with his cousin, of the *Bakersfield News-Daily*. The guy who hired his mother to write her petroleum industry column.

Whitman runs a finger carelessly over Reno's cheek. "Come on, boys. I'll take you into the kitchen and turn you over to Rodolfo."

Danny bares his teeth at Reno. His friend had told him this was a party: food, drinks, and drugs. Turns out the boys are hired help. Reno's neck and ears redden. They pass through the living room, where someone is playing a baby grand piano. The sound clashes with country music that drifts down from upstairs. Whitman touches one guest on the shoulder, greets another. Danny wishes the older man were focusing on him.

The huge, white-tiled kitchen is dominated by two black, six-burner stoves. Men in aprons dart from stove to shelf, arranging food on silver trays. Two others in striped vests haul cases of glasses and liquor to a full bar in the dining room.

A bald Hispanic with a cherubic face introduces himself as Rodolfo and hands each of the boys a pair of red satin shorts and matching vest. "Change in the bathroom around the corner, then see me."

"You prick," Danny whispers to Reno as they wait outside the bathroom for Kevin.

"There'll be money. Lots of it. Just go with the flow. We'll be back to High Endeavor before wake-up call."

"I'm not turning tricks."

Reno sighs, as if Danny is trying his patience. "Suit yourself, but these guys got clout. If you connect, they'll do things for you."

Kevin opens the door. The shorts squeeze his groin and the vest is widely cut to display tufts of red chest hair.

"I'm not a bugger boy," Danny says to Reno.

Kevin snorts. "Get real. The murder trial is coming up, and you need people looking out for you."

"I haven't noticed anybody looking out for me. I didn't say shit about that night at Reggie's, but instead of home supervision, I got High Endeavor."

Stepping between them, Reno raises his hands in conciliation. "Come on, Kev, cool down. Danny's free to do what he wants."

Somewhat mollified, Danny puts on the shorts, which cut into his crotch.

Rodolfo instructs the three boys to circulate throughout the house with trays of salmon tartlets, paper-thin beef slices on baguette rounds, slivers of brie, and cayenne-spiced pecans. When that's done, Danny is assigned to gather drink orders from guests around the pool.

As soon as he approaches the first cluster of men and begins jotting orders, he feels the force of someone's gaze. Glancing up, he sees Vinson across the pool, looking like a fool in a flowered shirt and Bermuda shorts while everyone else is naked. His eyes are unwavering, and the gravitational pull of his gaze makes Danny look down, to assure himself his feet are rooted to the ground.

The night Reggie died, Vinson had kissed Danny, the cigarette taste thick on the older man's tongue. Danny hadn't liked him and kept his distance after that, but Vinson had become increasingly tense and angry, alternately drinking alone at the kitchen table and bickering with Reggie. Danny thought Vinson was just some lawyer guy, so when he appeared in juvenile court, he was stunned.

Tonight he gets it—the prosecutor's opposition to home supervision, his insinuation Danny was involved in Reggie's death, and the sentence to High Endeavor, they're payback. From his chair at the pool, Vinson nods twice at Danny. Decorative lights reflect off his glasses like lightning flashes.

The thrall is broken when an old man with wattles under his chin reaches out to stroke Danny's crotch. Taking a step away,

Danny scribbles the drink order. By the time he returns with the glass on a tray, Vinson's gone.

After the encounter, Danny is so rattled he forgets orders and spills drinks. Rodolfo barks at him to take a break, and he wanders into the quiet living room, where he perches on the edge of a sofa, studying an oil painting of Yosemite in a heavy gold frame. The artist used a break in the deep green pine trees to highlight a waterfall. Danny steps nearer. The feathery mist that drifts off the falls is delicate and iridescent. He imagines the artist mixing the color on his palette and dipping fine brush hairs in the pigment.

"Like it?" Whitman stands behind him; his chest brushes Danny's shoulder.

"Yeah, a lot."

"It's a Thomas Hill, done in the 1880s when he was living in California. It wasn't until later he became famous."

Danny nods as if he's heard of the guy. He reminds himself to look up Hill once he's released from High Endeavor.

"There's another in my office. Want to see it?" Whitman leads the way across the black-and-white marble entry where a curved stairway rises to the upper stories. On the far side he opens a door to a walnut-paneled room dominated by a mahogany desk.

"This was my great-uncle's desk," Whitman strokes the satiny surface. "He founded the *News-Daily* and used it in the newspaper office for forty years, beginning in the 1870s."

Two framed photographs perch on the desk, placed at angles to a high-backed leather chair. One is a professional portrait of Whitman and a woman posed on a garden bench. The other is of three teenage girls. "My wife and stepdaughters. They're spending the summer at our Tahoe house." He flips both pictures face down.

A tremor rises inside him, fear or excitement, Danny is unsure which.

With a hand on Danny's elbow, Whitman guides him toward a river scene with the same waterfall in the background. "This is it, probably more valuable than the one in the living room because it's so clearly Yosemite Valley. Hill was broke and starving, and my great-grandfather got it for a bag of groceries."

Danny inches closer. "He really knows how to do water. I have a lot of trouble with it."

"You're an artist?"

"Not really. Well, sort of. I've taken some classes." Danny scans the room. In the spaces between the tall bookshelves, Whitman has hung his art collection: landscapes, figure studies, abstracts, even some drawings. To Danny, they are windows on a stunning view, like seeing real mountains or sunsets compared to reading about them. He's pored over art books with photos of pieces this good, but only seen them for real in museums. His fingers feel extra sensitive, itching to reach out and touch a bit of thick paint or handmade paper.

One piece particularly calls to him. Without thinking, he brings his hand within a few inches as if blessing it. It's a small ink drawing of a rabbit with a willow switch in his paw chasing a panda. The artist's strokes are bold, confident. How would it feel to have a brain so clear and fingers so obedient?

"It's Japanese. Twelfth century," Whitman says.

Tears spring to Danny's eyes, and he blinks in embarrassment.

Whitman's voice deepens. "H.G. Wells said, 'It's art that makes life.'" His gaze is heated and direct, and Danny notices that his brown eyes have lighter spots in them that glitter like gold flakes.

Danny tries to remember the last time someone studied him so closely, really looked as if trying to see beneath the skin. His mother, maybe, when he was little, long before his father died.

Funny that he should think right now about his father, who hated queers and was always saying, men do this and men do that. Meaning, not queers. Party sounds are muffled, the beat of the music upstairs is a dimly-felt vibration in his ear. He breathes quickly through dry lips.

Whitman steps close until inches separate them. Danny catches the mingled scents of minty aftershave, freshly ironed clothes and warm skin. He touches the silky fabric of Whitman's shirt and imagines what this wealthy, cultured man would look like naked. Beautiful, strong. Whitman's demanding hand strokes the satiny front of Danny's shorts. Danny groans at the surge of urgency and fire. His clothes chafe his skin, and a bead of sweat runs down his cheek. Whitman tilts his sharp chin downward until Danny feels his breath on his lips. He pushes his tongue into Danny's mouth.

Danny has been kissed before, but it was never this thrilling: loose and wet and unrestrained by guilt. Whitman's hand brushes Danny's nipple as he slides the satin vest off his shoulder.

Danny closes his eyes and behind his lids sees flashes of magenta, viridian and cobalt. When Whitman pushes Danny's shorts down around his ankles, he sighs in relief. He tries to unfasten the zipper of Whitman's slacks, but catches a fold of fabric in the zipper. Danny feels like an inexperienced rube and tries unsuccessfully to free Whitman's pants. Whitman laughs and untangles the placket. Danny thrusts his hand inside and touches wiry hair and hot skin.

"No, no, this is my show." The older man grasps Danny's wrist. He kicks at the chair and rolls it aside. He swings Danny around. With his hand on Danny's neck, he bends him over the desk. The wood is cool on Danny's cheek.

Whitman's fingers make a leisurely exploration. Danny groans, and his legs tremble so violently he can hardly stand. Whitman presses in. Danny cries out, his body stretched, invaded, hurt. He humps his back, frees his feet from his shorts, and kicks out, but he can't stop the pain. His cheekbone thumps rhythmically against the desk and a deep, mahogany red flashes before his eyes.

He focuses on the color, concentrating with every speck of his will, imagining a painting with a large red pool given depth by dark, congealed shadows, a bloody pool surrounded by blurry patches of white and brown, and by small strips of other pigments that appear to be oscillating to a certain degenerate beat. He invokes the smell of paint and linseed oil. He forces himself to feel the sweep of his hand, plan the movement of the brush, hear the quiet tock, tock of bristles on canvas.

Danny doesn't move after Whitman finishes. Clothing rustles, and in a moment he hears the office door open and close. The desk top is slippery with sweat from his face, eyes are hot and gritty with shame. The pain is his fault. If only he'd stayed at High Endeavor, if only he'd stuck to serving drinks, if only he hadn't trusted Whitman. If only he hadn't succumbed to longing.

There is a movement behind him. Has Whitman returned? On trembling legs, he turns to see the limo driver sitting in the leather desk chair. How long has he been watching? His tattooed hands are spread on the armrests, and he lifts one skeletal finger at Danny, beckoning him closer.

"I'm not...I'm not." Danny lurches as he tries to scoop up his clothes, but the driver plants one thick-soled boot on top of them.

"You'd better. These rich party guys aren't the only ones with powerful friends." The man digs his nails into Danny's arm. Danny kicks frantically at the chair's casters. It humps backward, and the driver smashes into the glass-fronted bookcase. Danny grabs the satin shorts and runs.

14

In May, Wade Thurston's trial for the murder of Reggie Roman opens in Courtroom Five. Newly sworn jurors clutch their paper tablets and sharpened pencils like college freshmen on the first day of class. Suzanne is the opening witness.

Sitting in the witness box is a freaky experience. She fidgets in the chair, situated above the attorneys and jurors, but below the judge. All eyes are on her. She straightens her back, trying to look like a middle-class chick, not a scruffy kid who knows only about derricks, well bores, rock bits, and pump jacks, whose education is two years at Taft's community college, who wrote for the *Midway Driller* newspaper before she moved to Bakersfield.

Jerry Cole, the high-ticket defense attorney hired by Thurston's got-bucks San Diego family, leans over to whisper in his client's ear. Thurston looks about twenty-one, as soft and white as Wonder Bread. She tries to imagine his plump fingers, interlaced on the tabletop, clutching a knife and then some unknown heavy object to stab and beat Reggie to death. Thurston is in custody, but for the trial he's been allowed to shed the orange jump suit and don a charcoal gray suit, white shirt and necktie. No handcuffs on his wrists.

Suzanne is sworn in by the court clerk and states her name. Judge John Simic flashes her a smile, teeth so perfect they've got to be fakes.

Deputy District Attorney Stanley Osterman clears his throat. She glares at him. He's the idiot who allowed Vinson, his boss, to manipulate Danny's auto theft case in juvenile court. Danny's still at High Endeavor, not to be released for another couple of weeks.

"Mrs. Ricci, I'd like to call your attention to January 4 of this year. Did an unusual event occur?"

"Yes."

"And what was that event?"

"I found a body."

"Did you know this person?"

"Yes." She keeps her answers as short as bitten fingernails.

Haag slips into the courtroom, easing the door shut so it doesn't slam, and takes a seat in the back row.

Osterman's voice rises as if to jar her loose from one-syllable answers. "And who would that be?"

"Reggie Roman."

"How did you know the decedent?"

Haag gives her a discreet thumbs up. He and Suzanne spent yesterday evening rehearsing her testimony, hoping to skirt the issue of Danny's presence at the scene. She considers each answer, not offering one word more than requested: the cat's bloody paws, Reggie's unlatched front door, her discovery of his body, and the telephone call to police. Osterman asks questions that establish the mess from the party, absence of any guests. She testifies she didn't touch anything other than the telephone while she waited.

Her guilty hand burns in the fold of her skirt. The key's gone, thrown in a trash can. When Osterman finally finishes, he mops his bald head with his handkerchief.

Cole plods over the same trail Osterman just traveled; then flips to a new page of the yellow legal pad filled with notes. "Mrs. Ricci, let's go back to early that morning. What time did you get up?"

"About 7:30."

"Had you slept well?"

"Yes."

"Did you take medication to help you sleep?"

"Yes." Her voice quavers. Sleep had seemed like such a cheap way to escape.

"During the night, did you hear or see any sign of partying next door at Mr. Roman's?"

"No."

He strolls out from behind the defense table and slides his hands in his pants pockets. "So you were unaware of what your son was up to that night, Mrs. Ricci?"

"Up to?"

In the back of the courtroom, Haag straightens in his seat, chin thrust forward.

"Yes. Did you know how he spent the evening?"

"No. I mean, yes, he was home when I went to bed, but I didn't check on him after that. He's fourteen. I don't need to tuck him in at night."

The spectators chuckle.

"Would you say Danny—that's your son's name, isn't it—Danny and the deceased were close friends?"

The wooden sides of the witness stand seem to contract around her, as if she's in a packing case. She takes a long breath. Jurors are watching her closely.

"Objection," says Osterman, "relevance."

"The young man lives next door," Cole says to Judge Simic. "He was home the night of the murder and had known the deceased for years."

Simic's attention drifts; a few seconds tick by before he refocuses. "Sustained."

"All right. We'll go at this from another direction," Cole says. "Mrs. Ricci, in January of this year, did police access certain of your bank records?"

"Yes."

"And did those records involve ten cancelled checks you had written for your son's art classes at Sampson Brothers Art Emporium?"

"Same objection," says Osterman.

Cole assures Simic he will show how the information is relevant, and the judge grants him leeway.

"The checks were for classes, yes," Suzanne says.

"Do you have personal knowledge what happened to those checks?" Cole asks.

"No."

"Did you have a conversation with police about them?"

"Yes."

"What was the substance of that conversation?"

"That the owner of Sampson Brothers hadn't received the checks nor endorsed them." Heat creeps up her neck, and she feels naked, as though her gullibility is on display for the world to see.

"Did you ask your son what happened to the checks?"

"He said he didn't steal them; he just didn't give them to Mr. Bosch."

"Like an armored truck driver who doesn't deliver the money sacks to the bank?" A couple of jurors laugh.

"Objection, your honor, the question is argumentative," Osterman says.

"I'll withdraw it." Cole preens a little. "Did you ask him if he forged his teacher's name and convinced the deceased to cash them?"

In the back row Haag is drawing his finger across his neck, but Suzanne's heart is beating quickly, and she can't stop. "He gave the money to a friend who needed it. That is, the friend's mother needed it to pay the rent."

"So would it be fair to say Danny and Mr. Roman were very close?"

"Reggie lived next door to us for a long time. Sometimes Danny worked at his store, sweeping up and moving furniture." Her mouth is dry, and she struggles to swallow.

"And over a period of nearly a year, Mr. Roman cashed checks with forged endorsements—a clear violation of the law—for his fourteen-year-old neighbor?"

Suzanne nods, and Simic reminds her to answer aloud.

"Yes."

"Did your son attend Mr. Roman's party the night he died?"

"I don't know."

"Because you slept very heavily?"

"Yes."

"Did Danny tell you he was a party guest?"

"Objection, your honor, heresay," Osterman says.

A juror coughs. Simic, staring at the courtroom's crown molding, blinks at Osterman, who repeats his objection. Simic sustains it, and Cole returns to his chair.

When her testimony is finished, Suzanne is allowed to sit in the audience. Only four spectators occupy the visitors' section: Maude Hedges, her permed hair frothing around her head like soapsuds; two court watchers—retired men who shuffle between trials—and the News-Daily's court reporter, a woman in a cheap wraparound skirt. Where is Reggie's family? Where are the clients who heaped praise on him for his exquisite taste, and the other neighbors who lived near him on Filbert Street for fifteen years?

Detective Barton occupies the witness stand for the remainder of the day and part of the next. As the trial rolls along, Suzanne camps out in a dark corner of Courtroom Five. At night, she returns home, stokes herself with coffee, and pounds the IBM to keep money coming in.

The facts pile up like chunks of ore. The coroner reports on Reggie's wounds and the drugs in his system. An evidence technician testifies glasses were wiped clean and describes a bloody shoeprint on the floor beside the body. A taxi driver tells how he drove Reno and Reggie from Filbert Street to the Bakersfield Rancho about 7 p.m. The cabbie returns to the motel at 9:30 p.m., picks up Thurston and Reggie, and delivers them to the house. The Bakersfield Rancho's desk clerk confirms Thurston was a guest, falsely listing his profession in the register as an agricultural chemicals salesman.

Suzanne absorbs these details as though she's seeing the dark side of the moon. Nothing she's heard matches the man she thought she knew: his wry sense of humor, elegant taste, or impulsive kindness.

Carlo's death was like this. The reality of his life was a broken landscape of lies and evasions. He'd been sleeping with the woman a year. Men who worked for him knew about it and lied for him. During the funeral, the other woman, sobbing loudly, huddled in the back row dressed in black. For Suzanne, shame and anger erased the Carlo she'd known, someone who took pride in his work, never questioned her spending on steak or shoes or gasoline, and sheltered them in a house better than anything she'd ever dreamed of as a girl.

Next, Osterman calls the resident at 1722 Filbert, four doors down from Suzanne, who was awakened at 2 a.m. by a stranger knocking on his door. The stranger asked him to call a cab and waited on the front steps for it to arrive. The next morning, the homeowner found a sterling silver spoon beneath a camellia bush. It was one of two dozen pieces missing from a set of Reggie's flatware. The neighbor completes his testimony with the dramatic finger-pointing moment, identifying Thurston at the defense table.

The prosecutor is about to call his final witnesses when Haag slips into the seat beside her.

"How's it going?" he whispers. He's finished with court appearances for the day, and his tie is loosened.

"No bloody clothes, no weapon, no witnesses."

"Doesn't look good for old Stan." Haag smacks his lips, relishing the possibility the district attorney's office will endure a rare defeat.

A Bakersfield Rancho cleaning woman identifies a pair of white leather tennis shoes as ones she fished out of Thurston's wastebasket the morning he checked out.

"What a dumbass," Suzanne mutters.

"Murder doesn't require a doctorate."

Planning on giving the shoes to her grandson, the cleaning woman hid them in her lunch sack and carried them home. Two days later, she called police, and detectives confiscated them from the sixteen-year-old. The evidence tech confirms the tread on the shoes matches the bloody footprint on the linoleum near Reggie's body.

Osterman rests his case. The syrupy slowness of a Friday afternoon has spread over the courtroom. It's warm and stuffy; one juror's chin rests on his chest. Because Cole will begin the defense case on Monday, Simic dismisses the panel for the weekend. When the twelve jurors and two alternates have filed out, the judge rocks back in his chair.

"All right, Mr. Cole. You have some issues?"

Thurston clasps his soft hands on the defense table.

"It's concerning our witness list, Your Honor. It's our contention that the two boys who stole the victim's car following the murder were at the party that night. They've been offered immunity from the prosecution for their testimony, but the offer has been declined."

Suzanne twists a strand of hair until her scalp hurts. She rocks a little in her seat. Danny must know the older men who attended the party, but he's kept his lips locked. Immunity would protect him from criminal charges, but not revenge. Whoever the men are, they will lose their gold-plated standing in red-neck Bakersfield if they're identified.

Despite Haag's warning months ago not to press further, she wants their names.

"The two boys are potential witnesses," Cole says. "Their testimony may very well exonerate my client."

"Their lawyers have already said the boys will cite the Fifth." Simic swivels in his chair while everyone waits uneasily. "Am I correct, Mr. Haag?"

Haag scrambles to his feet and tightens his tie. "Concerning Mr. Ricci, that's true, Your Honor. And for Mr. Goulet also, I believe." Haag has worked this out with Reno's lawyer already.

Osterman takes a sheaf of papers from Barton, who sits beside him at the prosecution table. "May I speak to this, Your Honor?" He pushes himself slowly to his feet.

"Go ahead."

"We object to Mr. Cole's calling these boys as witnesses. Intensive investigation has failed to turn up any evidence these two youths were involved in death of Mr. Roman, or were even present at the decedent's home that night."

"The kids are friends," Cole says. "Reno Goulet was there earlier in the evening, and the movements of Danny Ricci, a close companion of the deceased, are unaccounted for. Jurors should hear it first-hand if the boys are unwilling to testify."

The judge glances at Osterman out of the corner of his eye, and the prosecutor gives a slight shake of his head.

"Objection sustained," he says.

Cole's shoulders slump. He hoped to create a suspicion in the minds of jurors that Reno, Danny, or one of the other guests murdered Reggie. Instead, Osterman prevailed.

Haag pats her shoulder as he leaves, but Suzanne barely feels it. Her eyes are dry and achy as she tries to unravel tangled thoughts. Osterman's case is weak. Why hasn't he tracked down the pair of unidentified adults who also attended the party, instead of betting everything on his meager facts?

She remembers the way Osterman bailed out of Danny's juvenile court hearing as soon as Vinson waved a pinkie.

———

On Monday, Cole presents the barest skeleton of a defense, calling Thurston's pastor and a professor at San Diego State where the young man works as a lab assistant. His closing argument Monday afternoon hammers the weaknesses in the prosecution's case. The jury Tuesday returns a verdict after three hours of deliberations.

Thurston is guilty of receiving stolen property, but not guilty of murder.

Outside Courtroom Five, jurors drift away, and the two lawyers stand well apart as they wait for separate elevators. The hall empties as she waits in the pay phone booth, on hold for Haag.

"It's nice to see Osterman get his ass handed to him," Haag says after he learns the verdict.

"What happens now?"

"Thurston does a couple of years, with time reduced for good behavior. Other than that, not a thing. The case has been put to bed."

She hears footsteps echoing on the stone floor and peers out of the phone booth. The hall is empty, but the door to the stairwell clicks shut.

On her way home, Suzanne stops at the grocery store. Danny will be out of High Endeavor tomorrow, and she's buying the ingredients for his favorite meal: Southern fried chicken, mashed potatoes with gravy, and steamed corn, food her Okie grandmother taught her to cook. Standing in the slow-moving line at checkout, she inches the cart forward.

With Danny back, her days will be jam-packed, ferrying him to art classes and his probation officer, nagging him about his summer school homework. Not only will she be busy with Danny, but she must recruit more clients to pay the remainder of Haag's fee. It's tempting to ignore the existence of The Club.

And after all, the legal system has limped to a conclusion. Thurston probably killed him, but not every case ends like a Perry Mason television script. His sentencing in three weeks will be a four-inch story in the *News-Daily*. Reggie's sister will sell the house, and a new owner will move in, redecorate, and change the landscaping as if Reggie never existed.

She remembers the door in the courthouse hallway wheezing closed. Someone had emerged from the cloistered hallway behind the judge's chambers and taken the stairs. Two unknown men at the party. Hidden collusion upsetting the sentence on Danny's auto theft charge. Her son's silence. A signal between Osterman and Simic. A secret visit to the judge.

Her body feels as if she might drift up, powerless to anchor herself. She's reminded of the gas that killed her father. It, too, had been elusive—silent, unseen, impossible to grasp. The explosion blew the house off its foundation and ruptured the blood vessels in his brain.

15

Like a scandal-seeking neighbor, Suzanne peers from behind the curtain to catch a glimpse of Maude setting out on her morning walk. Brushing toast crumbs from the corners of her mouth, Suzanne hurries out of the house and says hello.

Maude shoots her a startled look from under the brim of a floppy straw hat. "I don't often see you at this hour, Suzanne."

"I need to stretch my legs before I sit down at the typewriter." Suzanne stoops to pet Maude's pair of white toy poodles, which jump around the old woman's feet like popcorn.

"Jane is a little snappish this morning. I think she has arthritis." Maude was a first grade teacher before she married her late husband, and she's named the dogs Jane and Dick.

Suzanne searches for a way to start the conversation. "Can you give her Bufferin?" she asks. "My grandmother had arthritis, and she always took Bufferin."

"I have a prescription from the veterinarian," Maude says, the corner of her mouth twitching.

This is not starting out well.

They pass Reggie's, where the For Sale sign has a Sold placard splayed across it.

"I think I'll make a pineapple upside down cake for the new people when they move in," Maude says. "The husband is the manager of the Kern River Bank. Very nice people."

In contrast to the low-life Riccis, Suzanne supposes.

Maude's late husband, Roscoe Hedges, was county superintendent of schools and a bigwig in county Republican politics in his time.

In the two weeks since Danny's return home from High Endeavor, she's noticed the Filbert Street residents are distancing them. It's as though families she's known for years don't want their children to be infected with whatever juvenile-delinquent disease infected Danny.

"I haven't seen you since the trial," Suzanne says.

"A terrible miscarriage of justice." Maude tosses treats from her pocket to the dogs. "That vile man should have been convicted of murder. I don't know what the jurors were thinking."

"It *was* surprising," Suzanne says. Especially that the DA didn't call Reno and Danny to testify.

They stroll south on Filbert toward Wilson Park. Sun has burned off the morning coolness, and Suzanne feels the hot sidewalk through the soles of her flip-flops. She tries to psych herself up for the real reason she's intercepted Maude at this early hour.

"Poor Reggie. A nice man, even if he was . . ." Maude rocks her hand back and forth.

They walk in silence for a block. "How's Danny?" Maude asks.

"He's going to summer school and taking an art class." Danny spends most of his free time with Grace, playing eight-tracks in his bedroom or drawing on his sketch pad.

Since Danny's return, Suzanne's been obsessing about the men in The Club, imagines them driving their cars with smooth leather seats and no engine knocks, brow-beating their overworked employees, drinking vintage wine and eating steak dinners, then sneaking away in the dark to coerce defenseless boys.

A gust of laughter floats past her and Maude as they walk the path along Wilson Park. Three weed-smoking college-age boys perch atop a picnic table, convulsed by their stoner wit. Maude steadfastly ignores them, chatting about holes the dogs have dug in the backyard and the Sterling Silver rose she planted at her husband's grave on Memorial Day.

When they pass the toilets near the playground, Suzanne notices two cars in the parking lot. A man stands near the door smoking a cigarette. He cups his hand over his face, as if relighting. After they pass, Suzanne looks back over her shoulder. A kid's bicycle with banana seat and wide handlebars leans against the restroom's rear wall.

Before, such small details would have slid past her unnoticed. Now that she's wised up, she sees, not an idle smoker, but a lookout watching for police while a second man is inside having sex with a boy. A magma of anger swells inside her, burning her throat and drying her saliva. The bike is a similar model to Danny's, which sits in the garage with two flat tires.

"Wait for me, Maude."

She strides across the damp grass to where the lookout stands, his cigarette's menthol scent strong in the morning air. "Excuse me, don't I know you?"

The man is tall and thin, dressed for the office. His bow tie bobs as he swallows. "I've never seen you before."

"I work for the *News-Daily*, and I'm sure I've seen you at a City Council meeting," she says, raising her voice.

"I just stopped for a piss and a smoke." His face is pasty white as his heel grinds out the cigarette. He scurries to his car in an awkward, pigeon-toed stride.

The bathroom's interior smells of Lysol and urine. An Hispanic boy about thirteen stands at the sink, hands under the faucet. In the opening beneath the stall door, Suzanne catches a glimpse of pants cuffs and a pair of polished black oxfords.

"Get out of here," Suzanne tells the boy. He hesitates, eyes darting between the stall and her angry face, then turns and runs. His wet hands leave drops on the gritty floor.

A low voice slithers from behind the stall door. "Go away, you fucking bitch, before you get hurt."

There is a metallic click. She imagines a gun or a knife. Even more than the fear, it's the thought of lying wounded or dead on the filthy, piss-stained concrete that makes her back carefully away. Outside, the sun nearly blinds her.

"What in heaven's name was that about?" Maude asks.

Suzanne gathers her resolve, struggling against the fear that she'll say something wrong, that Maude will say no because Suzanne is the poor, potty-mouthed kid from Taft whose father blew himself up.

Danny needs her, she reminds herself, and feels a flow of energy.

"Maude, I read you were appointed to the county grand jury last week."

Maude sighs. "We were sworn in Tuesday. I'm really too old, but I think I was selected because I'm Roscoe's widow. He served two terms."

"I know something the grand jury needs to investigate."

"Oh, dear." Maude gathers the dogs close to her feet and looks wide-eyed at Suzanne. "We're not up and running yet. Our organizational meeting is in ten days."

"This could be your first case. It's something so bad, it needs an organization like the grand jury to stop it."

Maude touches Suzanne's arm. "What's going on, Honey?"

"It's about Reggie," she says, searching for where to begin. "Reggie and his friends."

Dry, spiky seed pods from the sycamore trees crunch under their feet. Suzanne tells her about Reggie, about his parties, about Danny and other boys snared by the district attorney's office and courts. About boys being coerced into sexual relationships. "They were weak boys, vulnerable boys, fatherless boys," she says.

"How can you say such terrible things about people I know, Suzanne? Judge Simic's wife, Sylvia, is in my bridge club. And I knew Judge Peña's mother when I taught at Lincoln Elementary."

She struggles to keep her temper. "Men in high places are committing crimes against vulnerable kids, but no one's being punished. It's the grand jury's sworn duty to investigate abuse of power."

"I'd be embarrassed to even bring it up such terrible things," Maude says. "What will people say?"

"Grand jury investigations are secret. And I assure you, this is true. You taught two generations of kids. You love them, and I know you want them safe."

"And you're saying Danny is one of these boys?"

"Yes."

"I don't mean to sound judgmental, Suzanne, but several times I've seen him climbing out the window. He's gotten wild since poor Carlo died. Isn't this Danny's fault?"

Suzanne tries to stay focused. She'll deal with the implication that she's a bad mother at night, when her guilt dances in the moonlight.

"The boys aren't perfect. They've got the flaws that boys this age have. But that doesn't give adults the license to coerce and abuse them."

"Young people today have sex all the time," Maude says. "At least that's what I read in the magazines and hear on TV. What are these boys doing that's any different?"

"Adults are ensnaring and forcing them."

"That's what you say, but maybe the boys and adults are in love with each other. My mother ran away and married my father when she was fourteen and he was twenty-three. They were married for forty-six years."

Suzanne feels anger rising and twisting, threatening to send her to her knees. It takes all her will to speak calmly. "These young people are twelve and thirteen, and their abusers are in their forties."

"Well, that's not good," Maude says.

"And tell me, did your father coerce or rape your mother?"

Maude looks shocked. "Of course not."

"Sex with children is illegal. These men, they're educated, some of them in law enforcement." Her throat is scratchy with repressed rage, and she can barely get the words out. "They should be punished, not protected, hiding behind their degrees and good jobs."

A helicopter beats the air as it passes overhead. She and Maude complete their circuit of the park and return to Filbert Street in silence. It's after eight, and the automated whirr of air conditioners begins, pumping cool air into houses closed against the heat.

"Danny's not a bad boy," Maude stoops to pet the dogs. "All right. Give me a letter to the jury, saying the things you've told me, and I'll submit it at our first meeting."

PART TWO

16

JUNE 1978

Pete and Grace Stannard snake their way through the line in front of the arena for tonight's Haggard concert, past the scent of booze and weed in the stifling air. There is defiance here, Pete thinks, a surly confidence that country music matters even when Springsteen, Seger, and Stewart are at the top of the charts. These are Merle's people, and Bakersfield is his town.

Pete touches Grace's back, guiding her toward the stage door. His daughter's body vibrates like a fiddle string. He waves his two VIP tickets at a doorman, who has an aggressive belly and wears eelskin boots. The man frowns at the tickets before he admits the two of them into a rear hallway.

"Can we go to the dressing rooms?" Grace asks the doorman. "My mom is Janis Jonas."

Pete swallows to rid his mouth of an unpleasant taste. Janet has dropped her real name. Now she's Janis. Since she ran away to join Haggard's band four months ago, she's donned her stage persona like a tight-fitting dress.

"Only band and staff before the show," says the belly-and-boots guy.

They descend a stairway and find their seats in the second row, so close they have to tip their heads to see the stage.

Grace squirms in the seat next to him. Janis had telephoned six weeks ago to tell Grace she'd be playing Bakersfield with the band and was sending them premium tickets. Their fifteen-minute conversation was the longest Grace had spoken to her mother since she walked out. After the call, Grace alternated between vomiting her dinner and dancing on her toes to a private beat.

Pete wants to climb onstage and howl. He's got his job as a fire captain, a daughter, but no wife, only a picture of her with the band in *People*. He can tell that Grace hopes Janis is coming home; her skin is flushed, and her blue eyes dart as though they're about to jump out of their sockets.

But *he's* got no illusions. Janis has an empty space inside that's temporarily filled when she stands at the mic and listens to applause. He should have noticed years ago when he first met her at the firefighters' union picnic. Entertainment was a country-and-western band, and the singer was Janis—blonde hair, full lips, and perfect breasts. He didn't take his eyes off her, and when darkness settled around them, he sidled up and asked her out for a drink.

It was one of those inexplicable miscalculations that in his profession can cost your life. They spent every free moment of the next month together, mostly fucking, and on day thirty-one, they drove to Vegas in his '63 Mustang and got married. Grace's unplanned birth didn't deflect Janis; on weekends she sang and played guitar at local clubs where wire around the stage protected the musicians from flying longnecks. She and Pete had been married fifteen years when she took off. Without her, he struggles to keep everything rolling: his job—twenty-four on, forty-eight off—the house, and Grace. He's hired Mrs. Messina, a fierce Sicilian widow, to stay with Grace when he's on shift.

Noise from the crowd surrounds them like an envelope. The Texas Outlaws, the opening band, prances onstage. The audience applauds politely but talks and nips from flat liquor bottles during the set.

Once the Outlaws are finished, Grace sits frozen beside him while audio crew rearranges the sound system. The Strangers enter, all but Haggard. Pete is imprisoned in a soundless bubble as he watches Janis take her place on a riser at the back of the stage. Her rhinestone-studded boots wink in the spotlights, hips swivel in the tight leather skirt, and hair puffs like cotton candy.

"And now, MCA records presents the most beloved country artist in the USA, a star in the firmament of country music, and a true son of Bakersfield, Merrrrle Haggard!" Pete doesn't hear the cheering, applause, or thunder of boot heels on the floor. The band launches into *Okie from Muskogee,* a tribute to the Bakersfield crowd of Dust Bowl descendents. On the third number, Janis comes forward to sing with Merle. Her husky voice blends with his, and she's transformed from the girl he watched at the picnic ground. Tonight, she *is* Janis Jonas.

Pete glances at Grace. Light glows from somewhere within and warms her skin. Her eyes are darker, bluer than usual, and her mouth hangs carelessly open.

Over the next two hours, the band rolls out the Haggard standards. Pete's shoulder touches his daughter's, and he feels Grace's body mirroring her mother's, as if she still floats in amniotic fluid. Before the encore applause dies down, Grace springs from her seat and races backstage, leaving Pete to elbow his way through the crowd. A security guard scrutinizes his passes before waving him through.

When he catches up, Grace is peering into the dressing room.

"Baby! What did you think?" Janis' puffy wig sits on the dressing table; her hair is loose around her shoulders. Against the dented walls and grimy floor, she is incandescent with triumph.

Grace takes careful steps as if she's afraid to take up too much space. "You were fantastic, Mom. Just as good as I remember."

"I'm nothing like I used to be. My coach says my voice has a whole new range and depth."

"I really noticed that," Grace says quickly.

"You've grown, Gracie. Changed."

"No, I'm not." She sounds terrified. "I'm just the same."

Janis clears a space among the dressing table's litter. "Sit here while I finish taking off my makeup. You're taller. Tits are bigger."

Grace slides onto the dressing table, legs dangling. "Maybe a little."

"Hey, Pete." Janis' voice is muffled as she peels off a set of artificial eyelashes. She lays them carefully in a little case that he remembers seeing on the bathroom counter at home.

"Hey, Janis." Anger and hurt from all these months squeeze his chest like a heart attack about to happen. He rubs his sternum.

"I missed you guys," she says.

"Yeah, your letters, calls, and visits were almost more than we could handle."

She gazes directly at him, a look that he realizes is the first honest one she's ever given him—or perhaps ever would. She's never coming back. The heat in the small room and the familiar scent of her *Charlie* perfume makes him dizzy. He feels a shift in the alignment of his bones.

"Why don't you two come on tour with me for a couple of weeks? We play Nashville on the twenty-fifth."

Blood pulses in his temples; his mind clears as it does sometimes before he plunges into a burning building. He's got to protect Grace. "I can't get off work. My backup's on a month's vacation."

"But I could go." The happiness on Grace's face is blinding.

"You start school next week."

"Come on, Dad. Please. I could get the assignments and mail them to the teachers."

"Not your first two weeks in high school. There's registration. Orientation."

"Lots of people start late. Migrant kids do it all the time."

"And they learn zip. No."

"I hate you." Grace starts to cry.

It's nearly 1 a.m. and he feels helpless, weary to the soles of his feet. Searching for a way to close this thing out, he turns to Janis. "Can we maybe take you out for coffee and some pie?"

Her gaze is almost sympathetic. "That works. It'll be another hour before the roadies are done."

They walk through the parking lot to his Cutlass. Janis slides into the passenger seat, and Grace gets in back like she used to. Pete stares out the windshield at the moon's strange red tint. It's the same moon, same Bakersfield sky, same woman sitting beside him, but everything's different.

At the all-night truck stop, Grace scoots closer and closer to Janis on the banquette until Janis says, "Sweetie, I don't want you in my lap."

Grace inches back.

"Hag is writing songs for a new album. It has a couple of solo bits for me. We'll begin recording after the tour."

Her eyelids are dark and her face slack with fatigue, but Pete hears a note of pride. This is her passion. Her life. How did the two of them stay together so long?

While they wait for two coffees, a Coke, and a piece of apple pie for Pete, Janis rests her head against the plastic back of the booth and falls asleep. Her mouth sags. Grace studies her with undisguised longing.

When the waitress delivers the order, Grace says, "Mom, come on. Your coffee's here." She shakes Janis' arm and pushes the cup close.

Janis awakens with a little convulsion, spilling coffee onto the front of her white shorts.

"Oh, God, I'm really, really sorry." Grace bites her lip.

Janis blots the brown stain with a napkin. "Lucky for my sex life it wasn't too hot."

Grace covers her mouth with her hand.

Poor kid, he thinks, my poor dumb girl.

17

The doorbell wakes Pete from a short dream-filled sleep. He scrambles up and reaches for his turnout clothes, then realizes he's at home. Most of the night, he and his crew struggled to extinguish a two-alarm in a restaurant kitchen. When he dragged in at seven, he let Mrs. Messina go home and ate a bowl of chocolate ice cream before he fell into bed.

His watch shows 10:30. The bell is still ringing. Where's Grace? Pete snatches a pair of cutoff jeans from the chair and hops into them. When he opens the front door he feels the reflected heat from the sidewalk. A tall, skinny kid mounting his bicycle turns when he hears the latch click.

"Is Grace here?" A sketch pad is stuffed into the pocket of his rucksack. A fishing tackle box similar to the one Grace uses for her art supplies hangs from the bike's handlebars.

Pete combs his fingers through his hair, which still smells of smoke. He's disoriented, as though for a few seconds he's in the alley behind the restaurant.

"You're the kid from Gracie's class?"

"Danny Ricci." The kid dismounts from his bike. "We were going to do some sketching."

"Actually I'm not sure where she is. I was asleep."

"Sorry."

Pete opens the screen. "Come on in. I'll see if I can find her."

Danny props his bike against the porch step. Before coming inside, he rubs his sweaty forehead with the hem of his shirt and wipes his tennis shoes on the mat.

Pete leaves him in the living room and checks Grace's bed, but it's empty. He phones Mrs. Messina. The housekeeper says she left without disturbing Grace. Jade Sandoval, Grace's school friend, doesn't answer. When he returns to the living room, Danny is studying one of Grace's still lifes that's propped against a candlestick on the mantel. It's an oil painting of a raw steak, three eggs, and a bunch of green chard.

"I remember when we did this in class. Hers turned out great. Mine sucked," Danny says.

"I don't care much for it." Looking at the painting only makes Pete more uneasy. Green vegetable leaves and white eggshells seem so pure against a raw, glistening steak. How did a girl Grace's age gain the life experience to portray the violence of everyday things? He sees it often at work: bacon grease catches fire, a penny sticks in a child's throat, a cherry bomb blows the hand off some damn fool.

He shoves his hands in his pockets. "I don't know where she went, and she didn't leave a note. Are you sure you had the time right?" He keeps his voice low to hide his alarm. That's how he works with his crew, as much to calm himself as to reassure them.

"I talked to her last night. She said 10:30."

"You go to Highland with Grace?" Pete asks.

"No, Bakersfield High." Danny looks amused at the interrogation.

"You met at Will's classes?"

"A couple years ago."

"Sit down," Pete says. "Let's have a Coke."

The boy slowly lowers himself into an easy chair.

Pete brings two cans from the refrigerator There are twin sounds as the tabs pop. "How come Grace never talks about you?"

"She's speechless in the presence of my greatness."

Pete laughs, and some of his tension eases. "Okay, tell me this: did you two hang out much this spring?"

Danny hesitates. "Not all that much. I was gone for awhile. Just got back."

"Gone? Gone where?"

"I was . . . sick for a few months. Out of school."

They sip in silence. Danny tilts his head to the side, studying Grace's painting. "I like the frame."

"Will said this one with the gold flecks would set it off."

"I'm working on some new stuff, now that I'm…well again."

"Not meat and eggs, I hope."

Danny smiles. "Pen and inks, kind of Japanese. Will says they're good."

"I wish Grace would start again." Pete sets his drink on the coffee table. The carbonation burns his stomach. Should he take a chance? From the way the kid holds his elbows and shifts his hips, he's probably gay. Danny reminds Pete of his brother, Hugh, who lives in San Francisco with his young lover. This kid seems nice enough, and at least he's not going to try to get into Grace's pants.

"I guess she told you about her mother," Pete says.

Danny nods. "That she's joined The Strangers."

"Have you noticed anything different about Grace since then?"

"No, sir."

"About her friends at Highlands? Know any of them?"

"Not really." Danny hefts his backpack onto his shoulder. "I gotta go. Thanks for the Coke." The screen door slams. He wheels his bike toward the street.

Pete realizes he's fucking this up royally. From the porch, he says, "She's good, don't you think? Real talent."

"Better than me."

Pete follows him down the walk and says pleadingly, "Is there anything you can tell me that might help? Her grades last semester were all D's and F's, and she's grounded."

Danny shakes his head and wheels off.

Pete gathers the two soda cans from the living room, empties them into the kitchen sink, then stomps them flat. While he stands at the counter, the smell of rotting garbage drifts up from the overflowing wastebasket, which Grace is assigned to empty every morning. He carries it outside and dumps it in the trash can, then cleans it with a gush of water from the backyard hose.

The smell is still on his hands. He swipes them against his shorts. How satisfying it would be to paddle her behind, like he did when she was little. A mixture of worry and anger grips him. Her last semester at school was bad enough, but since the Haggard concert, she's as remote as a dark star.

The sliding screen is open, and he's about to step inside the house when he catches a movement in the corner of his eye.

Grace is lying on the patio lounge. It's dark under the awning, shaded by azalea bushes and a huge elm tree. Flashes of light shoot through the branches, and he has a sudden memory of a fire in a dental surgeon's office, where canisters of nitrous oxide threatened to explode. Strange thing is, the other time, he wasn't afraid.

She utters a low, broken cry.

"Grace? What's going on? Where have you been?"

She lies on her side, facing away from him, with arms wrapped around her knees and drawn tightly to her chest. Her shoes lie on the patio, and the soles of her feet are dirty.

"Go away." She screws herself up tighter.

"Look at me!" He tugs her around to face him. Against the coarse fabric of the cushions, her smooth arms are covered from shoulder to wrist with bruises, dark as rot on a white peach.

A murderous wave of fury closes his throat. He struggles to breathe. Whoever did this, he'll kill the bastard. His fingers want someone's neck, and without thinking, he squeezes her bicep.

She screams and wrenches away.

Pete captures her face and holds it carefully between his hands. "Who did this?" His voice breaks.

"No one, Daddy." Her pupils are dilated, inky in the dimness.

A deep breath steadies him. In the kitchen, he dumps two trays of ice cubes into the sink. Ice sticks to his skin, but he tears it off without noticing and bundles the cubes into towels. When he presses them against her arms, she groans.

"Tell me who it was."

She twists her head from side to side. "Nobody, nobody did it. I fell down the stairs at Jade's house."

"Bullshit. Someone grabbed you and held you. Were you raped?"

Her tears drip onto his hands. "I'm telling you the truth, Daddy."

"I've seen thousands of injures. No way this was a fall."

"Call Jade. Ask her, she'll tell you."

"The little slut who only comes to the house when I'm gone?" He scrambles to his feet. Grace falls back onto the cushions.

"What time did you sneak away?" he says.

"About eleven-thirty. Jade and I wanted to hang out. Nothing bad." She shivers at the touch of the ice packs.

His fingers tighten into fists with the urge to shake her. Her wide eyes remind him of Janis, cornered but determined. He never hit Janis, but there were times when he wanted to.

"I'll call her, but don't move until I come back."

Jade's number is scribbled on a scrap of paper thumbtacked to the bulletin board above the telephone.

He dials non-stop until at last someone answers. "Jade?" The telephone crackles in the silence, as if she's straining to identify his voice. "Pete Stannard, Grace's father. I've just seen her. She's a mess. Bruises all over her arms. She says you can confirm what happened."

"What does Grace say?"

Pete hasn't met the girl, but Grace has talked to her on the phone for hours since the disastrous Haggard concert.

"You've got thirty seconds to tell me, or I'm going to have a heart-to-heart with your parents."

"They don't care." Her brash tone is more tentative.

"Twenty seconds."

"All right, don't get hemorrhoids," she says. "We were fooling around in the kitchen dancing to the BeeGees. The floor was a little slippery, you know, from some lard. Grace backs up, backs up, doing this funny step, and I yell at her to stop, but she doesn't.

Bump, bump, bump, she falls down the basement stairs, all the way to the bottom."

There's a space deep in his chest where he knows she's lying. Nobody gets bruises like Grace's from falling down a flight of stairs. It's the ribs, the thighs, and the calves that absorb the impact, not arms and wrists. But he also wants to believe it was an accident. He aches to have things simple: Grace is going through a rough period, but she'll pull out of it. She's going to laugh again, pick up her art supplies, and hang out with the Ricci kid. Eventually, she'll stop hating him because he's here and Janis isn't.

He closes his mind, like switching off the TV, to terrifying images of large, meaty hands grabbing her and thick fingers with dirty nails digging into her skin. Maybe Grace *did* try to break her fall by absorbing the shock with her arms. It isn't impossible.

"So what happened then? How'd she get home?"

"I drove her."

"Wait a minute, you aren't old enough."

She laughs. "My mother was sick, Mr. Stannard. Would you rather I leave her at my house, than take the keys and drive a mile?"

"What about the drugs?"

"We didn't drop anything."

"Her pupils are dilated," Pete says.

"I wouldn't know about that."

He reminds himself to check the medicine cabinet for the codeine-laced cough syrup. "Don't ever contact Grace again."

"Whatever you say, Mr. Stannard."

He returns to the patio. She's thrown the ice bags on the floor and buried her face in the cushion.

18

"What's the matter?" Pete asks.

Danny wipes his palms on his jeans. "I'm a little nervous."

"It's not hard. Let the clutch out slowly, and at the same time press the accelerator."

Grace props her elbows on the seat back and leans over Danny's shoulder. "Don't worry. Daddy will only kill you if you wreck his big, bad Cutlass 442."

In the two months since Pete discovered Grace terribly bruised, the purple-blue marks have disappeared. He's stopped obsessing over each phone call and forcing her to account for every minute. Nearly all Grace's free time now is spent with Danny. He's a likeable kid. The two of them sketch, listen to the new Strangers album with Janis on it, cruise the Valley Mall. Saturdays, they attend art classes at Sampson Brothers.

Now it's late August, a week before Grace and Danny start back to school. They're parked in the empty lot at Centennial Methodist Church, where Pete and Grace attend Sundays when he's off work. Because Danny turned fifteen in June, Pete has offered to give him enough instruction to get his learner's permit.

"Shifting gears is a matter of coordination, like playing the guitar," Pete says.

"Last time I tried to drive, I didn't do very well." Danny's face is pale and his forehead damp.

"Relax. You didn't have me as your driving instructor."

Danny tries again. The car lurches forward, tires squeal, and the engine stalls. Pete rubs the side of his face to keep from flinching. This is the beautiful car he washes and polishes himself. "Make sure you push the clutch all the way in," he says.

This time Danny shifts smoothly and guides it in a loop around the blacktop. Pete unclenches his fingers from the door handle long enough to switch on the air conditioning. The afternoon sun has turned coppery red as it struggles through the smog.

He props his arm on the sill. "Okay, put it in reverse and look over your right shoulder. Go slow. Back right, now left."

Grace tugs his sleeve. "When do I get a turn?"

"I didn't know women were legally allowed to drive in California—ouch!" He bats at the hand that snakes from behind to pull his ear.

"Come on, when are you going to let me?" Her breath warms the side of his face.

"Danny's older. He's eligible for a permit."

"Seventy-two days. That's how much older he is. Practically nothing. The time it takes a potato to grow, or something."

Pete wishes she would stay young, his little girl who dressed her Barbie dolls and wobbled on her mother's high heels. Grace's ankles have lost their baby fat, and she totters on her platform sandals like a hooker. The way her breasts fill out her halter top reminds Pete of Janis. This womanly Grace frightens him. Whatever happened back in June—he tries not to think about what actually occurred—he feels completely inadequate to parent her. How is he to cope with PMS, sexuality, and boys hanging around, swimming in testosterone?

He sighs. "All right. Danny, pull up into one of the parking slots."

The kids trade places. Grace slides the seat forward and adjusts the mirror. Her palms measure the wheel as if she's doing a pre-race check at the Indy 500. Pete squirms.

"I can't believe it. I'm actually in the driver's seat."

"I was afraid of this. Give you some horsepower, and you'll think you run the world."

Grace shoots him a sly look. She seems determined to convince him she's recovered, teasing him and joking with Danny, but he senses a dark knot inside her that hasn't dissolved.

She shifts into first, accelerates, and downshifts to second. As the end of the parking lot approaches, she rotates the wheel to the left, at the same time upshifting to third. Pete's rib cage expands in pride.

"Jeez, is this fair?" Danny says. "I drive like a girl, and she drives like a guy."

"Poor, poor baby," Grace says.

Pete touches her shoulder. "Not bad."

"I'm an effing Mario Andretti." She flicks him a look.

"Not in my car, and don't say effing. Now put it in reverse."

Pete recalls his first experience behind the wheel. His father, a commercial fisherman out of Morro Bay, had been out in the boat all day. Usually, Pete's brother, Hugh, trucked the catch overnight to the wholesale market in LA, but Hugh was sick. So his dad gave Pete the briefest of instruction on operating the box truck, then fell asleep with his head cocked against the passenger window. Pete drove south on Highway 101, through Arroyo Grande, Buellton, and Santa Barbara, the truck vibrating under his thighs, the balky gears making him tremble and sweat. He was fourteen.

Grace backs up. Pete notices the cuticle around her nails is raw and torn. He doesn't remember seeing this before. As she shifts into first, a police black-and-white turns into the lot.

"Shit." Pete glances over his shoulder. Danny has slouched down in back until he's barely visible.

"Turn off the engine and open the window, Grace."

A female officer climbs out. Her streaked blonde hair is pulled into a French braid, her weapon strapped around a thick waist. She props her hand on the door. "May I see your license, Miss?"

Pete leans across Grace. The officer's name tag over her breast pocket reads L.L. Theuss. "I'm her father. We were just practicing her driving skills."

She parks her sunglasses on top of her head. "Does this juvenile have a permit?"

"She's just a few weeks from the proper age," Pete says.

"Almost isn't good enough."

"She's not on the street. It's a vacant parking lot on private property."

"But without permission," Officer Theuss says.

"That's correct, Ma'am."

She taps the cover of her leather citation book with a ballpoint pen. "Aren't you a captain at BFD 14?"

"That's me, Pete Stannard. This is my daughter, Grace."

Without ink touching the page, her citation book closes. "Sorry, to bother you, Captain. We had a call from a neighbor that teenaged kids were spinning donuts in the church parking lot."

Pete is about to reply when Theuss peers into the back seat.

"Danny, is that you?"

"Yes, Ma'am."

In the rear view mirror Pete sees the white moon of Danny's face.

"You and this girl are pals?" asks Theuss.

"Yeah."

"How is everything going?" she says.

"Really great."

"Say hello to your mother." She slaps the window sill with her palm.

After the black-and-white pulls away, the car smells of perspiration. Pete walks around the hood and sends Grace to the passenger seat. An uneasy pulse beats behind his eyes. "How is it you know this cop?" he asks Danny.

"She and my mom are friends from when my dad died."

Pete gets behind the wheel and flicks the radio to a rock-and-roll station. "Romano's Pizza is calling us."

———

Romano's bakes the best pizza in Bakersfield. It's not quite six o'clock, but the restaurant is nearly full. They commandeer one of the scarred wooden picnic tables that give the place its shabby charm. Grace and Danny, sitting on one side of the table, unite against Pete on the other side, to veto mushrooms.

"Yuck, fungi, growing in your belly, eating your vital organs," Grace says. Pete orders a separate pizza for himself. He'll eat leftovers tomorrow for lunch. A trio tunes up on the small stage, an odd combo for Bakersfield: guitarist, drummer, and flautist.

As they eat, Danny whispers something to Grace, and she laughs, cupping her hand over her mouth to keep food from falling out. Pete separates a strand of cheese from his slice of mushroom pizza. Despite the hassle with the policewoman, he's pleased at how the driving lesson went. Lately, there have been times when every parental move he makes seems ham-fisted, but not today. He wishes he could talk to Janis, but she's on tour, and his messages on her manager's answering machine in Nashville must have filled a tape.

Grace and Danny toss their pizza crusts on the metal pan. He can't help himself; he recites the story about how, as a kid, he ate every scrap, even pizza crusts, to survive the ravages of Hugh and his older sister, Leslie. Grace picks up a crust and offers it to him.

On stage, the flautist begins a solo. The notes seem odd and displaced, as though she is lonely and searching for a melody. Benches scrape. Six people sit down next to them at the long table, three men and three teen boys. The man beside Grace is Galen Franzen.

"Commissioner." Pete nods.

Franzen widens his eyes as if it will help identify him. "Oh, right. Pete Stannard."

The last time Pete had seen Franzen was years ago when the older man was the training director for the PD. The two of them taught an arson seminar together, but Franzen is no longer the trim police science instructor in a flawlessly pressed suit. His body is flabby, his eyes rheumy, and his shirt marked with cigarette burns.

"Sorry to hear about your wife," Pete says.

Tears swim in the old man's eyes. "She was a saint, God bless her."

Pete suddenly is aware that Grace is huddling close to Danny, away from Franzen and the other two newcomers on her side of the table. In a voice as thin as smoke, she excuses herself and scurries to the restroom.

Pete studies the group more closely. A restless, finger-tapping teen with red hair sits next to Franzen. Further on, a pony-tailed man rests his hands on the tabletop. Each finger is tattooed with the image of the bone that lies beneath the skin.

Next to Pete is a slim youth with peroxided hair who reeks of aftershave although his cheeks show no evidence of an adolescent beard. A heavy-set man with wire-rimmed glasses beside him blocks Pete's view of the third boy.

The kid with the bleached hair leans across the table. "Hey, Danny. Long time, ya know."

"You back, Reno?" Danny rattles the ice in his Pepsi glass.

"Just this week."

"Good luck." Danny scoots toward the far end of the table, as though the newcomers smell bad.

"Come to the skateboard park on Saturday. Some of us are getting together."

"Don't think so."

Pete speaks to Franzen, sitting diagonally across from him. "What are you up to these days, Commissioner? Still teaching?"

Franzen is watching the tattooed man, who has handed something to the red-headed kid from a half-closed hand. When Franzen turns back to Pete, one eyelid is twitching. "Dennis and I try to help out Probation with kids coming out of juvenile facilities. Provide some male influence in their lives."

He introduces Pete to Assistant District Attorney Dennis Vinson. Pete is taken aback by the prosecutor's malevolent stare behind his thick glasses. Pete glances over his shoulder to see if someone behind him has incited Vinson's animosity, but the area is empty except for Danny, who has turned his back towards them.

Pete tosses his half-eaten pizza wedge on the pan. "I'm done," he says to Danny. "What's taking Grace so long?"

Vinson lights a Virginia Slim. Haze swirls around them, like air around a smoldering fire.

Grace emerges from the restroom and heads for the door at a half-run. Pete throws a tip on the table and hurries after her. From the corner of his eye, he sees the pony-tailed man stop Danny and whisper in his ear.

Outside, Grace is standing beside the car. In the parking lot's floodlights, sweat shines on her upper lip.

"Grace, what's the matter? Is it those people?"

"They're Jade's friends. I just don't . . . don't want to have anything to do with them."

He has trouble getting the car key in the lock. When it's open, she stumbles into the back seat. The engine is running when Danny jogs across the lot and climbs in. His eyes are wide and unblinking.

"You okay?" Grace asks.

Danny nods. He's quiet on the way to Filbert Street. Suzanne Ricci is out on the lawn in a pair of short shorts and a tube top, chatting with an elderly neighbor. Danny slips out of the car without saying goodbye. On the sidewalk, he stumbles on a piece of broken concrete, recovers his footing, and goes inside.

Suzanne frowns in the direction of the house, then walks over to the car. Pete rolls down the window.

"How's he doing?" she asks.

"Driving instructor probably isn't one of his career options, but he's catching on."

She grins. "You guys want to come in? I've got vanilla, chocolate or marshmallow mint."

As she leans in to say hello to Grace, her shoulder and the round flesh of her upper arm are close to his face. He catches the warm scent of her skin.

It would be nice to spend the evening with this attractive woman. The lighted house looks inviting through the open curtains. He glances at his daughter. She's bent as if her stomach hurts.

Down the block, boys kick a soccer ball back forth; the thump of feet against leather is excessive, unsettling. "Not tonight. Another time, okay?"

Suzanne steps back from the window. Grace climbs in the front seat and pulls one leg under her.

"Fasten your safety belt."

At home, Grace closes herself in her bedroom rather than join him watching television. The telephone rings, but before he can answer, Grace snatches the extension. If he eavesdrops now, she'll hear the click. Actors move on the screen, but he pays no attention.

On the job, he battles fear by being prepared. He's made weight lifting mandatory on every shift. His crew conducts equipment checks and drills every morning. With Grace, he's had no training. He stares at the screen. The narcotic stream of dialogue and hypnotic flashes of light soothe him, and he falls asleep.

When he awakes in the morning, Grace's bed is empty.

19

After Pete drops him off, Danny's feet are so heavy he can't negotiate the stairs. Instead, he sits on the bottom step. Despite the cool breeze from the dining room windows, sweat drips down his back and soaks the waist of his Jockeys.

His mother pounds the IBM, carriage thumping on the return. Her column for the *Tulsa World* has to be in the mail tonight to meet deadline. They never eat in the dining room anymore; her freelance work has sucked up every foot of space.

In the midst of the clutter, perched regally on a stack of papers, is Narcissus, who prowled the yard, mewing ceaselessly, after the murder. Danny adopted the animal, as if giving it a home could make up for what happened.

"Are you packed for the weekend?" she asks, without looking up.

For a moment, a black spot settles in his brain. He can't think what she's talking about.

"The trip to San Francisco, remember?" She props her elbow on the table.

Pain darts across his forehead as memory returns. They're driving to the Bay Area tomorrow for a three-day getaway to visit art galleries and museums. They've been planning it since he got out of High Endeavor.

"Be sure to pack a pair of nice slacks and a dress shirt. I have reservations at the Hayes Street Grill tomorrow night."

When he doesn't answer, she says, "What's wrong?"

"Mom, could I go away to school this fall?"

"Away?"

"Not in Bakersfield. Somewhere else."

"Like Harvard or something?"

"Funny," he says.

"Well, what?" Lines between her eyes deepen.

"To Outward Bound in Colorado, or that hippie place, the Waldorf School in Sacramento."

"Of course not. You're on probation."

"I could be transferred to another county's jurisdiction. Kids from High Endeavor did it."

"No. I'm your mother, and I want you here with me. Besides, I can't afford to send you to a private school."

"How about Palm Springs? It wouldn't you cost anything, because I'd be living with Aunt Luanne and going to public high school."

"She drinks too much since she and Bernie split up. What's the matter with this home? Am I a bad mother?"

"Please, Mom." He feels like a balloon, stretched to bursting.

A red blotch appears on her cheek. "Are you afraid you're going to be harassed at school? If so, I'll get the principal on the phone before you set foot in the door."

"It's not about school. It's just I hate this fucking town. I want to get away, as far as I can, and never see it again."

"Did you have a fight with Grace? Did her father say something?"

"No, no." With more strength than he thought he had, he moves his cheek muscles into a smile. "Things are good with them."

Her eyes drop to the typewriter. "Let me think about it, okay?"

Upstairs in his room, he locks the door, sinks down on the edge of the bed, and buries his face in his hands. He groans, remembering

Jack Stone's low whisper at Romano's. Tell the girl, Stone said, there's a party at Franzen's. We want the two of you there. 11:30.

Danny hasn't attended any of Galen's parties, but at High Endeavor Reno whispered the details: a lavish smorgasbord of liquor and drugs, and sex with poor old Galen. But there is something else he heard, not from Reno but from Grace.

A couple of weeks ago, Danny and Grace had been hanging out in her room, both of them trying on her new lamb's-wool sweater. When he pulled it over his head, the sweater was too short to cover his midriff. Danny mimed trying to cover himself, and she laughed until tears came. It wasn't as if she were sad or anything, but all at once she began crying for real, sobs that doubled her over like stomach cramps.

What exactly happened in June, Grace? he asked. She told him, in a whisper almost like a hiss. She and Jade were the only girls among the kids who went to a party at Galen's. There were plenty of reds, whites, and booze, but instead she took a Quaalude someone offered her. It made her feel relaxed, sexy, and desirable, as if she were the sun, and the planets couldn't help but revolve around her. First, she danced in front of the cameras, and the hot, bright lights didn't bother her. Then someone held her arms with stony fingers while Jade did things to her. When a strange man unzipped his pants and pressed into her, she heaved, screamed, kicked, and bit to free herself. After awhile Kevin had squeezed her arms so tightly she couldn't move.

The scene an hour ago at Romano's plays back to Danny in a warped color palette, like something from *Scream* comics. Stone's face glows acid green and Reno's hair, not white-blond, but blue. The company that shoots porn at Galen's is owned by guys with connections, Stone told him. Danny knows what that means: Galen's connected to police, Vinson to the DA's office, and Whitman to the media.

Danny is nauseated at the thought of going to the party. It's been a relief to hang out with Grace in the last weeks. He can be innocent with her—not that he doesn't think about sex all day and dream about it at night—but they know each other's secrets. They pretend they're virgins. Laugh at themselves. Be goofy and uncool. They dream that someday Bakersfield will be far behind them, and they'll live as poor artists in a tiny apartment in Paris.

Grace won't be the only one expected to perform tonight. After the rape in Whitman's study and his confrontation with the tattooed limo driver, Danny is pretty certain they'll make him do things. Maybe he could hide or be sick. The pizza feels like it's going to come up any minute.

He carries the telephone, black cord trailing behind him, into his closet so his mother won't hear him, curls among the shoes and dust. Dials Grace.

"Oh God, Danny, I was so scared, I hid out in the restroom. What did Stone want?"

"He says to be at Galen's at 11:30. There's a party. He said it would be different than last time."

"No! I'm never going near those people again."

"If you don't, he said he'd send your father the film from last time."

Danny hears small, choked sounds. He's pretty sure she's got a fist in her mouth so Pete won't hear her cry. Finally, she says, "If he does that, no way will Dad let me go on tour with Janis."

"Maybe Stone's bluffing," Danny says.

"And maybe there are fairies and leprechauns."

"It might not be so bad if your dad knows," Danny says. "The tour won't be all that great. You'd be sitting around a lot, while your mom rehearses and stuff."

"Danny, I've got to go on the tour. This is my last chance. If I go another year without seeing Mom, it'll be like, Grace? Grace who?"

From Grace's end, Danny hears Rod Stewart singing about someone loving you as you grow old. His eyes sting, thinking of Grace with no mother to brush her hair or kiss her forehead.

"Your mother's real busy right now. She'll want to see you more often once the tour's over."

"She could get married again and have another baby. Then I'd be nowhere."

"Gracie, you're talking yourself into the party. Don't do it. Stay home."

"But Stone promised it wouldn't be like last time, didn't he?"

"Don't believe him. He's a super bad dude." Above him, clothes brush his head like remnants of scary dreams.

The telephone crackles, and silence coils around him. "If you come, you can protect me," she says.

He pulls a shoe out from under him and throws it through the closet door. "How? Punch them in the face with my powerful right arm? Use a knife or nunchuks? Get real."

"If things start to go bad, you can call . . ."

". . . police, yeah, right."

"Your mom's friend. The officer at the church parking lot."

"I don't know how to get ahold of her. It's not like we're buddies or something."

"Get it from your mom's Rolodex, you donkey."

"Why should I? This is shit-kickin' dumb!"

"Because you love me, that's why. You're the only one in the world that really cares."

"Okay," he says finally. "I'll go over to 24th Street and hitch a ride."

He flops on his much-washed yellow bedspread. It smells of laundry soap, which he associates with his mother. For a week or so after his release from High Endeavor, he spent almost every free minute in his room. He's hung a poster of Mr. Universe, Arnold Schwarzenegger, in a Speedo. How different his life is, now that his mother knows he's gay. The trip to San Francisco is her way of saying, *it's okay.*

But his muscles ache, and he feels sick. His joints creak as he rises from the bed, pulls his running shoes from the closet, and forces his feet into them. It's early, only a little after nine, but sometimes it's hard to catch a ride if it's late. He pushes up the window. His foot's propped on the sill so he can tie his shoe when there's a knock on the bedroom door. Quickly, he steps away from the window.

Suzanne pokes her head in. "Danny? Oh, good, you're not in bed yet."

He turns his head away from her to hide what feels like a smear of guilt on his face.

"I've got another hour's work on the column," she says, "but it's got to be at the post office before the last pickup at eleven."

The floor shifts under Danny's feet.

"I need you to bike over to Bill Murdock's," she says. "He's got a photo of early oil exploration in McKittrick that will dress up the story. By the time you're back, I'll be done and can still make it to the PO on time."

"I don't know," he says.

Her eyes narrow. "What? You've got an engagement?"

"No, no. It's just that I'll be out after curfew. I could get picked up for violating probation."

"It's Friday. Curfew is 11, and you'll be back by 10:45, easy."

"It's really dark out."

"For God's sake, there are street lights. What's the matter with you?"

"All right, I'll go."

When the door closes, and footsteps on the stairs fade, he dials Grace. The phone rings and rings. Two more tries without an answer. Grace must've slipped out early.

Danny can't help it—he's glad his mother's errand gives him an excuse. By the time he gets back, traffic on 24th will be thin. Too late go to the party. He knows he's betrayed Grace, but he warned her.

20

Suzanne waves at Nadine, the *News-Daily's* receptionist. She and Danny arrived home last night after three days in San Francisco, and she needs to talk to Hedges. At this hour of the morning the newsroom is nearly empty. Reporters are out on their beats, covering the county board of supervisors, canvassing the courtrooms, making the rounds at the sheriff's office and police headquarters.

Carl Hedges peers at the computer screen. He was a big shot editor at the *Los Angeles Times* for ten years, but moved to Bakersfield after his father died to be closer to Maude.

"I've got an idea for Friday," Suzanne says.

"Oh, no, I have to replace 'Newsy Notes from Kernville' with a real story?" Hedges asks in a falsetto.

A misfit on the *News-Daily,* Hedges isn't trusted by the higher-ups, who are suspicious of his background on what they regard as a liberal rag. Currently, he edits the paper's loose ends: weekly food section, religion page, community news from outlying areas, and Suzanne's petroleum industry column.

Hedges' hangdog personality usually irritates her, but today she's mellow. The trip's left her feeling like she's opened up a new world for Danny. He was on edge during the drive, chewing his nails, picking at a pimple on his forehead. But once they settled into their hotel and headed for the Asian Art Museum with its collection of ivory netsuke, the deep lines between his eyes smoothed out.

In the Castro District, he bought a copy of *Christopher Street*, a magazine featuring gay writers. They threaded their way through the crowds, past gay art vendors, boutiques selling leather chaps, feather boas, and size thirteen heels. Life there seemed terribly wrong to her, like the aftermath of a flood, where everything familiar had been swept away. From the bars and coffee shops, men spilled onto the sidewalks, drinking, dancing, and flirting. One man whistled at Danny, who suppressed a half-smile.

But at dinner that night, she caught a snapshot of the man he might become. His scanty beard was dark on his chin and upper lip; his eyes shone with a thousand new thoughts. He sketched on the placemat, the napkin, and the cash register receipt. Seeing him so intent, his curly hair flopping across his forehead, allowed something to loosen. Her anxiety, clinging like a leech for years, seemed to ease. Danny was going to be okay. She was going to be okay.

Today she's returning to the grit and grease of the petroleum business. "How about a retrospective piece on the oil well blowout in the Santa Barbara Channel?" she asks Hedges.

"A nine-year retrospective? That's a lame idea; ten years, maybe."

Not hot news, but over the weekend, she hadn't spent a second thinking about work. She's scratching her brain for another idea when she notices Hedges staring past her. Harris Whitman stands in his office doorway.

"Suzanne, I haven't seen you recently." He wears a sport jacket of soft wool that makes her want to stroke it like a dog. His slacks break perfectly over his imported shoes.

Such perfection reinforces her bad decision to wear jeans and flip-flops, reminding her of the years when she was the too-tall girl with bony elbows whose old man was blown to bits. "I come in every week when I turn in my column."

"Oh, right," Whitman says vaguely. "What's new with the oil barons?"

"Still rich and powerful." Does he read his own newspaper?

"Come on in." He slides into a chair behind his desk while Suzanne perches uneasily on the edge of the visitors' chair. The last time she was in his office was four years ago when she pitched the column to him. Scrabbling for money, she'd followed up on Reggie's tip and proposed the idea to Whitman, who read her sample column: a piece on the massive Lakeview Oil gusher of 1910.

He bought it and suggested she write weekly on developments in the oil and gas industries. The small but steady income from the *News-Daily* kept the house out of the bank's hands and served as a base to build her list of clients, including her highest-paying publication, *Oil and Gas Weekly*.

Whitman's glass and aluminum desk holds one small pile of papers stacked beside a Mount Blanc pen. No fingerprints cloud the surface. Is his skin ever oily?

"How are things going for you?" He leans back in his chair, one ankle crossed over the other knee.

She flashes a quick glance at him. Is he unhappy with something she's written? "Great. I've developed some moles in the oil business who call me with tips. Saves time chasing leads."

"I have a column idea for you. Have you heard of Connie Fitzgerald?"

"The oil equipment mogul who developed polymer-enhanced slurry?"

"I think that's it," he says.

"He drives the gold-plated pickup truck?"

"Not quite that fancy, but I'm told it has leather seats and a mahogany dashboard. The story would be on his new invention—a coating that restores worn-out drill bits. He's in the manufacturing phase, I'm told."

"I'll get on it."

"Use my name when you call," He steeples his fingers and touches them to his lips for a second. "Are you and your son managing all right?"

"We're fine." A telephone buzzes in the newsroom, and her fingers twitch with the impulse to answer it.

"That's good. Your boy's in high school now?"

"At Bakersfield High." Maybe he's heard gossip about Danny. The newspaper's editorial stance is very conservative. Could he be morally opposed to gays? Considering the city's homophobia, it's possible he'd drop her column.

He nods. "Not far from my house." He opens his mouth to say something else when a series of telephones buzz, one after another.

From the office, she sees Hedges pressing buttons to put lines on hold. He trots over to Whitman's office and stops in the doorway. "Photog heard on the scanner a body's been found near the Wagon Wheel Cafe on Whitman Highway. Teen girl."

"The missing kid from Highlands High?" Whitman taps his thumbnail on the glass desktop.

"Possibly," Hedges says.

21

"Here to identify an unknown female subject?" The medical examiner riffles various piles of the paperwork on his desk, finds his glasses, and jams them on his face. "Yes, right. This is it."

Pete sees the examiner's lips move, but can't hear. This stunned awareness has struck him a couple of times before, once when a gas line exploded, and again when he discovered a baby dead of smoke inhalation. He's momentarily deaf and unable to speak. In this state of suspension, he notices the medical examiner, B. Kramer, has pinned his name plate upside down to the pocket of his white coat.

Sheriff Detective Harry Strong's eyes dart around the cluttered office, which stinks of strong liniment. "I called two hours ago and left a message I was bringing in the next of kin. This is her father."

"Busy morning—drowning, vehicle fatality, and a couple of violent deaths. Nothing we can't handle, of course."

"Let's get this over with," Strong says.

Kramer pats three pockets before he locates a pen. "We're off," he says brightly, as if the three of them were embarking on a fishing trip.

Pete's been to the morgue before, but he's surprised again that the viewing room isn't cold and vile-smelling. The air is neutral, scraped of feeling like flesh from a deer hide.

Kramer lifts the sheet from the victim's face and nests it around her shoulders.

Relief buckles Pete's knees. He grabs the edge of a desk.

"What the hell?" Strong glares at Kramer, then at the dead black woman in her late 30s with a dense afro. Visible is a single bullet hole in her forehead.

"Where's my victim?" Strong bellows.

Pete collapses into a chair and covers his face with shaking hands. He's happy. Glad the poor woman whose dark skin has paled to an ashen gray is not Gracie.

Kramer fans himself with his clipboard. "Staff must somehow have been given the wrong information. Wait here. I'll have this cleared up in a jiffy." He wheels away the gurney.

"Sorry about this, Pete. Things have gone to shit since the new coroner came on." Strong taps Pete's shoulder with his knuckles. "Unfortunately, this is another deceased female, but I was at the scene. They'll find that one shortly."

Pete's known Harry for years, since he was a hose man and Harry, on patrol. They encountered each other regularly at crime and accident scenes, over corpses and at arson fires. The detective seems like a stranger now, no more familiar than B. Kramer.

In less than five minutes, George Ball, the elected county coroner, hurries in, the hem of his vented suit jacket flapping. "Paperwork was diverted at some point, not by us, of course. I have a call in to the sheriff."

"Everything was fine when my victim left the scene," Strong says.

Pete pays little attention. The next one could be Grace.

In fifteen minutes, the same gurney is back. "Is this your daughter?" George Ball carefully inches the white sheet down to her chin.

When he sees her, Pete is split with a terrible cleaving stroke.

"Is this your daughter?" the coroner says again, more gently.

One part of him sees his child and knows it is she, once-perfect skin so thin it looks as though it will tear if touched. Dirt and dried blood cake the hair around her ears. A red crust lurks in the corner of her mouth. He sees her smooth neck, the sweet throat of a girl whose tendons have yet to become sinewy with life's disappointments. Her eyes are closed, revealing blue veins on her lids, deprived of oxygen on their wandering course to her heart.

His other self refuses to believe. The white sheet slips another inch, exposing a cotton bra strap that droops over her naked shoulder. This small, still form, this child, this girl in her underwear isn't Grace, his beautiful Grace whose strong young bones sizzle under his hands when he hugs her, who smells of a pure soap and clean skin when she is ready for bed, whose spirit hums in her fingers when she grips a paintbrush. This body with skin the color of smoke that, when the sheet is removed will reveal devastation, this is someone else's child. Not his Grace who might be home now. It's a mistake; perhaps she told him she was staying with a friend, and he forgot. He is ashamed for a moment that he's been so frantic with worry. She will be home when he returns from this mistaken errand, she will pour herself a glass of cranberry juice, eat a Ritz cracker, watch *Emergency*.

"How?" he asks in a high, reedy voice. His eyes are dry.

Kramer thumbs through a stack of papers on a clipboard. "We won't know for certain until after the autopsy. Preliminarily, we've concluded she died of stab wounds."

"Where? I want to see."

"Pete . . ." Strong says.

The pity in the detective's voice infuriates him.

Pete gestures, and the coroner lifts the sheet to expose Grace's torso. Her padded bra and bikini panties are unmarked, as if they have just come from the dryer, but the white skin of her cleavage, her torso, her ribs, and the firm smooth swell of her thighs are covered with wounds. They don't look that bad; the skin surrounding the cuts is blue and collapsed along a small depression traced by a thread of red. They seem so trivial that Pete cries. He digs the heels of his hands into his eye sockets but he can't hold back the tears.

"The major blow may have been from the back, with the blade going between the ribs," Kramer says. "We'll be able to give you a better answer soon." Ball lets the sheet fall back over her face.

Soon, Pete thinks, means after the autopsy. His jaw goes slack, and he's unable to close his mouth. The muscles that hold his face together are gone. He knows he won't be staying for the autopsy— only those directly involved with the case attend—but he saw enough of them when he worked arson investigation. Images come flowing back now, and he hears his own sobs. The ME will take her apart until only her scraps are left.

Strong grasps Pete's elbow so tightly that he deadens the nerve. "Steady, Pete. Let's go outside."

The detective drives him home, but when they arrive, Pete's unable to move.

"We need to talk." Harry climbs out and walks around the hood to hold the door for him. Another white county car is parked at the curb, and a younger detective, Gary Muñoz, hops out.

On the porch, a pair of pink flip-flops rest beside the door mat, one overturned. He sees a clump of mud mixed with strands of grass clinging to the sole. She wore them last Sunday when she washed his car. Her toenails were painted with blue polish.

Strong clears his throat. Pete tries to fit the key in the lock, but his hand is shaking badly. Strong takes the key and lets them inside. The house is stifling, and Pete struggles to breathe.

"You got instant coffee?" Strong asks. When Pete nods, the detective goes to the kitchen.

Pete sinks wearily onto the living room couch. He never liked this room. The furniture, heavily carved fake Mediterranean chosen by Janis, is pretentious and uncomfortable. The one genuine thing here is Grace's painting, still propped against the candlestick on the mantel as if it were temporary, not important enough to be hung on the wall.

Muñoz steps closer to study Grace's signature in the right-hand corner. "It's very … interesting."

Stumbling past Muñoz, Pete snatches the painting off the mantel and hides it behind an end table. His hands are trembling.

Strong returns with three mugs and sets them on the coffee table. He gestures Pete back to the couch, commandeers the only comfortable chair, and leaves Muñoz a straight-backed one with slippery upholstery.

Pages flutter in their notebooks. "This is going to be very, very hard, Pete, but hang in there, because we're going to get this guy." Strong's jowly face is flushed, and his voice a little unsteady, maybe thinking of his own daughter, whom Pete met years ago.

Strong reads from notes, looking up at Pete every few sentences. Grace was discovered about nine that morning. A motorcycle gang member stopping to piss in the weeds along Whitman Highway near the Wagon Wheel Café had spotted her body face down in the dirt. He told the café manager to telephone the cops, then roared off on his Harley. Detectives are looking for him.

Strong takes a deep breath. "We believe she was nude when the wounds were inflicted, but subsequent to the attack, someone bathed her and put her underwear back on."

Muñoz straightens, tight as a wire. "It's as though the killer knew her and didn't want strangers to see her naked."

The two detectives exchange a long, complicated stare before Strong resumes his narrative. There was no blood, weapon, or sign of her outer clothing at the scene, which led him to the preliminary conclusion she'd been killed elsewhere, then dumped. Her body was covered with shallow knife cuts. The apparent cause of death looked to be two deeper wounds, including one that entered between the ribs on the left side of her back, probably entering the heart.

"Did you hear something?" Pete asks.

"What? No." Strong raises his eyes.

"I thought I heard the back door close."

"Muñoz, go see, will you?" Strong sips from his cup and studies Pete over the rim.

The younger man returns and gives his partner a negative shake of the head.

Strong clears his throat. His voice seems distant to Pete, like a bad phone connection.

"Another thing. She had a baggie of hash worth about $300 stuffed in her panties. The medical examiner's initial estimate, based on a visual examination of the tissues, is that she's been deceased about three days. You reported her absence to the PD on Saturday morning when her bed hadn't been slept in. She probably was dead when you called."

Pete barely listens. He's tuned to another frequency, and in that separate realm he hears quick, light footsteps. He closes his eyes and presses his fingers to his temples.

A noise in the hall. This time Pete goes to look himself. It's dark and empty, except for narrow wedges of light from the bedrooms. When Grace was small, she'd run with little footsteps down the hall to his and Janis' room. He remembers her cold feet against him in bed.

Strong puts a hand on Pete's shoulder, but he shakes it off.

"Come on, Pete, work with us. You want to catch whoever did this, don't you?"

"Right." Pete struggles to put the memory aside.

"I know you're upset with the PD." Strong returns to the living room. "You wanted a juvenile investigation opened immediately, but it looks as though there was nothing they could have done. She was already gone."

Pain beneath his sternum bends him almost double. Briefly, he imagines the men on his crew pressing the electric paddles to his chest. After a minute, the spasm subsides.

"Maybe we were wrong," he says unsteadily. "It could be . . . it could be some other girl that looks like Gracie. I'm not certain now, not at all."

Muñoz slaps his notebook on his thigh. "Captain, please stay on track. It *was* your daughter; everything matched, down to the moles and childhood scars. If we don't move quickly, whoever did this will walk. We need you to tell us everything, everything you can remember, about the night she went missing."

Back on the couch, Pete massages his breastbone. He's gone over every detail until his memory is worn thin and dangerous. "She's on summer vacation, so I took her and her friend to an empty church parking lot yesterday afternoon for a driving lesson. While we were there, a female BPD officer came by to check out a complaint we were spinning doughnuts, but that wasn't true. We were doing slow circuits around the blacktop. Nevertheless, we left and went to Romano's for pizza."

Pete describes the group adjacent to them at the pizzeria that night, but he can't articulate clearly the strangeness of it: the man with tattooed hands, the boy with bleached hair and hard eyes, the assistant DA staring through a haze of cigarette smoke.

"Franzen was there? The police commissioner?" Muñoz asks.

"With two other men and three boys."

Strong nods. "Franzen heads up a Big Brothers-type group. They mentor at-risk kids."

Pete sips the coffee. It's terrible, and he makes a face. "After just a few minutes, Grace went to the bathroom and stayed there for quite a while. When she came out, she almost ran out to the car."

"Did they speak to Grace? Threaten her in any way?" Strong asks.

Pete shakes his head.

"Okay," Strong says. "Let's back up. What's the name of Grace's girlfriend that came along with you?"

"It wasn't a girl; it was Danny Ricci, a friend from art class."

Strong's eyebrows go up. "I need his number. What happened then?"

"I dropped Danny off, and we came home. Grace went to her room, but during the evening, she received a telephone call. After that, I fell asleep in the rec room watching TV and didn't wake up until five the next morning."

Muñoz looks skeptical. "You don't know who called?"

"No." Inwardly, Pete curses himself. He should've eavesdropped.

"You didn't hear her leave?" Muñoz asks.

"The rec room is in the back. She must've gone out the front."

Her room was clean, he tells the detectives, clothes folded and hung up, school books stacked on her desk, bedspread smoothed and tucked neatly under the pillow. Alarmed, he called the Riccis', but no one picked up. When he phoned her friend Jade, her mother answered. She cursed and slammed the phone down. On the redial, there was no answer.

Streets surrounding the house had been empty. He remembers having the odd thought that everyone was dead.

"I got in the car and drove for blocks around, asked people, but they hadn't seen anyone."

Muñoz taps his notebook with his pencil. "Does she often disappear on you?"

A hot flush creeps up the back of Pete's neck. Good cop, bad cop, he thinks. "She's had problems this last year, what with her mother taking off, but she's straightened herself out."

"What kind of problems? Bad grades? Drugs? Sex? Did she run away?"

"No, of course not," Pete says. "Well . . . yes, she sneaked out a few months ago, but it was just that once. She's been good ever since."

Muñoz loosens his tie. "Just once, or once that you knew about?"

"Once."

"When she sneaked out that time, you were very upset, right? She could've gotten raped or abducted. What did you do?"

Pete withholds mention of the mysterious bruises. "I grounded her."

"Did you threaten her with a more severe punishment if she did it again?"

"No, I assumed she wouldn't."

"But she did."

Strong intervenes, easing the tension. "We need a list, Pete.

Names, addresses, and phone numbers of anyone she's been close to over the past year, especially if she's acquired new friends. I'm going to contact her school teachers and counselors. Is there a pastor she's close to?"

"Ron Crawford from Centennial Methodist."

"What about her mother?"

"Janis is on the road with Haggard's band. I left a call with her agent when Grace first went missing, but lo and behold, her mother is missing, too."

"What?" Muñoz's pencil jerks on the page.

"A figure of speech. It's been damn hard, the waiting."

"You two are on bad terms?"

"We aren't on any terms. She never calls either of us."

Strong shoves his notebook in his blazer pocket. "We need to search Grace's room. There may be something there that'll help."

"The bathroom, too," Muñoz says.

"I already went through everything: her desk, schoolwork, drawers, closet."

They insist. Muñoz, wearing gloves, rifles through the bathroom medicine cabinet and wastebasket while Strong in the bedroom shakes her books, peers under the mattress, and delves in pockets and shoes. When he opens her dresser drawers and touches her panties and bras, Pete can't stand the thought of the invasions visited on her: Autopsy. Mortuary. Every nuance of her life, mind, and lovely spirit.

"We'll get the phone records, Pete. Find out who called. Meanwhile, we need the list," Strong says.

After the detectives leave, the wind chime on the patio tinkles. Pete searches the backyard, sweat soaking his shirt. She could be here; it's possible. The sun has scorched the grass, and soil in the gardens has cracked and turned ashen. He gathers the cushion from the chaise where she lay that morning months ago and stuffs it in the trash.

22

Suzanne slides open the van's passenger door and hefts out two bags of groceries. After she left the *News-Daily*, she bought the fixings for tacos and Mexican rice.

Next door at Reggie's, the new gardener guides his roaring mower back and forth. She starts up the driveway to the side door, but stops when a black-and-white brakes in front of the house. Liza rolls down the window and peers out.

"Come on in—I've got groceries." Suzanne calls over her shoulder.

Liza climbs out, leaving the door open. The police radio crackles. She trots up the driveway. "Something's happened."

"Tell me after I get the ice cream in the house." Suzanne props the door open with her knee, but turns back at the odd note in Liza's voice. Her friend's hair, usually in a tight French braid, straggles out of its plait. The armpits of her uniform shirt are stained with sweat.

Liza takes a deep breath. "Grace Stannard is dead."

"Impossible. I saw her last week."

"It just happened. They. . . "

Liza continues to talk; the lawn mower sputters and stops. Narcissus slides sinuously out of the house through the half-open door.

Suzanne flashes back to her visit with Harris Whitman this morning at the *News-Daily*; he inquired about Danny, and gave her an assignment. Then the telephones rang, one after another, like buzzards over a rotting carcass.

"Suzie?" Liza jiggles her arm.

Suzanne drops the bags on the garage floor and scrambles inside.

"Danny?" He isn't on the first floor. She takes the stairs two at a time. "Danny?"

He's not in his bedroom. She rattles the bathroom doorknob, and when it doesn't yield, she runs at it with her shoulder. Pain shoots up her neck, but Liza joins her, and together they slam the wood panel until the lock gives. The air is saturated with the tinny scent of blood. She rips aside the shower curtain to see Danny lying naked in the tub.

His arms, chest, and white abdomen, darkened by a vee of curly hair, are smeared with blood. He's unconscious, but his eyes are half-open, giving him an odd, secretive look.

A silvery razor blade glints in the soap dish. She hefts him to a sitting position, trying to awaken him and liberate him from the tub coffin, but his head falls back and arms flop. The blood is warm and silky on her hands.

"God, oh God!" Suzanne shakes Danny and screams at him. His cheek twitches in unconscious pain.

Liza grips her shoulder. "Suzie, listen! Wrap towels tightly over his wrists. I'll radio for an ambulance and wait for it at the curb." Her heavy boots pound the stairs.

Suzanne lowers Danny back into the blood-smeared tub, her hand cradling his head to keep it from hitting the porcelain. By the time Liza returns with paramedics, she's bound the spongy, gaping cuts, but blood has soaked the towels.

One paramedic kneels beside her and presses a stethoscope to Danny's chest. "He's got a faint heartbeat. Lucky he cut crosswise. If he'd slit the vein vertically, you might have lost him."

"Shut up, shut up!" She staggers to her feet, catching the edge of the sink to keep from falling.

"Careful, Ma'am. Don't faint on me." A second paramedic grabs her around the waist, but she shakes him off without taking her eyes off Danny.

"Please, sit in the hall," he says firmly.

She hovers outside the bathroom while the paramedic team struggles to maneuver Danny out of the tub, around the sink and toilet, and onto a gurney in the hall. They tuck a blanket around him, covering his nakedness.

The creases in Suzanne's hands are rusty with drying blood. The torn and bloody shower curtain, wet, shredded towels, and matted rug look like a murder scene.

"I saw her last Thursday." Her voice comes from a strange, removed place. "She said hello from the back seat of her father's car."

"I saw them, too—her dad, Grace and Danny." Liza guides her downstairs and opens the passenger door of the black-and-white.

"No, you weren't there. I walked over to talk to Pete." Suzanne feels guilty now, that she'd wanted to trace the length of Pete's tanned arm, propped on the sill of the open car window.

"Earlier that day," Liza says.

Suzanne holds up three fingers. "We were gone three days. Seventy-two hours."

———

She sinks into a chair in the empty hospital canteen and rests her cheek on folded arms. Smells of cigarettes and bad coffee taint the air. It's 10 p.m. Although she's nearly paralyzed by weariness, her eyes won't close. Doctors sewed Danny's wounds with more than two dozen ugly, black stitches and gave him blood. He's in a single room on a morphine drip. His skin was gray, and his eyes, before he closed them, looked like the pits of hell.

The canteen's pay phone jangles for some visitor who's long since left. The sound goes on and on, stirring paranoia that until now she's held at bay. She digs the heels of her hands into her eyes. How did Danny know about Grace's death before Liza, who has her police radio tuned to every hum of police news?

The phone rings again; she picks up the receiver and slams it down. On the dirty tile floor is a copy of the *News-Daily's* evening edition. The story about Grace is Page One, accompanied by two photos; one a high school yearbook picture, and the other, detectives searching the scrubby bushes along Whitman Highway. Suzanne tilts the paper to get more light on Grace. She looks very young, cheeks still with a hint of little-girl roundness, but her smile is troubling, lips stretched tightly over her teeth.

This was her son's best friend. Why didn't she know her better?

About a month ago, Suzanne returned from an errand to hear the two of them playing Rod Stewart's new album. Their laughter was delicious, and she peered around the corner to see Grace, who had arrived in a leotard and wrap-around skirt, take the skirt off and shake it at Danny like a bullfighter's cape. He pretended to be the bull for awhile; then they traded places, raucous spirits free for an afternoon.

Yet someone hacked this girl as if she were a slab of meat. Suzanne rolls the paper in a ball and crams it in the waste container.

She plucks her address book from her purse and feeds a dime into the telephone's coin slot. Pete Stannard's number rings for a full minute. She hangs up and calls a taxi.

23

Cars line the curb for half a block on either side of the Stannards' house so Suzanne parks around the corner. A station wagon with a radio station logo on the door hovers across the street, and a television van directly in front loads up to get back to the station for the eleven o'clock news. Lamps burn in the house, but the porch light is off, as if it's Halloween and they're out of candy.

She knocks.

The man in the doorway takes a long look and wrinkles his nose like he smells dog shit. "Janis and Pete aren't available. Any information will come from the Sheriff's Department."

Suzanne looks down at her T-shirt and jeans, stiff with dried blood. "I know I look terrible, but I'm okay, really. My son, Danny, and Grace were best friends."

"Services are pending; once arrangements are firmed up, it'll be in the newspaper." He's a Lawrence Welk wannabe in a leisure suit and white shoes. She can't imagine how Pete and this guy are connected.

"I've got to talk to Pete."

"Janis and Pete are very distraught. They aren't seeing anyone."

She gets it now. Janis is back—with a Nashville entourage. Through the doorway Suzanne spots her, hair lying on her neck in greasy clump and clothes limp and wrinkled. She's talking on a Princess telephone.

"Please. My son may be in danger too." Suzanne's head aches, and she blinks against the pain.

The door begins to close. A juicy anger flows through her. She slaps the door back with her palm, whacking him in the nose. He cries out, and Janis pauses in mid-sentence.

Pete strides from the back of the house. Compared to the night he dropped off Danny, he's gaunt as a scarecrow. His eyes take refuge deep in their sockets.

"I heard...that is, a friend from the PD stopped by late this afternoon to tell me about Grace. I can't tell you how sorry I am." Her voice catches.

"I appreciate your condolences, but this is a very bad time for us. Can you excuse me?" He starts to turn away.

"Have they arrested anyone?"

"No."

Anxiety overtakes her; she clutches his arm. "Are there suspects?"

"My daughter is dead, Mrs. Ricci. Please go away."

Nearly his height, she leans close to his ear. "I need to talk to you about Danny—Danny and Grace."

He stares at her. "Five minutes."

With a hand on her elbow in an odd, old-fashioned gesture, he leads her to the rec room at the back of the house. It's decorated in browns and rusts that Reggie used to say were "earth-toned, you know, like dirt." Seven or eight men, a couple of them dressed in navy pants and light blue shirts of the Bakersfield Fire Department, talk quietly. As she follows Pete to a corner sofa, the deep-voiced conversation stops for two beats. She smells masculine sweat on ironed cotton.

Windows in the brightly lit room face the dark backyard, and their reflection in the glass makes them look like actors in a play. The men resume their conversation, but the deep timbre of their voices seems foreign. It's Pete's world, guys who stand with their arms folded across their chests the way her brothers do, the way

Carlo did. As if it'll keep their feelings from falling out. They're on a different planet from her and Danny.

Pete sinks down beside her. A plate of hamburger casserole, dried around the edges, sits untouched on a side table near his elbow. He rubs the back of his neck and closes his eyes wearily. "What's so damn important?"

Anxiety, like a pursuer's breath on her neck, makes her shiver. "Danny tried to commit suicide early this afternoon."

He's silent, probably thinking, *At least your kid is alive.*

"Thing is, police and the *News-Daily* knew about her murder at the time he cut himself, but the public didn't."

She bends toward him. His nose is scabbed and red. "Because Liza Theuss stopped by, I knew about Grace's murder sooner than just about anyone. But at that same moment, Danny had already slashed his wrists. He knew Grace was dead much earlier."

He snatches her arm like a drowning man. "He was told by someone who already knew she'd been murdered?"

"Yes."

"Is he going to recover?"

"He's in the hospital, stitched up, under sedation."

"I'll get the detective, Harry Strong, over there right away." Pete half-rises.

Suzanne lowers her voice to a tense whisper. "No way."

"Someone stabbed my girl and tossed her alongside the road like trash. Why the hell are you here, if it isn't to help?"

She feels his angry heat, and reacts with rising fury of her own. "I'm trying to save my own child. Whoever killed Grace could be after Danny, too."

"Whoever told him about Grace isn't the killer. A witness, maybe. He's the one in the cross hairs, not your son."

"Is there a suspect? Is the department close to an arrest?"

"They don't have any idea who it is. That's why we need Danny."

"Then he's not safe. I need to get him out of town."

"Absolutely not. He could be a material witness."

"So what? Danny's alive, not like your daughter" It's crude, to say it like this, but fear isn't allowing for smooth words.

For a heartbeat, his hands clench into fists. The sharp smell of sweat and anger rises off him. She trembles, but doesn't lean away.

He exhales a long breath. A calculating look crosses his face. "Let's do this: Strong's giving me a briefing in the morning. When I'm done, I'll call you."

"As soon as you hang up," she insists. "Word of honor?"

"Agreed, but I want something in return. When Danny wakes up, I get a chance to talk to him."

"Whatever information Danny gives you must not, under any circumstances, have his name on it."

"It's a deal." He sinks back on the couch and closes his eyes.

One of his firefighter posse appears beside them and frowns at Pete's exhausted face. "I'm Jon Camacho," he says to her. "I'm afraid he's done for tonight."

24

Pastor Ron Crawford closes the Book of Psalms and dabs his forehead with his handkerchief. Pete is sandwiched between his brother and sister, Hugh and Leslie. His skin burns beneath the starched white shirt. It's stifling in the Methodist church. Every row is full, mourners squeezed thigh to thigh on the wooden pews. His black suit, which he hasn't worn since his father's funeral five years ago, smells of stale nicotine. Grace would have pinched her nose and reminded him of the lectures he'd given her about fires ignited by cigarettes.

The organist plays the final hymn, *Amazing Grace*. Even those who didn't know her well—firefighters in navy blue dress jackets, boys with sideburns, girls with long, ironed hair—sing with choked voices, and the few people she was close to, like Mrs. Messina and Will Bosch, cry openly. Pete's all-encompassing pain has dried up any tears he might have shed. His knees, elbows, the joints in his fingers, all throb with the loss. Bending to tie his shoes this morning was almost more than he could bear.

The chancel holds no coffin to be carried out by pallbearers. Pete decided to free her poor body. All that's left of her—soft black ashes and bits of bone—are cupped in a small brass urn in the cemetery's columbarium.

Before the service, he spotted Strong and Muñoz in the rear corners of the sanctuary. Pete bumps Leslie's shoulder as he turns to scan the church again for Suzanne. He's telephoned a dozen times since he talked to Strong and left messages on her machine, but hasn't reached her.

The swelling notes of the final hymn, meant to be uplifting, jar his bones. His arms ache, down to the tip of each finger. He glances into the side chapel where Janis leans on her mother. How wrong it is, that this self-centered woman is shedding her tears, while Grace is gone.

Smoke flutters from the snuffed-out candles. Every day on the job, he smells burning: vinyl car upholstery, redwood fences, shake roofs, ceilings, walls, tables, curtains, cats and dogs, human hair, human flesh. Sweat drips down his cheeks and off the end of his nose. He doesn't wait for the benediction, but slips out the side door.

On the front sidewalk, television and radio reporters heft their cameras and tilt their microphones to interview Marty, Janis' media guy, who is providing a couple of sound bites. Pete sinks into the driver's seat of the Cutlass and strips off his jacket, tie, and soaked shirt. As mourners pass the car on their way to the parking lot, they stare curiously at him, flushed and dripping in his sleeveless undershirt.

Janis bends to look inside the car. With her face so close, the odor of her breath is strong and familiar, a reminder of all he's lost.

"Why aren't you dressed? People are coming to the house," she says.

"Go ahead without me. I need a few minutes."

"I need a few too, Pete."

"Leslie and Mrs. Messina will be there. They know where everything is."

The congestion in the parking lot thins. TV reporters do their standups. Pete slumps in the seat, so tired he hasn't the strength to fit the key in the ignition. A VW bus emerges from the back lot with Suzanne at the wheel. It turns right into the street. A passenger scrunches down in the seat.

Pete twists the key and guns the engine, maneuvering between the remaining cars. Springs groan as the Cutlass bounces over curb, but the VW has disappeared. He races in its direction and scans the side streets until he spots it.

The VW accelerates, but it's no match for the muscular Cutlass. He noses the van's rear bumper, but she doesn't pull over. He lays on the horn. The VW clatters along, belching exhaust into Pete's air-conditioning. Heart pounding, he races alongside, then stops in front of her. After jumping out, he hammers on Suzanne's window. Her eyes widen when she sees his reddened face, damp undershirt, and flattened, sweat-soaked hair. After a few seconds, she lowers the window an inch.

"Why the fuck haven't you called? I kept my part of the bargain. As soon as I heard from Harry Strong, I phoned you." He bends awkwardly, mouth close to the small window opening.

"I've been busy." She looks straight ahead.

The engine is still running, and the window vibrates against Pete's cheek, revving up his desperation. "I've been busy too, Suzanne. Planning a funeral. Taking calls from asshole reporters who want to know what it *feels* like. Listening to detectives say they've got nothing."

Danny is hunkered so low in the passenger seat he's barely visible above the dashboard. Pete circles the van. "I want to talk to you."

Suzanne switches off the engine and leans across Danny. "I asked him, but he's scared."

A passing car honks at the Cutlass, which is partially blocking the street. He pays no attention. "The detectives have zip. Kids from school are giving us zip. There's zero physical evidence. The more time passes, the less chance we have."

Danny's voice is muffled. "I'll talk to him, Mom."

She throws Pete a furious glance.

"Mom, it was my fault." The kid wipes his nose. His sleeve falls back, revealing bandages on his wrist.

Suzanne shakes Danny's shoulder. "You had nothing to do with it. Some monster got ahold of her, a sick, sick, man who preys on children."

"I said I'd come with her, but instead, I let her go alone," Danny says.

"What the hell are you talking about?" Pete asks.

Suzanne slowly raises her hands. "Okay, Pete. Okay."

He follows the VW, barely wasting a thought on Janis or the reception for the mourners.

At Suzanne's, the three of them gather in the kitchen. It's dim, one bulb in the ceiling fixture burned out, leaving shadows in the corners. White takeout cartons of Chinese food litter the long, rectangular table.

Suzanne grabs a wastebasket from under the sink and sweeps the mess into it. While she plugs in the percolator for coffee, Pete rubs a painful spot over his ear that radiates down to his tight jaw.

Danny sits with his back to them, looking at the window sill where two mangoes are ripening. His shirt sleeve hides the bandages.

"To hell with coffee." Suzanne switches the percolator off and removes a half-empty jug of Gallo burgundy from the refrigerator. She pours wine into two jelly glasses, handing one to Pete without asking whether he wants any.

Pete scoots his chair close enough to Danny to trap him between the table and the wall. He doesn't want the wine, not when he's got the kid in his sights. "Okay, Danny, you're at bat."

Danny's leg jiggles, and his breath comes fast.

"Come on, give." Pete waits, but the only sound is Danny's rapid breathing.

Danny sways, his eyes rolling up in his head.

He grabs the boy's shoulders to hold him upright. "Get me a paper bag," he shouts at Suzanne. He's seen hyperventilation before, when survivors are under extreme stress.

She fumbles in a couple of drawers, cursing her clumsiness, until she finally snatches one out. Pete holds the open end of the wrinkled brown sack against Danny's mouth and nose.

"Breathe into it, long deep breaths."

The bag contracts, then balloons.

After a few minutes, Danny's ready.

"You don't have to talk to him," Suzanne warns.

As the boy spills the details, Pete is dragged back to the night at Romano's. The subtext screams at him now, flashing signals ignored.

"You remember how Grace took one look at Galen and ran for the restroom?" Danny asks.

"What does the commissioner have to do with this?"

"The party. It was at his house." Danny tosses the paper bag on the floor. "The guy with Galen, the tattooed one, he told me to come to Galen's that night and bring Grace."

"That's ridiculous. A guy who's been in law enforcement for thirty-five years, partying with a bunch of kids?"

Danny's face is a landscape of contempt. "She had to go. She'd been there before."

Pete feels as though he's falling. "When she was beaten up? That was at Franzen's?"

"And that's not all that happened."

Suzanne interrupts. "You were there in February?"

"No, Grace told me later. There were people there, Galen and other people, who did things to her."

"Things?" Suzanne asks.

"You know." Danny looks out the window, past the mangoes on the sill.

"She was raped." Pete is suddenly clear. Bruises, purple-green prints of fingers on the inside of her arms.

"Not exactly. Somebody gave her some 'Ludes."

"Rape, and you didn't tell anyone?" Pete asks.

Danny's lip curls. "Who was I going to tell? The police commissioner? And I didn't see you telling anyone about her getting all beat up."

"She said she fell," Pete says.

"And you believed her?"

"Get back on track, both of you," Suzanne snaps. "Danny, what happened after you talked to the tattooed man?"

"Wait a minute. Who's the guy with the tats?" Pete says.

"Stone. He drives a limo."

"And the others?"

Danny turns his face away. "Kevin who's Galen's boyfriend. The DA. Reno and Jesus."

"Okay, what then?" Pete says.

"You dropped me off, and as soon as Grace got home, I told her what he said, but she was really scared after last time. I told her…" His throat contracts.

"Get it all out," Suzanne says.

"I said I'd meet her at the party. Make sure nothing happened. But I didn't go. Remember, you made me go to pick up the photos?" he says to Suzanne. "I got the pictures, but by the time I got back, the buses were done. Hardly any cars were on the road so I couldn't hitch a ride. I cut out on her when I promised. She went by herself, afraid not to, and it's my fault she died."

His mouth twists, and he begins to cry.

Suzanne attempts to wrap her arms around his shoulders, but he shakes her off and runs outside.

Pete sees the kitchen, not the real room that once might have been pleasant: long table covered with a checked oilcloth, cast iron Dutch oven on the counter, fruit on the windowsill. In other times he might have run his fingers under Suzanne's thick hair and touched the nape of her neck. Instead, it's a miserable, broken place with cracked counter tile, spilled food on the oilcloth, cat hair on the linoleum. He visualizes clearly the unseen dirt and grease around him, the bacteria in the kitchen drain, dried lipstick in the corner of Suzanne's mouth, his sweaty feet in dress shoes, a rotten tooth in his mouth, the rind of dirt under his fingernails.

He feels the dark creep of events throughout his body, until his sight narrows and the only thing he sees clearly are the mangoes, a bruised yellow-green as they ripen on the windowsill.

25

While Pete decides what to do next, the Cutlass idles in front of the Riccis's. During his confession, Danny'd looked terrified, as if his telling opened a black hole. Grace must have experienced that kind of fear, amplified a thousandfold.

He's agreed not to name Danny in order to harvest what the boy knows. Honor sucks, he thinks.

Pete calls Strong from a telephone booth, but he's out. He drives to Panorama Heights, a housing development on the Kern River bluffs. The expensive homes look down their noses at the oil derricks and pumps of the oil field to the north. He passes Assemblyman Conklin's and turns onto Rollins Street. Franzen's is second on the right, across from Sizemore Park.

Pete's never visited Franzen, but he has the address, and he memorized every street in town as a rookie fireman. Back when the two of them taught arson investigation, Franzen often asked Pete out for a drink after they locked up the classroom, but Pete never took him up on it. Grace was small then, and Janis hated being tied down during the evening. Soon after, Franzen was appointed to the commission, and by that time he was too high on the ladder to invite Pete anywhere.

The Cutlass cruises past the house. In the park, a group of teens clusters around a picnic table. High-pitched, girlish laughter hovers in the air, reminding him of Grace when she was in junior high. He blinks quickly, cranks the window up, then circles the block and leaves the car at the curb.

Franzen's house was once a showplace with a fountain, junipers lining the driveway, beds of roses and gardenias along the flagstone walk. The gardenias have turned brown for lack of water and fallen leaves cluster around the base of the rose bushes. Yellowed newspapers are scattered on the porch. Pete wrinkles his nose at the odd odor about the place, very personal, like the scent of unwashed shirts and pants in an old man's closet.

He imagines Grace climbing the stone steps. He rings the bell. As he waits, he rocks on the balls of his feet, first doubting Danny's story, then believing him. It's too bizarre not to be true.

Pete thumbs the doorbell. It rings somewhere deep in the house, and within a few seconds two dogs begin an operatic duet of furious yapping. Claws rake the other side of the door. No one answers from this or several additional tries. He pounds, then kicks repeatedly, but the door must have an iron core, because it doesn't yield. He's about to step off the porch when someone yells from inside the house.

"Get the hell out of here, or I'm calling the cops!" It's a boy's voice, loud and belligerent. It must be one of the kids from Romano's.

"I have to see Galen." Pete shouts at the door panel.

"Go away. He's asleep."

The noise would have awakened anyone within fifty yards. "You tell him it's Pete Stannard, and he'd better get himself out here."

The boy curses the dogs, who finally stop barking.

A new voice, weak and shaky. "I've got the PD on the phone. Go away or go to jail." It's Franzen.

Pete backs down the steps. "You're going to jail for what happened to my girl, Galen!" His temples throb as if he's about to stroke out.

In the park, a group of high school girls perches on children's swings. They turn the chains until they're wound tight, then lift their feet and whip counterclockwise, screaming and laughing. Near them, three boys show off by traveling hand over hand across the monkey bars.

Pete's about to unlock the Cutlass, but instead shoves the keys into his pocket. If Franzen used drugs and alcohol to lure teens to his parties, he might have recruited them from this convenient gathering spot across the street.

The sun has set. The air cools and wind rises, stirring the playground dust. The kids fall silent as he approaches. He doesn't like their looks. Two of the girls wear miniskirts that skim their crotches, and another's oversized breasts threaten to tumble out of her halter top. The boys' hair falls to their shoulders.

He walks over to where the grass ends, and the playground gravel begins.

A girl is wearing *Charlie* perfume. After Janis left, Grace began using it. When he sees all the young people who aren't Grace, his eyes fill with tears. His mouth tightens and he blinks, feeling moisture on his cheeks. The girls giggle; the boys scorch him with contemptuous stares.

"What's the matter, old man? Wish you were young again?" says a kid with a few scraggly lip hairs.

"He's slobbery drunk." A boy in a muscle shirt kicks dirt at him.

Pete gulps a lungful of air. "I just want to talk." He chokes on the words.

"Shove off, you faggot. We're not on the market." The boy with the wanna-be mustache glances at the girls to assure they're watching, then shoves Pete's shoulder with the heel of his hand.

Pete raises his palms. "I'm not . . . that. I'm her father. All I'm asking . . ."

"Give us money, old man." The kid's fist aims for the center of Pete's chest, but when Pete lurches sideways, the blow lands on his shoulder instead. Pain burns away the moisture in his eyes.

Fists raised, he squares off against them. He's in good shape, but he's not sure he can prevail against three teenage boys brimming with testosterone.

"Wait guys, he's not one of the pussy men." The girl with the D-cup slides out of the swing. "I know him. It's Grace's dad."

The boys don't hear. Pete stands his ground, and when the ringleader lashes out with a right jab, Pete blocks it with his forearm.

She inserts herself between them and Pete. "You retards, it's Grace's old man. He's just being freaky."

"Jesus, mister, get ahold of yourself. Go home." The kid in a muscle shirt drops his fists in disgust.

"I want . . . what I want," he says, stepping back, "is to know about it. If any of you saw her. Who she was with, that is. Did she come here? That's it, all I wanted."

"We already told the cops. We don't know nothin' about Grace." The kid with the lip hairs speaks with such sincerity he's got to be lying. "Real sorry, old man."

"Is there anything? Any rumors?"

In seconds, the kids scatter. "Hey, wait," Pete calls, but they're crossing the grass and climbing on their bikes.

The only one left is the big-breasted girl. She sits on the end of the slide with her hands in her lap, watching him. One of the abandoned swings creaks to and fro, as if still under the spell of its absent occupant.

"You know me, sort of," she says. "I'm Jade."

26

Pete and Jade cruise east toward the mountains. Headlights from oncoming traffic brush the car's interior, illuminating her smooth brown legs. Her back is turned to him as she stares quietly at the dark hills.

"I got to Galen's first," Jade says. "Grace wasn't there yet, so I washed down some reds with tequila shots."

Guests were the usual—boys from Franzen's work with at-risk youths and their adult male "friends".

"No other girls?"

"Usually a couple more are there, because one of the regulars likes to film both girls and boys doing it, but not that night."

"Doing it?" The car swerves with the involuntary twitch of his hands.

Jade tosses him a pitying look. "You know."

After Grace came home bruised, he assumed Jade was a teenage slut overloaded with sex drive. But now he sees how vulnerable she is.

"When Gracie got there, she was dressed really weird, like a grandma or something, jeans and this baggy shirt."

Jade says Grace immediately swallowed some reds. "The first time, that's why we went, for the goodies. I could forget about my mom and all the other stuff. School. Snotty girls."

"That was February. Why even think about going back, after what happened?"

"Stone said he'd send the film to our folks. We were scared shitless."

"Did you see who killed her?"

"I didn't see. I was…" Jade flips her fingertips as if to brush away a fly.

"You were messing around?" Pete refrains from using the word "fucking".

Jade looks away.

"Where were you, and where was Grace?"

"I think I was in the garage, where there was a mattress on the floor. I was pretty out of it, but I think Grace might have been in one of the bedrooms."

"Who was at the party?"

"Kevin, of course. Reno, and Jesus, and a kid named Diego. Other boys, too, but I don't know all their names."

"What about adults?"

"The old guy, Galen."

"And…"

Jade shrinks until Pete imagines she might collapse her bones like a mouse slipping through a crack.

"I can't. They'll get me."

"Grace is dead because of those men," he says.

Jade mumbles something. He leans across the gear shift panel to catch what she's saying: "I don't want to die."

He's still in his undershirt, and a breeze from the open window brushes her long black hair against his bare arm. He catches the scent of *Charlie* again. He's stirred, in an odd, sad way. The last time he had sex was months ago with an old girlfriend at his twentieth high school reunion. Before that, it had been with Janis, when she was still Janet.

It isn't so much Jade's sexuality that draws him as her loneliness and isolation, a reflection of his own. "Listen, stay at my place tonight. In the morning, we'll go to the sheriff's office, and you can tell them what you've just told me. They can find a safe place for you and provide protection."

Her eyes are in shadow; he can't tell what she's thinking.

"Okay," she says finally.

At the next turnout, Pete makes a U-turn back toward town. The road burrows between the treeless hills, lights gleaming below them like an island in a dark ocean. Toward the west, the last of the sun touches cloud. He glances at her, but she stares at her fingers, twisted in her lap.

The funeral earlier in the day seems years ago, down a long road of events. He remembers that mourners may still be at the house. His mind grapples with the complexities of getting rid of them and bringing Jade there to spend the night. Janis and her entourage are staying at the Rancho Bakersfield.

Traffic thickens as they return to the city. Pete stops at a traffic light, and just as it turns green, she jumps out of the car, darts through oncoming traffic, and disappears down a side street. By the time Pete disentangles from the two lanes of cars and drives in that direction, there is no sign of her. The small shops are closed and parking lots are empty. No one answers when he knocks on the door at her mother's place five blocks from home.

———

Pete can't get close to Franzen's house the next morning. A sheriff's patrol car, a tech van, and three white Dodge Aspens—Strong calls them *ass pains* because they tend to stall—crowd the curb. Pete hovers in the playground and watches.

Last night, Janis, her entourage from Nashville, and Hugh and Leslie were still at the house when he arrived home. Ignoring their strange looks at his wrinkled undershirt and rumpled hair, he made excuses and shut himself in the bedroom. It was close to midnight, but Strong sounded alert when he answered the phone. Pete wondered how often a late night call interrupted the detective's sleep. Their conversation continued for an hour. After Strong hung up, Pete had lain awake, eyes aching. The detective was headed for the office to draft a search warrant, roust his staff from bed, and alert the crime scene technicians. His plan was to swoop down on Franzen's house as soon as a judge has signed the warrant.

This morning, Pete sees Kevin open the side gate and walk down the driveway with two leashed Chihuahuas snapping at his heels. The boy trots across the street, with a snap of the leash to hurry the dogs along and waits while they relieve themselves in the grass. A uniformed officer emerges from the house next door, murmuring into his walkie-talkie. In a moment Strong meets the officer on the sidewalk and they talk, heads close. On the way back inside, the detective gives Kevin a long, unfriendly look.

Pete dozes in his car as the day wears on. He eats a handful of broken cookies left over from the wake and uses the park's toilet. Evidence technicians raise Franzen's garage door and back his Jaguar into the driveway. Pete watches them spend half an hour vacuuming the interior and emptying ashtrays into cellophane bags. They peel up the carpet from the trunk floor.

Pete tortures himself reconstructing Grace's last hours, imagining what she saw and suffered, every detail, how she looked, what sounds she made. What she felt.

As if by reliving it he can shift her terror and pain to himself.

Strong takes a break for a smoke; before he returns inside, he scans the park. When he spots Pete's Cutlass, he stiffens. Pete climbs out and meets him at the edge of the playground. A young woman in cutoffs and tennis shoes pushes her two children on the swing, her arms pumping to keep the boy and girl in the air.

"What've you found?"

"I'm not saying until the lab works on the stuff," Strong says. His skin is flushed, and an envelope of excitement surrounds him.

Pete blocks his way. "I deserve it, Harry. If anybody should know, it's me."

"I told you last night, I'm moving slow." Strong frowns. "The BPD commissioner, for God's sake. If anything goes wrong, I'll need a testicle transplant, because for sure I'll get my balls handed to me. And Franzen's not the only one putting pressure on. Got a call this morning from the exec office. Word's leaking out, and the sheriff is feeling the heat."

"You're tiptoeing because my daughter's murder involves some fat cats?"

Strong kicks a divot of sod into the air. "Don't you ever, ever accuse me of lying down for the brass. I'm telling you, I need to be absolutely sure every piece of evidence is properly gathered and preserved."

The kids on the swings, about two and four, scream at their mother to push them higher, harder.

"How soon will you arrest him?"

Strong's fingers stray toward the cigarette pack in his shirt pocket. "Three, four days and I should be able to send the case to the DA for review."

"Review?"

"Make sure we have the staples on the right corners." He taps Pete's shoulder. "Relax, I've got this."

A uniformed deputy approaches. "Yes, Merrill, what's up?" Strong says.

The deputy tilts his head toward the sidewalk and draws him away. The older man listens, draws a handkerchief from his pocket and wipes his forehead. "Okay, time for me to chat with him. I'll let the sheriff know."

27

Heat has softened the asphalt on Highway 119. The van doesn't have air conditioning, and Suzanne cranks the window down. Her blouse is marked with a diagonal stripe of sweat from the shoulder belt. Oil derricks rear up from the treeless hills bordering the Taft Highway, silhouetted against the dark blue sky. She spent her girlhood with those derricks on the horizon, and they suck her back to that terrible time.

Conrad Fitzgerald finally has returned from peddling his recoated drill bit in Iraq. This morning she's meeting him at his office before he takes off from the Taft airstrip in his Beechcraft Baron. She veers off the road to stop and think, just a few miles short of Taft, near a cluster of ramshackle houses.

Maybe she should scratch the interview. Three weeks have passed, but the sheriff's department hasn't arrested Grace's murderer. Danny's been monumentally angry, not at the inaction of the detectives, but at her.

"You made me. I didn't want to; I told you, but no. 'Do the right thing, Danny,' you said." His lips were dry and cracked.

"It won't be long now," she told him. "They have to answer all the questions. Get all the facts."

Actually, she's just guessing; the reason for the delay is baffling and fills her with unease.

She rests her forehead on the wheel. Hedges called last night, saying he's scheduled her column on Fitzgerald for tomorrow's paper. Whitman is anxious to run the story, Hedges said, before another publication snatches it.

Alienating the *News-Standard*, a major client, isn't an option, so she sighs and maneuvers the floor shift into gear. The van climbs the hills, stirring long-forgotten memories of riding beside her father in his pickup on this same stretch of road. She'd felt so safe, the scent of his skin strong in the enclosed cab, sun-bleached hairs shiny against his forearm, scarred fingers loose and confident on the wheel. What would her life have been like if he'd lived?

It's a mile farther to Fitzgerald's compound, buttoned up with an eight-foot chain link fence and identified by a sign hanging from the gate, Star Petroleum Equipment. A voice speaks through an intercom. She leans out to give her name, and the gate hums open.

A dozen trucks sit in the lot, looking downmarket compared to the sleek, custom GMC painted in gold flake, sitting in kingly splendor directly in front of the building. The truck has no door handles to mar the smooth contours of the body, making her wonder how Fitzgerald gets in. She tries to peer inside, but the glass is deeply tinted. All she sees is the reflection of her face, which seems changed, crow's feet and worry lines deeper in the harsh sun.

Inside the building, air conditioning on steroids makes her shiver. A male receptionist sitting at a large computer keyboard and monitor holds up a finger and taps three numbers on a nearby telephone. In a moment, Fitzgerald emerges from his office, footsteps soft and catlike in eel-skin boots.

"Mrs. Ricci? I'm Fitzgerald, but everyone calls me Connie." His gold pinky ring is cool against her palm. He's several inches shorter than she, but that doesn't strike her as much as the hair, not only on his head, but brown and thick in eyebrows, ears, nostrils, and on the digits of his fingers. A shadowy trail of closely-shaved stubble extends from his chin down his throat and under the collar at the back of his shirt.

Suzanne feels a twinge of disgust, but covers it with a cough.

His voice is light, with a hint of joviality; he seems unaware of her reaction. "Come back to my office, and I'll tell you everything you need or want to know about the Fitzgerald tungsten-coated bit."

His office is an engineer's, filled with blueprints and specifications, a Commodore computer, T-squares, slide rules, and equipment catalogs. Suzanne's attention is drawn to the wall behind his desk, where he's hung ten black-and-white photos of workers in the Midway-Sunset field of the 1920s, their faces blackened by oil. Lace-up boots cling like refugees to their feet. Scruffy fedoras tilt on the backs of their heads.

Her father looked like this when he came home after a night shift pulling a string out of a well: the creases in his hands black with oil, fingernails crescents of grime. "I'm the devil, honey," he told her once. "I'm black as sin. Nothing will make me clean again."

One photo depicts a splintered oil derrick lit by the eerie glow of a waning blowout fire. Teetering in front of the wrecked superstructure is a man, a boy really, of eighteen or nineteen, covered with oil. Her eyes lock on him and won't let go.

Fitzgerald's feet shuffle on the carpet behind her. "That's the 1924 blowout. Bought those pictures from Standard Oil. Cost me a grand."

She breaks away and walks unsteadily to one of the wing chairs in front of his desk. It takes her several minutes to set up her tape recorder.

"Tell me about yourself first," she says, pulling a notebook from her purse.

Fitzgerald doesn't sit, but wanders around the office as he talks, touching various objects: a large tri-cone drill bit on a Plexiglas pedestal and a pool cue in a velvet-lined case.

A lot of what he says she knows already. He came to Taft as a child after his father, a Texas wildcatter, went broke during the depression and escaped to California with creditors on his heels. Connie graduated from Taft High, attended Cal Tech on a scholarship, and returned to his hometown to carve out a multimillion-dollar oil equipment business.

Suzanne taps her pen against her lip. "Let's talk about the tungsten bit. It seems like a risky venture. Carl Jimson landed in jail two years ago for peddling a scam recoating process. What's different about yours?"

Fitzgerald plays with a set of keys attached to a chain on his belt loop. "Let me tell you something, Mrs. Ricci. I sold equipment last year to the oil minister of Saudi Arabia. This is a guy who's half brother to the king. Think I'm going to ruin everything by peddling a piece of junk? That's what Carl Jimson had. Crap."

"Didn't he work for you at one time?"

"Years ago. But my bit is totally different. Say you're out in a field, drilling into valley hardpan. Depending on the underlying strata, companies spend a lot of money replacing the drill bits. So, rather than selling them for scrap, I've invented a process that dips them into an electrolyte solution, charged with tungsten particles."

"Aren't companies going to be suspicious, after they threw money away on Jimson's bogus ones?" Suzanne asks.

Fitzgerald struts in front of his desk. "Companies are standing in line. Standard Oil alone could save millions."

Her father was like this, always with a scheme, a plan. But all of his were failures. Another unsuccessful scheme meant a year eating Cheetos for breakfast and beans for dinner.

Fitzgerald speaks into his telephone intercom, and in a moment his chief engineer arrives with a stack of papers. "Here's the analysis done by our consultants at Cal Tech," Fitzgerald says. As he thumbs through them, his shirt cuff slides back, exposing the thick, dark hair on his wrists.

Suzanne asks for Xerox copies.

"Those are yours. We've got the originals," he says.

This afternoon, she'll phone Cal Tech to assure herself the paperwork isn't bogus.

"It's too bad you can't watch the process. We're doing final testing at a plant in LA. You could fly down with me in the plane," he says. While he talks, he shuffles a stack of pink phone messages as quickly as a Las Vegas dealer. He's signaling her he's done, and she's glad. Deadline is hours away, and Danny's home alone.

"I've got what I need," she says. "I'll talk to some industry folks by phone when I get back to Bakersfield. It's scheduled to appear in tomorrow's issue."

"Send me a copy."

"Sure." He's got a multimillion-dollar business, but can't afford a newspaper subscription?

"Can I use your telephone? I need to check on my son. He's home sick."

"Be my guest." He seems to forget about her as he stuffs a notebook and a stack of papers into his leather briefcase, slams the door of a large safe, and spins the dial. He settles a Stetson on his head, checks its tilt in a mirror.

No one answers at home.

They walk silently down the hall, steps muffled by thick carpet, past offices where men are bent over drafting boards, and through the lobby with its polished black floor and stainless steel counter. Outside, the brightness makes her eyeballs ache. She shakes his damp hand, feeling the wiry hairs on the back. She promises to call him at his Los Angeles office if she has any questions.

On the trip back to Bakersfield, clouds of hovering insects smash against her windshield, leaving smears on the glass. The temperamental radio intersperses heavy static with wailing Spanish love songs. She spins the dial to the "Praise and Blessings Hour."

As soon as she arrives home, Suzanne runs upstairs. A muffled rhythm comes from Danny's room and when she opens the door, he's lying on the rug in his pajamas, a headset plugged into his eight-track player. The vibration in the soles of her feet tells her music is blasting in his ears. When she waves at him, he barely blinks.

Her watch shows that deadline is four hours away, so she leaves him sprawled on the floor, putting off their talk until later.

At her dining-table office, she calls Cal Tech. "The technology's good," the consultant says. "I was skeptical at first, but my tests show the process works. The challenge will be quality control in the recoating process."

She learns that five companies, including Wickwood Oil, have signed contracts, and are stockpiling used bits waiting for Fitzgerald's factory to open sometime next month. Keys click as she types the column, and it isn't until the last page is finished she realizes Danny didn't come down for lunch.

With the envelope containing the story in her hand, she calls up the stairs. "Danny, there's leftover chili in the refrigerator. Eat something. I'm going downtown."

There's a faint grunt of assent. At the *News-Daily*, Hedges gives her his usual mournful look.

"This better be good. It's listed in the news budget, and His Eminence has inquired about it twice."

"Don't get your Jockeys in a twist, Carl. It's fine. What's not to like about the expansion of a local business?"

She uses a vacant office to call Pete. His phone rings for nearly a minute, and while she's waiting, she surveys the newsroom through the window. The computer system has been down all day, and women's section writers, who should be gathering their purses and heading home, are still proofing pages.

She hangs up and redials. For the last two weeks, Mrs. Messina in her menacing Sicilian accent, has taken Suzanne's messages, but Pete hasn't called back. This time, he answers. She hears a television in the background.

"Danny hasn't left the house for days," she says. "I think someone blabbed, and he's been threatened."

Pete's sigh flutters over the line. "I wish I knew what's going on, Suzanne. I telephoned Strong the same night we talked to Danny. I didn't use the kid's information, because I got his story and a lot more from Jade. The next morning, the sheriff's people combed Franzen's car and every inch of his house. Strong was positive Smithson would file within a day or two."

"That was three weeks ago."

"You think I've lost track? I can tell you to the hour how long it's been. The fucking DA is stalling."

"Where's Jade? Is she safe?"

There's a long silence. "She's gone into hiding."

"She's in danger too?"

"Strong promised, absolutely, to keep their identities under wraps until there's an arrest."

"You donkey, someone up the chain of command violated confidentiality." If he were close, she'd kick him in the nuts.

"I *had* to tell Strong in order to get Franzen. I thought if they arrested him, both the kids would be safe."

"Could have been that pussy-faced sheriff, Hap Monroe," Suzanne continues. "He's running for election next year. Maybe he owed a favor."

"Wait a minute. If we're talking blame, how about your newspaper? Not a single story naming the obvious suspect in the murder of my girl."

Now that computers are back up, she can see the newsroom moving sluggishly into action. Reporters argue with editors or stare at computer monitors the size of portable television sets while they keyboard their stories.

"I'm only a freelancer. I don't know how the news decisions are made." A nerve in her neck twinges. Why hasn't Tug Garrity, the pit-bull managing editor, assigned a reporter? It's common knowledge among the journalists that Franzen's the suspect.

"Hold on a minute," he says.

As she waits, Suzanne watches Garrity emerge from his office, face wrinkled in anger. He shakes a forefinger inches from Hedges' nose. Is he upset about her column? Whitman's office light is off and blinds half-closed.

Pete's back. "There's news."

"Oh, my God, an arrest?" Her legs go weak. She sinks into the squeaky desk chair.

"It's in the works. That was Strong on his way home. Smithson's scheduled a press conference for tomorrow morning at ten."

"I'm . . ." She presses her fingers against her lips. Tears threaten to leak into whatever she was going to say. "I've got to tell Danny."

"Good." He clears his throat. "When you're done, come over to my place. Let's have a drink."

28

Suzanne kicks off her flip-flops and perches on the edge of Pete's swimming pool. It's not a fancy one with decorative tile and waterfalls like Reggie's, but nice nonetheless. The cool water makes her feet tingle, and the concrete is warm under her shorts. Sunlight flashes between the houses and creeps over the roof, touching the top branches of the big sycamore. The atmosphere shimmers. Water at the deep end glitters, sapphire against the gray decking.

A musical clink of ice accompanies Pete as he carries two glasses from the kitchen. "Here you are." Suzanne is pleasantly surprised when he hands her a JD, a taste she inherited from her father.

Suzanne gazes up at him, seemingly seven feet tall from this angle. He doesn't look happy, exactly, but he moves more lightly, like somebody off work on a Friday night. He slips off his tennis shoes and plops down beside her, his arm high to keep his drink from spilling.

He touches her glass with his. "'To some sense out of a fucking mess."

They sip their drinks. She fishes for something to say. Despite the murders and the friendship between Danny and Grace, she doesn't know Pete very well. She scoops handfuls of water and trickles it over her calves.

"Do you think the case is strong enough?" she asks.

"The search warrant yielded some damning evidence." He rolls the glass between his palms.

"Why didn't you tell me that? I've been going crazy with worry."

"It's bad. I haven't been sleeping, thinking about it." He looks at her, his irises nearly black in the waning light. "Neighbors saw Franzen's carpeting and plumbing fixtures being replaced the day after Grace disappeared."

She touches his shoulder. His skin burns under her hand.

"They found blood matching her type in the house and on carpeting from the trunk of his car. And . . ." His voice trembles with anger. ". . . his pubic hair and hairs from his dogs were found on her body."

A long swallow of JD burns her throat. "Those are terrible things to hear. But it's good, too. It means they can get a conviction."

"It's a way to look at it."

"I can't wait for tomorrow. I'm relieved, but also afraid," she says.

"There's a lot at stake. I think after tomorrow, Gracie might be able to rest. I can feel her; she's been in constant motion all this time. I can see the possibility she could be at peace."

"And Danny can get on with his life," she says.

The scent of barbequing steaks drifts from the neighbor's yard. Children laugh, and a ball thumps against the fence. After this is over, she'll repair the creaky fence at her place and replace the rusty barbeque.

"When he's convicted, I'm going to take Gracie's ashes home to Morro Bay and scatter them in the ocean. But not until then," he says.

"She'd be happy, not only that Franzen's convicted, but that Danny's safe." Suzanne feels the freedom she'll have, to enjoy small things or even be irritated by inconsequential stuff. She rolls a sip of whiskey around her mouth. Her taste buds have been dulled for awhile. Her mother drank a lot when Suzanne was growing up. Still does. Maybe she needed it to raise five children on a laundress's pay. No more about her mother. Don't ruin the evening. Pete collects her glass and goes into the house to fix two more. She hasn't eaten all day, and her intoxication meter is creeping up.

He returns with the drinks and a bag of chips. "Sorry, I don't have any food in the house."

Suzanne rips open the bag and stuffs a few in her mouth. "You're talking to a girl who ate Cheetos, the poor kids' breakfast, when she was growing up." She lies back, the sky overhead pricked with a few stars.

"What will you do, once it's over?" she asks.

"I honestly don't know." His feet stir the water. "What about you?"

"I've got my hands full until Danny's out of high school." She's immediately sorry she spoke. Grace never will graduate.

A mottled gray-green lizard scuttles across the deck and falls into the pool, where it scrabbles frantically with its long, clawed toes.

Pete gets a blue skimming net from behind the diving board. "I dreamed for years of buying a little place on the coast—in Cambria, maybe—and using it on my time off. Retiring there one day. I could buy a little boat."

The net swirls in the water. He scoops up the reptile and shakes it into the garden. "Have you ever thought of remarrying?"

"God no, I'm not right for it."

"You have a secret imperfection? Something really terrible?" He looks amused.

Heat from her body dampens her clothes. At the shallow end, she descends the steps and lets the water lap against her legs. With too much to drink, the words just seem to flow out of her mouth. "Fact is, I'm a lousy fuck."

"You're kidding."

"Sad, but true."

"Your husband told you this?"

"Many times, between affairs."

The old ache comes back, like a stubborn stain. She plunges into the water, dives deep, cold water sliding through her clothes, touching her nipples. The pool lights are off, and down here in the dark she's invisible. Not too tall, not awkward. Protected. By the time she breaks the surface, her lungs are begging for air. She treads water and swipes her hair out of her eyes.

Pete jumps in. The splash rains drops on her face. "I haven't done a water rescue for awhile," he says.

"I don't need rescuing."

They bob up and down, hands brushing each other. His hair is flattened, and his sleeveless shirt clings to his shoulders. With lazy strokes, they swim to the shallow end and sit half-submerged on the steps looking at the red autumn moon. Television murmurs in a nearby house.

She feels cold and hot, like a swallow of JD on ice.

"I've got an idea," he says.

"No."

"What? You don't know what I was going to say."

"Yes, I do," she says. "You're not going to get me out of these wet clothes."

"Drive home in your wet clothes. That's what I was going to say." He cocks his arm on the step.

She tips her head back, letting her hair float on the water.

"Second idea," he says. "How about another drink?"

"I'm already hammered." It isn't true, but she says it anyway.

"Okay, forget that one. Last and best idea. Are you ready?"

"Yep."

"We go to bed with our wet clothes on."

She laughs, and they climb out. Water streams from their shirts and shorts, puddling on the deck. He touches her shoulder and turns her gently toward him. He looks proud yet needy, like a beggar too ashamed to ask. His eyes seek something, understanding perhaps, and she sees that he's had no one to confide in; he's dealing with his unbearable loss alone, as if he were on a barren moon. Just as she's been. Tears spring to her eyes, and she's moved by the red moon, the drops clinging to his lashes, and the plea on his face.

Suzanne strokes his wet arm, water running ahead of her finger, the wiry hairs smoothing, then springing back. She doesn't want to relent, yet she does. Tenderness for him wells up in her mixed with tenderness for herself.

She leans over and licks a drop from his cheek.

In his bedroom the covers are smooth and pillows arranged neatly. At first, she feels like a burglar. His wallet, a jackknife, and a dish full of change sit on a tall dresser. Another low, wide dresser has a bare top and dusty mirror. Has Pete gotten rid of the clothes Janis left behind?

He comes close, and she catches the scent of his wet clothes and skin. His fingers struggle with the buttons on her damp blouse. Finally he loses patience and tugs it over her head. She slides her hands under his shirt, feels his heat. As they kiss and lick, he rocks her hips against his erection. The room tilts, and she's disoriented, unaccustomed to the way their bodies fit together. Pete is taller than Carlo. With her chin almost even with his, she realizes how good it feels not to hunch over, not to make herself small as she did with Carlo, but to look into Pete's eyes with her back straight. They undress each other, and when they stretch out on the soft sheets, their toes, legs, arms intertwined, it feels so fine she groans in his mouth as they kiss.

He slides down her, his tongue tracing a line to the slippery moisture between her legs. "You taste like sex. And chlorine," he says.

29

Pete wakes as the dove gray dawn slips around the edge of the window shade. He doesn't see Suzanne at first, his face half-buried in the pillow, just feels the difference in the tension of the mattress. It's weighted, sloping away from his thigh and chest. For an instant, a wrinkle in his memory fools him into thinking it's Janet here beside him.

His beard scrapes against the pillow; he turns his head and sees the tangle of Suzanne's hair against the elegant curve of her spine. His eyes move down, and it seems he's never really seen a woman's back before, the soft expanse of white skin, the globe of her buttocks and the secretive cleft.

Sliding closer, he slips his arms around her and cups her breasts in his palms.

"We don't have time." Her voice is husky.

His thumb and forefinger pinch a nipple as plump as a cherry.

"I have to go home and change," she murmurs. Her hips move against his erection.

"We'll be quick."

But they aren't. He presses into her from behind, a long, slow, slick, hot entry that's even better than the night before when their skin was cool from the swim. They burn with sleep heat, sex heat, the fire of newness. Their hips rock, his cock between the fleshy mounds of her ass, the knobs of her spine against his torso, and he revels in the perfection of their fit; in the midst of the sweat and scent.

When he's almost there, Suzanne pulls away.

"What?" He struggles to catch his breath.

"Shhhh." She presses him back against the mattress, straddles him, and guides him inside her to the sound of slick, wet flesh. Pete cups her face and pulls it to his. Her hair tents around him, and she's so close he can see the mole beside her right eye and the rose color of her lips. In the midst of his climax, she seems like a lover from long ago, known yet foreign.

While Pete showers and shaves, Suzanne puts on her damp clothes from the dryer. She zips her shorts and slips her toes into her flip-flops. "See you in a couple of hours." She wipes a speck of shaving cream from his cheek and kisses the spot.

He dresses carefully in slacks, navy blue blazer, and tie. On the way to the press conference, he stops at 7-Eleven for a cup of takeout coffee. The first sip burns his tongue, but it doesn't bother him.

"We're going to get him, Gracie. The bastard is going to prison," he says.

In the lobby of the county administration center, the press is gathered in a cluster, waiting for Smithson, the DA. Microphones line the podium like a row of teeth, and camera tripods are set up on a platform. In the crowd, Pete sees his friend Jon Camacho and his wife. The Camachos's daughter died in a drunk-driving crash that Smithson's office never prosecuted. There are other familiar faces: Liza Theuss in civilian clothes, Strong and Muñoz, and Deputy Coroner M. Kramer. Pete scans the crowd for Suzanne, but doesn't see her.

Smithson emerges from the elevator with a couple of staffers hovering at his back. His white hair straggles untidily, and the knot on his necktie is slightly askew. It might be an indicator of the pressure he's under that he dispenses with the formality of thanking people for coming.

He reads from a written text. "When I was elected without opposition in the June primary, it was because the people of Kern County felt safer. Their children are safer. They knew that in the last four years, more suspects have been charged. More have been brought to trial. Convictions under my watch increased twenty percent."

TV and radio reporters shift restlessly. They're waiting for a quote, and this isn't the three-sentence sound bite they need.

Smithson continues with filler. Pete shifts uneasily from foot to foot. The DA doesn't need election rhetoric; the June primary confirmed him for another term. If Franzen were under arrest, Smithson would open with it.

Finally, he gets to the point. "Three weeks ago a young girl was murdered. She was raped, stabbed multiple times, and her body abandoned alongside the road. It was a despicable crime that deserves swift and severe punishment."

Pete spots Suzanne standing near the elevator. Above her head the light blinks as the car moves, like a meter registering her anxiety about Danny.

His fingernails bite into his palms.

"The sheriff has investigated. Search warrants have been issued on one of Bakersfield's best-known law enforcement professionals, even though he has protected citizens for more than thirty years." Smithson attempts a righteous, ringing tone, but can't bring it off.

A spider web sways in the air conditioner current. Pete takes a deep breath and clings to the memory of Grace as she was her last afternoon, confident and cocky, as though the future were a strip of smooth highway, rolling out in front of her.

Smithson licks his lips. "We know that Police Commissioner Galen Franzen hosted a party for his young friends the night of April 7. Someone, we don't know who, brought drugs to his house. But despite what rumors you may have heard, there is no evidence Grace Stannard died there, or that she even died that night."

Pulse thrums against Pete's temples. What about the new floor in Franzen's bathroom? What about the blood in his car? What about his pubic hair on Grace's body? What about Jade's story that Franzen provided drugs on many occasions?

Strong sidles up beside Pete. His sport jacket hangs loosely around his torso, and skin bags under his eyes.

"Unfortunately, there have been some investigative missteps that have erected substantial barriers in the prosecution of this case," Smithson says.

Pete grasps the detective's bicep. Strong grimaces and shakes him off. He inclines his head toward the podium. *Listen*, he's saying.

"When the victim was examined by the coroner's office, forensics officers neglected to take the temperature of the body. Without it, we have no evidence to corroborate when the crime actually occurred."

The elevator doors open with a soft wheeze. Vinson emerges, and Pete's breath comes faster.

"So, while we'll continue to vigorously investigate Grace Stannard's murder, my office has determined there is insufficient evidence to file homicide charges at this time."

Reporters shout questions at Smithson, but the one from talk radio with the loudest voice gets the nod. "Why didn't the coroner's technician do the test?"

"You'd have to direct that question to the sheriff," Smithson says. "The coroner's deputy tells me it's done at the request of the investigating detectives."

"Fucking son of a bitch," Strong says under his breath. "It's a murder, and I gotta ask?"

The reporter from the NBC affiliate asks, "Is your refusal to file charges against Commissioner Franzen because he's a powerful, well-known public figure?"

"I made the decision, in consultation with my office's charging committee, on the basis of sufficiency of evidence for a conviction. Our consensus was that evidence is lacking."

A late reporter hurries in and sets up a tripod for the cameraman. The others glare at him. He's messing up their sound. "Have you and Sheriff Monroe discussed where the case goes from here? What's next?"

"I notified him of our decision last night, but any further action depends on new evidence."

Radio wants to ask another question, but the TV networks heft cameras off tripods and circle around Pete.

Blood was congealed in her hair, Pete remembers. Her eyes were open, but dull and fogged. Fingers on one hand spread. The knife wounds looked like thin lips, deadly kisses all over her body. With a tremendous effort, as if he were hefting the dead weight of an unconscious victim, he pulls himself together. Camera lights snap on, and he feels their heat.

"Are you giving up, Pete?" Someone asks.

"There'll be no letting up, no stopping until someone is jailed and convicted."

"What's your next step?"

"I'm not at liberty to say right now, but stay tuned. You'll be seeing a lot more of me." After four or five queries, he cuts them off, exhausted by his burden of self-control. He aches to smash the soft cartilage in Smithson's nose or wrap his fingers around the coroner's neck.

He longs to howl. To cry.

When he was fourteen or fifteen his dad took out a party of sport fishermen. While Pete reeled in a customer's line, one prong of a triple-barbed hook sank into his hand. It penetrated more and more deeply, ripping the fleshy part of his thumb. As he struggled to extract it, amidst the boat's heaving and the blood dripping down his arm, he cried. His dad used a knife to cut it out.

Across the room, he sees Suzanne, face chalk white, whispering to Liza. He searches the lobby for Vinson. The *News-Daily's* political reporter, Mike Gwaltney, hovers nearby, hoarding his questions until the other media are gone, angling for an exclusive.

Before Gwaltney closes in, Camacho intercepts Pete, his eyes red-rimmed. He's pinned a large button on his lapel with a photo on it of his daughter and the years of her birth and death.

"I can't believe it," Pete says.

"It was the same with Sarah. That bastard waits and waits, and then comes up with some reason, any bullshit thing, why the guy should go free."

Camacho tugs at his right ear, a nervous gesture which has stretched its lobe longer than the left. "After Sarah died, I'd look in the mirror when I shaved. I'd say, seventeen days today, forty-five days today. Finally, I said, a hundred and fifty-seven days. That's the day Smithson abandoned her case entirely."

Pete shoves his hands in his pockets to hide their trembling. "We're going to get them, Jon. We're going to squeeze that gutless whore Smithson. We'll send Franzen and everybody else involved to prison."

Gwaltney, who's been eavesdropping, taps Pete's arm.

"Isn't this really a case of bad investigative work, like Smithson said? The sheriff and the coroner dropped the ball?"

"There's a mountain of blame to go around, Mike. Maybe you should look in your own backyard. The *News-Daily*, for instance, never reported that warrants had been served to search Galen Franzen's home and car. He's been the number one suspect since a few days after Grace died, but there's been no mention of him in the paper. It's a conspiracy at the highest levels of power in this town."

Gwaltney shifts from foot to foot. "That's a little strong."

"Not nearly strong enough."

Pete catches a glimpse of Vinson and Smithson, heads tilted toward each other at exactly the same angle, deep in conversation. "How does Vinson fit into the picture?"

"He's head of the charging committee," Gwaltney says.

30

Suzanne sits in the passenger seat of a sound truck three days later with a microphone in her hand. Her friend Colin, who owns the truck, agreed to donate his time for tonight's protest.

Two hundred people pack the street in front of Franzen's house. Across the street in the park, volunteers at folding tables gather signatures for Smithson's recall. It's dusk. A line of palm trees in the park casts shadows like prison bars. Maybe it's a sign Franzen is headed for the lockup. Microwave trucks from the TV stations hover in the playground parking lot. The protest will be over in time for the ten o'clock news.

Colin steers his truck cautiously through the crowd. "Come on," he says under his breath, "get out of my way, mister. You want to end up a grease spot?" He likes fiddling with his equipment, rearranging the wiring, and choosing the music. People, not so much.

Suzanne spots Strong standing beside one of two unmarked Ass Pains parked down the block. Closer to the house, two sheriff's deputies sit in patrol vehicles with engines running.

"Turn on the amplifier. We're ready," Suzanne says. Colin clicks the dial and frowns as *Tragedy* by the Bee Gees pours out of the roof-mounted loudspeaker.

"Bad choice," he says.

"Why the hell not? A murdered girl and no one in jail sound like a tragedy to me."

At the end of the block, he makes a U-turn. "I've worked campaigns since 1950. People don't want to hear about tragedy. They want to feel good. Hear upbeat music, like marches."

"Losing a kid is everybody's worst nightmare. No smiley faces here." Suzanne spent a couple of hours last night listening to eight-tracks searching for appropriate music. "Anyway, this is the one I chose."

Colin sighs.

As the truck glides back toward the crowd, she spots Kevin. He's standing beneath a crepe myrtle tree on the corner lot, watching and smoking. He holds the cigarette between his thumb and forefinger like an habitual smoker, which seems so wrong, considering his boyish, freckled skin. Months ago at the skateboard park, Franzen had bought him candy and a Coke. She tilts the rearview mirror so she can watch him. He tosses the cigarette into the gutter and grinds it out with his tennis shoe.

Music echoes between the houses. On the street and in the park, Pete's supporters slip flyers under the windshield wipers of the vans and station wagons to pump up support for Smithson's recall.

When the sound truck makes another pass in front of Franzen's, Pete is standing on the sidewalk holding a bullhorn. Blackout shades shield the interior of the house from prying eyes.

That night following Smithson's press conference, Suzanne couldn't sleep. Downstairs, Danny huddled in a blanket on the couch, the television rolling through a dreary menu of 1950s cowboy shows and bad comedies. She swallowed a sleeping pill and gulped a JD on ice, but her eyes refused to close.

She reviewed the wall of official betrayals that has risen brick by brick, thwarting each of her efforts to keep Danny safe. Vinson intervened to send Danny to High Endeavor. Superior Court refused to open up testimony in Reggie's murder trial. The grand jury never responded to her demand for an investigation of the district attorney's office. Now Grace's murder will go unpunished. The Club will slither away unscathed.

At 3 a.m. that morning, she had called Pete. "We're going to start a campaign to recall Smithson. The first shot will be a demonstration in front of Franzen's house."

"A recall?" Pete was awake, but his tongue sounded thick. "You're crazy. He won outright in the June primary."

"We're not serious about the recall," she says. "We just want to squeeze Smithson's nuts hard enough to make him file charges."

"Then why not Smithson's place?"

"Because Franzen's the story."

On the sidewalk, Pete signals her to cut the music. Raising his bullhorn, he exhorts the crowd.

"April 9, the man who owns this house held a party, where he gave drugs and liquor to kids. The next day this man, a law enforcement official, completely familiar with investigative techniques, had the carpeting and fixtures torn out of his bathroom. My daughter, who attended the party, was found dead April 12 with over thirty stab wounds in her body."

His voice over the bullhorn escalates until it hurts her ears. "The rug in the trunk of this man's car is stained with blood that matches my daughter's. On my daughter's body were hairs from this man's dogs. On her body were hairs from his private parts."

The crowd is still. Suzanne smells Bakersfield oil in the air.

"Yet Ian Smithson, Kern County's elected district attorney, the man sworn to prosecute criminals to the fullest extent of the law, says there's no evidence."

"If it can happen to my child, it can happen to yours. Criminals must be shown that they can't get away with abusing and murdering our children. We've got to make punishment swift and sure again."

He exhorts them to write letters, call radio stations, post flyers, and slap bumper stickers on their cars for Smithson's recall.

Suzanne signals to Colin, and he switches on *Ain't No Stoppin' Us No*w by McFadden and Whitehead. The crowd claps, chants, and sings the words.

"Okay," he says. "Maybe you do know what you're doing."

Suzanne can hardly believe it's working. She's never tried to organize anything. Her job has been reporting yields, citing statistics, quoting what government officials and industry analysts say about the oil business. She's been safe, hiding behind the print.

But in the last two days she's stepped out from behind the typewriter, intent on squeezing Smithson until he puts Franzen on trial—a trial that surely will break open The Club's protective shell.

The music fades in anticipation of Pete's wrap-up. "Ian Smithson must file charges against Galen Franzen, the criminal who lives in this house. Franzen's been free twenty-five days. During that time my daughter has been cremated, but he's slept in his soft bed, eaten meals, and taken a trip to the ocean."

Pete's got too much fire under the message now. If the protest gets violent, the effort will lose credibility. Suzanne throws open the door of the truck.

"Ian Smithson has told the sheriff he might consider filing charges against Franzen for contributing to the delinquency of a minor and furnishing marijuana. Both are misdemeanors—no worse than littering or trespassing."

She hasn't heard about this pitiful concession on Smithson's part. Where has Pete gotten his information? Strong was here earlier. She glances around, but the mass of people is too dense to spot him.

The sun is low, and shadows give Pete's face a vengeful look. She perches on the running board, above the crowd, and draws her forefinger across her neck. *Wrap up.* He shakes his head.

"Is a year in jail enough punishment for stabbing a child thirty times?"

The crowd yells *No.*

"Is one year a fair exchange for a girl's life?"

No, no!

"Let's kick Ian Smithson out of office and put this child killer in prison!" Pete strides onto Franzen's porch and hammers on the door. He's trespassing now, subject to arrest. She struggles through the tightly packed crowd.

Protesters surge toward the house, grinding the dead grass under their feet. The deputies clamber from their cars, one shouting into a hand-held radio extender. Rage darkens and twists Pete's face so that he seems unrecognizable as the man she made love with a few days ago.

The concussion of a gunshot clubs everyone into silence.

31

After an endless moment, women's high-pitched screams begin. Men's yells fill the air as protesters trip over bushes and trees, scratching their arms and legs. They push, shove, and stumble into the street. A boy loses his grip on mother's hand. The child falls, but Pete snatches him from under stampeding feet as he fights his way toward the park, where he hands the child to his mother.

Suzanne's body twitches with the urge to run, but something more substantial roots her in place. She struggles toward the house between sweating bodies. Police are trying to force Franzen's door. Harry Strong runs through the side gate into the backyard. Meanwhile, police cars approach from both ends of the block, their forward reds flashing and sirens wailing. Suzanne cowers under the sensory overload.

Officers jump from their cars and use batons to push the remaining crowd across the street into the park.

She's bewildered. No one lies in the street; the pavement is free of blood. Pete appears, grabs her, and pulls her to his side. Her arm feels the pressure of each finger.

"Someone took a shot at us," he says. "I didn't think this could get any uglier." Sweat drips from his jaw, leaving spots his shirt.

"You were stirring them up. Advocating vigilante justice," she says.

"What? No, I—"

Franzen's door splinters. Police lunge inside.

In a brief silence, an ice cream truck's bell tinkles at the other end of the park, blocked from cruising the street by patrol cars angled to form a barricade. The truck pulls up behind the television sat trucks and raises its awning, ready for sales.

Pete and Suzanne hover near Franzen's broken door. After a few minutes, Strong emerges from the house.

Pete strides alongside him. "What happened?"

"He ate it. The gun was next to his hand." Strong sounds admiring, as if he respects the decision of a fellow officer to wrap up the case so neatly.

"That doesn't mean anything," Pete says.

"You think I'm a rookie? Of course, it doesn't, but *we're* out of it. The PD will follow up; it's their case."

Strong turns toward the waiting media, but Suzanne stops him. "Was the boy there?"

"What boy?"

"Cut the bullshit, Harry," Suzanne says. "Kevin, Franzen's boy lover. I saw him down the block earlier."

"So what? Grace's murder case is closed. It's off my desk, now that the old guy's dead."

Pete steps between Suzanne and the detective. "What if the kid was jealous and killed Grace because Franzen was interested in her? Kevin might have murdered Franzen, too."

Strong sighs. "The commissioner didn't like girls, Pete."

"Franzen was married for forty years," Pete says. "Grace could have caught his eye. Despite the evidence—her blood in his house and car, Franzen's hair and the dogs' fur on her body—none of it says he was the only one responsible."

"As far as I'm concerned, Franzen was the sole killer. Remorse made him commit suicide."

"Then who lifted Grace into the trunk of his car? No way the old man could have done it himself."

Creases deepen between the detective's eyebrows. "Not my problem."

The sun has dropped behind the palms and ash trees bordering the park. Franzen's dead landscaping and broken door are indistinct. Suzanne feels the slow spin of events moving against them. Grace's murder investigation is ending too neatly. Without a spotlight on law enforcement corruption, Danny remains caught in the net cast by The Club.

"What if Kevin killed them both?" she asks.

"I'm going in to write my report," Strong says.

32

Without thanking Colin or saying goodbye to Pete, Suzanne races for home. The house is dark, but next door at Reggie's, the new owners are entertaining.

It's all wrong. At Reggie's people are starting a fresh chapter in their lives while she and Danny are being sucked relentlessly into a shadowed, murky world. The hopeful feeling that buoyed her while she organized the demonstration is blown to bits. With Franzen dead, there will be no show trial to spotlight The Club's crimes.

Nothing is being done to protect Danny, who identified the players. He's a rabbit fleeing a pack of coyotes.

Her heart beats quickly as she enters the house. "Danny, are you here?"

She climbs the stairs, replaying the morning Reggie was killed. The outcome is the same. His bed is rumpled, but empty.

She makes a call to Tito's Restaurant in Taft. "Lucky? It's me."

"Hey, Sis. What's up?" Nights, he works there as a fry cook.

"I need you."

"The kid's okay?"

"No."

"I'll be at the Olive Highway truck stop in an hour and thirty," he says.

"See you then."

"Don't smoke no fags," he says, their mantra for *keep safe* since the day their father blew up the house.

Her stomach growls. She hasn't eaten all day, so she heats two leftover tacos and a can of refried beans. Once the food is on the plate, it smells like garbage.

The phone rings.

"I hear you were out at Galen's tonight," Liza says.

"In the street." Suzanne is cautious, remembering that Liza knew Franzen and was close to his late wife.

"Danny too?"

"Your cop buddies didn't give you a list of everyone in the crowd?"

"Chill out, Hon. Just checking on the kid."

"That's *my* job, Liza. Back off." Anxiety and guilt, combined with the food odor, are making her nauseated. Weeks ago, she'd been naïve enough to reassure Danny he'd be protected. If she hadn't insisted he talk to Pete, he might have been safe now.

It's after eleven when she heads for the truck stop. Suzanne spots two cop cars on the way and wonders if patrols have been added after the mess at Franzen's. She parks at the truck stop in view of the street. The VW shakes as a truck-trailer hauling fresh tomatoes rumbles to the pumps. The tomato scent mingles with the smell of gasoline vapor. The trucker descends from the cab, and slides the nozzle into the big aluminum fuel tank. While he waits, he leans against the cab, strikes a match, and lights a cigarette.

Suzanne watches the cigarette tip, her eyes locked on him, as he sucks it into a hot glow.

———

She'd been home sick from school. Not sick really, but miserable. The boys in her class, who at eleven were vicious little runts, teased her about her height. Girls pretended to admire her thrift-store clothes, then laughed behind her back. That morning after her mother yelled at her for the third time, she got up, went to the bathroom and stuck her finger down her throat. She lay in bed with her bogus stomach flu, while the boys left for school and mother for the laundry. Dad had been at the drill site for hours. Luxuriating in the quiet, she listened to radio soap operas and read her favorite sexy passages from a Readers Digest condensed book she found in her mother's bedside table.

By noon, her feet were itchy and her empty stomach growled. She walked the three blocks to the Dairy Queen and bought a soft cone, which tasted cool and sweet on her tongue. She dawdled, first in the library, then under a cottonwood tree, where a family of jays darted from a shaggy nest.

Half a block from home, Suzanne spotted her father's pickup in the driveway. The job had shut down waiting for a replacement part to arrive, she learned later. She stopped, unsure how to avoid punishment. No memory remains of the sound, only the force that slammed her to the hard-packed dirt street and knocked her unconscious.

When she awoke, the roof was blown off, the house a mass of ripped joists and rafters. Glass from windows lay between the weeds, glittered on the street, nested in her hair. Fire leaped twenty feet. Her father's body was recovered from the burned shell of the house. A fire investigator said his cigarette ignited natural gas vapors from a leaking floor furnace.

―――

The tomato hauler holds his cigarette between clenched teeth, squinting against the smoke, and hangs up the nozzle. As he clatters away, Lucky's Chevy Luv wheels into the lot. She locks the van and joins him in the pickup.

"What's up, Suzie?"

"Things are shitty."

"Tell ole Lucky," he says, slinging an arm over her shoulder.

The comforting weight brings on a trickle of tears. She knuckles them away and lets the events of the last few days spill out.

"Those fuckers." The scar on the side of his face reddens. He twists the key and starts the truck. "Let's get going."

They cruise the parks and the high school's baseball dugout. At the Greyhound station, Lucky leaves the pickup at the curb and marches inside. When he returns, he shakes his head. "I scared off some old fart trying to recruit a homeless kid, but no sign of him."

"This is a waste of time," she says.

He taps his fingers on the steering wheel. "Let me think a minute."

Since they were kids, Lucky had been the one with a talent for finding things. Once, she lost her watch, a gift from Grandma Marlowe. After Suzanne turned the house upside down and accused the Stooges of theft, Lucky had found it by shaking the watch out of the sofa coils.

He puts the truck in gear. They prowl the downtown alleys, which smell of rotting garbage, then the restaurants along 99.

"What are we looking for?" It's nearly one, and her skin is crawling with impatience.

"Danny's been gone for hours. Boys his age are always hungry, right? At Tito's, hungry folks gather by the back door at closing time in case we've got leftovers. I'm trying to spot people by the back door of restaurants."

"I've got an idea." She directs him up Columbus, where a local lawyer owns the Shamrock Grill.

The street is parked solid, but in the overflow lot out back, cars have thinned. A dumpster sits adjacent to the rear door, but nobody loiters close by. Lucky parks in the shadow of a tree and kills the engine.

"See the mark spray-painted to the right of the door?"

"It looks like the Greek letter psi."

"Not too many bums know Greek. It's a fork. In other words, 'Free food here.'"

They wait, tense and silent. Crickets chirp in the vacant lot behind them. Smoke from the grill curls out the kitchen door.

———

It was her fault back then. All these years, she's squeezed the memory small and hid it. The day she'd stayed home from school, it seemed only ice cream would make her feel better. She had no money; her brothers were broke. A search yielded no coins in the crevices behind the couch cushions. There was one other place. She attached a wad of gum to the end of a flat metal yardstick and shoved it through the grating in the floor furnace. At the bottom of the furnace box were a dime and two quarters. She poked and stabbed at them. Finally, a quarter stuck to the gum. Later she learned she'd knocked loose the coupling from the gas line to the furnace.

The coin went in her pocket, the yardstick lay forgotten on the floor, and she closed the back door tightly behind her. *You didn't know what you were doing*, she's told herself all these years.

———

During the next half hour, Lucky gets out and pees in the bushes. The lot empties. The sound of clanging pots and pans drifts from the kitchen, and a brown-skinned man in a white apron tosses garbage sacks into the Dumpster.

Two figures, a man and a woman, appear from the side street pushing a shopping cart. She has a shaved head and wears a pair of ragged jeans covered with patches on knees and ass. His face is hidden by a wide-brimmed hat pulled low over his forehead. Then a couple of girls, one with her blouse knotted under her small breasts, the other wearing a poncho, join the line. A minute later a rattling Ford pickup parks at the curb, and three men climb out. Their hair is long and tangled, and one wears a sheathed knife on his belt.

When the cook's helper reappears in the doorway, twenty people are milling around the door. He carries a set of tongs and cradles a big baking pan in the crook of his arm. The hungry crowd produces metal camping plates, paper cups, and small cardboard boxes. The three men push to the front of the line, which generates yelling and profanities, but no one challenges them. The cook's helper hands out what looks like fried chicken, then returns with a pan of leftover bread.

"Shit," Lucky says. "Looks like we struck out." He adjusts his seat back.

Suzanne clutches his arm.

"There." She holds her breath as she watches the two girls pause for a second or two in the yellow rectangle of light from the kitchen. She doesn't blink. The one wearing the poncho is tall, and long hair hangs in a curtain around her face. Her elbows jut out, and she stands with feet too far apart.

Suzanne slips out of the pickup. The two are absorbed with the food, pulling at hunks of bread with their fingers and gnawing chicken off the bone. They smell of sweat. She isolates Danny's odor, a scent she's known all his life.

"Danny, it's me," she says in a low voice.

He looks up. The long, honey-colored wig not only conceals his dark hair but creates the illusion of rounded cheekbones and curved lips. The poncho disguises his straight hips and wide shoulders to all but the keenest observer.

"Get out of here," he whispers.

"Come on. It's dangerous." She grasps his arm. Tears fill her eyes as she feels the weight of his bones.

His voice cracks. "You think home's safe?"

"I know things are bad right now, but I can get you away."

The crowd backs away from their whispered conversation as if to avoid contamination.

"You can go to Lucky's. Stay with him."

He combs his fingers through the wig's long hair, pulling it more closely around his face. "You don't get it. Taft is only thirty miles away. In the same county, where these guys control everything."

"Grandma Rossi." Suzanne is truly desperate to suggest Carlo's mother, who is half senile and lives in a camper beside the Salton Sea.

"You are so frigging dumb." A drop of spittle flies from Danny's mouth. "I'm not safe anywhere. I didn't want to talk to Grace's dad, but you made me. Said how we'd catch Franzen, put him in prison."

"He's dead now."

"Yeah, and it could be me or anybody else who knows too much." He scurries away, the girl a few steps behind. They're about to plunge through an opening in the oleander hedge when a BPD car jounces over the curb and squeals to a stop. A single side spotlight pins the young people like butterflies.

Two cops fling open the doors. "Stop. Hands up!" Boots pound, hoarse grunts and shouts bounce off the walls. Danny and the girl scramble through the tangled branches.

Suzanne plants herself between Danny and the officers. "No, no! It's my son. Leave him alone, he's my son. I was picking him up, just picking him up, he was at a costume party and I'd come to get him . . ."

One officer swerves, but the other collides with her, knocking the breath out of her. She struggles to inhale but can manage only small sips of air.

The girl disappears, and they converge on Danny. As he stoops to wriggle through a gap in the hedge, an officer snatches at the poncho. Danny kicks backward like a balky horse. The officer stumbles, but his partner grabs Danny around the torso, staggers, and brings him down. The wig flies to the pavement and rests there like roadkill.

Suzanne finally manages a deep breath. Blood seeps from raw spots on her knees and palms. Ignoring Lucky's outstretched hand, she staggers to her feet. One officer, face sweaty and paunch heaving, jams a knee into Danny's spine. He fishes at the back of his duty belt for handcuffs, but she hauls on his arm.

"Back, off, lady or I'll arrest you for interfering with an officer." This one is the rookie, his thin blond mustache closely trimmed.

"Get away from him! I'm his mother. I work at the *News-Standard*." Any ploy to free him.

"He's under arrest for possession of drugs." The overweight cop untangles the cuffs from his belt and snaps one loop around Danny's wrist.

"There's no drugs. He doesn't do drugs. He's a good boy who went to a teen party." Suzanne leans close to the cop kneeling on Danny's spine and smells his stinking breath. "Who said he had drugs? Somebody lied."

"Get back." The rookie reaches for his wooden baton. Lucky seizes Suzanne's arm, but she jerks free.

"You jackasses! He's a victim, not a criminal." She lunges for Danny to drag him to safety. This time, Lucky hauls her away.

"Shut your face, Suz, or you'll get beaten up and land in jail."

"I don't care." She kicks him in the shin as he drags her to the edge of the lot. Breath comes fast and rough.

The fat cop digs in the pockets of Danny's jeans. "Got it!" He holds aloft a plastic baggie of dried leaves and tosses it to his partner. The other metal cuff snaps around Danny's wrist.

33

Pete is pouring water into the coffeemaker when someone pounds on his front door. He winces at the pain in his temples. He was awake most of last night drinking with Jon Camacho, trying to make sense of Franzen's death.

It's Suzanne. She whirls inside like a Bakersfield windstorm, her hair tangled and face swollen. Before he has a chance to say hello, she's at him.

"You bastard. It's your fault!" Her fists fly, landing a solid punch next to his ear. It hurts like hell, and he has to restrain himself from hitting back. Instead, he grabs her wrists.

"What's going on? What's happened?"

"They've arrested him." She tries to kick his shins.

He's completely bewildered. "Kevin?"

"Danny, you moron."

Pete summons the calm voice he uses on the job, but his heart is beating way too fast. With his hands around her wrists, he edges her toward the kitchen, careful to avoid her feet.

"Come on, Suzanne, sit down. Tell me."

"Danny's in jail on a trumped-up drug charge."

Pete squeezes his eyes shut for a few seconds, trying to banish his headache and shift his focus to Suzanne's problem.

"It's bad news, but I didn't do it. How come it's me that gets a punch in the head?"

The story of last night's arrest tumbles out. "It was you. You interfered, leaked his name to that incompetent detective," she says.

Sun streams in the kitchen windows. His forehead is wet, and he mops it with a kitchen towel. "There's some conspiracy to arrest him? I don't believe it."

"You're daughter's dead, and you're still as dumb as a rock."

"Strong wouldn't put an informant in danger. He's one of the good guys." Even while he says it, a grain of doubt chafes at him.

"Somebody at the sheriff's department leaked Danny's name." Her voice rises again. "The Club wants to tidy things up, and guess who the loose end is?"

He backs out of range. "Jesus, Suzanne, my Gracie is dead. I had to do something. Her murderer must be found."

"Nothing's going to bring her back, but Danny's still alive." She wraps her arms around her chest and begins to cry.

He had a dream about Grace during last night's restless sleep. He was supposed to pick her up from school, but he couldn't find his car keys, he made a wrong turn, he went to the movies and forgot her. When he finally arrived, she was talking to friends and didn't recognize him.

"I'm sorry," he says. "I didn't know what else to do."

She slumps into a chair and rests her forehead on the kitchen table. "God, I'm so tired."

"Me too." He takes her hand and leads her into the bedroom, where they drop their clothes on the floor. The room is hot, and he throws the covers back. Suzanne stretches out, her back to him, and closes her eyes. He's drained of desire, but traces her curves, hand hovering just above her back and hip. The odor of their bodies, sweaty and faintly soiled, calms him until he falls into a heavy, dreamless sleep.

———

When Pete wakes, he's facing her across an expanse of damp sheet. It must be early afternoon—the sun has moved away from the window, light is dim in the stuffy room. From the window comes the sound of his neighbor's mower pulverizing the grass.

He touches his ear; it's still sore.

On the far side of the bed, Suzanne's watching him, head resting on her arm, body curved like a question mark.

"I'll take a shower," he says.

"No, don't." Her voice is low and hoarse.

She reaches over and scratches the stubble on his cheek, not exactly inviting him to jump her, but ready for something.

His penis stiffens against the sheet.

Like boxers approaching an opponent, they slide warily toward one another. He feels a residue from this morning, a restless pulse pushing him.

She traces the contours of his lower lip with her thumb. He nips it with his teeth, harder than he intended. Her breasts rise and fall, and he hears a hum in her throat. He takes her forefinger in his mouth, licks the knuckles, then bites the base of her nail.

The sheet rustles, and he feels her kneecap against his groin.

He raises his hands in surrender. "You're still mad?"

Her foot begins to caress the length of his erection. She whispers something, her eyes never leaving his. He feels the rough movement of her sole, imagines her forbidden words.

She slaps his cock.

"Bitch!" He scrambles to the far side of the bed.

"Isn't that what you wanted?"

"No. Yes. I don't know." He feels the residue of the slap: heat and excitement.

As he creeps toward her on his hands and knees, Suzanne's eyes follow him. Her breasts rise and fall; the sound of her breathing fills the space between them. They're sealed in a fragile arena, where they seem to be shielded from thoughts of their children, from the unbearable press of events.

"Lie on your back," he says. He rubs his scratchy face between her legs, his hands tight when she squirms, inhaling her morning scent, kneading and licking until he feels the coming heat of her climax, the thrust of her hips, her cry.

It's a minute or two before she comes back. "You win," she says, and eases him inside her. He cups her head in his hands, hungry to see her face, to imprint his image on her and own her, but when he comes, the force of it renders him helpless.

Lying back on the mattress, he feels stained, as though the violence done to Grace has seeped into every part of him, infecting even his pleasure.

He sighs and climbs out of bed. The neighbor has finished the lawn, and in the silence, Pete can hear his own footsteps on a creaky board. The refrigerator door huffs as he takes out two longnecks and pops the caps. When he returns, she's sitting up with the pillows stacked behind her back. The dark triangle between her legs is an ink spot on a white page. Pete touches her thigh with one of the cold bottles.

Suzanne yelps. "Give me that." She takes a long swallow, wipes her upper lip.

They drink side by side. The bathroom sink drips an uneven rhythm. He takes her hand and frowns at her long finger bones. "Have you seen him?"

"For a new minutes, after he was processed into juvenile hall. He's terrified. If they convict him of a second crime, he could be sent to a state facility." Her fingers curl until her nails dig into his palm.

"It's only a misdemeanor. Maybe he should plead guilty."

She rears up off the pillows, hair flying around her head. "He didn't do it!"

"Do you want to be right, or do you want to get him off?"

"I'll talk to Dutch," she says.

He can tell she's pissed. "When does he make his court appearance?"

"Tuesday. Dutch is afraid Vinson will interfere again."

"Jesus. That guy." Vinson is one of those ugly black flies that circles inches from your face. After the press conference Vinson patted Smithson on the arm as if he were a mother praising a child. Gwaltney from the *News-Daily* said it was Vinson's influence over the charging committee that resulted in the refusal to charge Franzen, his pizza parlor buddy.

It seems preposterous that Grace was killed because she refused to have sex with Franzen, or because the old man erupted into jealous rage over her attention to someone else. As far as he can tell, Franzen and his circle have no sexual interest in girls. It's equally unlikely Grace, who was too terrified to tell Pete the trouble she was in, would have threatened to expose the clique.

He rolls the longneck between his palms. "How long have you known Danny is gay?"

"Why?"

"I was thinking, how hard it is to figure out your kid."

She curls her toes tightly, like a boxer flexing his knuckles. "Probably for a long time, but I finally got honest with myself in January after Reggie Roman died." Draining her beer, she arcs the bottle into the wastebasket. "He was our next door neighbor. Danny was there that night, but I don't think he's told me everything."

"Like Grace. I could write a book about what she didn't say."

34

Danny watches as Officer O'Malley, the asshole who planted the weed on him, saunters over to talk to the court reporter as if the ground should thank him for walking on it. Danny expected him to be here, but anger swells in his chest nevertheless, enough to crack his ribs.

Danny feels again the scrape of his cheek as O'Malley shoved him against the pavement, the pain of the officer's kneecap jutting into his kidney, and the whispered words in his ear, "Gotcha, you little faggot."

Anger blurs his vision, so it's a while before he notices the fear on his mother's face. He turns to see Vinson unsnapping the latches on his briefcase at the prosecutor's table.

"Shit, he's here again," Haag mutters.

The taste of breakfast egg rises in Danny's throat. Vinson was at Reggie's, again at Harris Whitman's party, and then across from them at Romano's. He recalls the solid feel of Grace's arm as they sat side by side at the table that night, and the pain of losing her floods him once again. He presses his knuckles against his mouth to keep it from trembling.

"In the matter of Daniel Marlowe Ricci." Judge Peña's stubby fingers page through the case file. "The charges are possession of marijuana for sale. How do you plead, Mr. Haag?"

Danny tenses.

"Not guilty, your honor," Haag says.

During their meeting at juvie after his arrest, Haag urged Danny to plead guilty, but he balked. The charge was bullshit.

The lawyer's eyelids had drooped, as if he'd seen too many guilty clients who tried to shine him on. "How about breaking and entering the vacant house?"

"Jade had permission to stay. The lock was already broken before we got there."

"Too bad we can't find Jade," Haag said.

Danny reminded Haag that his mom and Lucky were at the arrest scene to back up his story the weed was planted. Lighting was poor, Haag had shot back. Two biased witnesses testifying to events in the dark didn't make a strong defense.

Peña peers at Suzanne cautiously over the tops of his glasses. Even though he's elevated by the raised bench, he seems intimidated by her height. "Has counsel discussed the implications of a not guilty plea with you, Ma'am?"

Suzanne nods, but realizes her mistake and speaks aloud for the record.

"Mr. Vinson, I assume you've made some offer to dispose of this matter."

"Yes, your honor. We suggested six months as a ward of the court."

Peña's eyebrows rise. He gestures with his gavel toward the defense table. "Very generous, Mr. Haag, considering this is a second offense."

"I understand, your honor," Haag says.

Peña sighs. "Okay, your first witness, Mr. Vinson."

"Before that, your honor, I request that the defendant's mother be excluded. She's a potential witness."

Something dangerous flashes over her face, and Danny feels like a little boy again, sure his mother will find a way to rescue him. Then her features smooth out like an ironed handkerchief and she disappears into the hall.

O'Malley unfurls his story, using a monotonous tone: neutral, inhuman words like "subject" for Danny; "incident" for the indignity of lying helpless with his nose in the asphalt's smelly oil; and "contraband" for the plastic bag of marijuana that appeared in the officer's hand.

Danny doesn't blink, as if his stare will force O'Malley to stumble, but the tale is perfect.

Someone called dispatch, O'Malley says, reporting two kids had broken into a vacant house. The informant said officers could find them hanging around the Shamrock Grill's back door at closing time begging for leftover food.

"And did you, indeed, find the suspects there?" Vinson is deep in his phony lawyer talk.

O'Malley says he spotted Danny, who fit the neighbor's description. A search turned up an ounce of marijuana in a plastic bag.

Fear pinches Danny's breath, as if a pillowcase is being tied over his head. He escaped The Club the last time he was in court, when he'd endorsed those checks and driven Reggie's car. But now, when he hasn't done anything, they're closing in.

It's time for the defense. Haag calls Lucky, but Danny sees right away his uncle's not going to do him any good. Lucky stretches the truth, claiming the girl stuffed the weed in Danny's pocket. He wants to scream at Lucky to shut up and stop making things worse.

His mother is better, but not much. She uses good grammar, and she's dressed okay. Problem is, she tries too hard, not giving the bare minimum answer like the asshole cop.

Peña finds Danny guilty of possession for sale.

Danny lowers his forehead to the table. Blood pounds behind his eyes. He *is* guilty, in a way. Grace might've been saved if he'd kissed off his mother's errand and gone to the party. Grace was frightened, and he assured her he'd be there. Whatever The Club does to him now, maybe he deserves it.

"Probation shall prepare a report and disposition recommendation." Peña leans across the bench to consult with the court clerk who runs his calendar. "Three weeks from today."

"Your honor, I'd like to make a suggestion to be considered by probation." Vinson's voice is soft. "A group of Kern County citizens has come together to combat juvenile delinquency by providing mentorship and guardianship to local youths involved in gateway criminal activity. It's my understanding the defendant fits the profile the citizens' committee is looking for."

Sweat runs down the depressions on each side of Danny's spine. His cotton jumpsuit is damp and cold in the courtroom's air conditioning. He feels like a mouse he found once nested in a box of shredded paper in the garage. He trapped it in a shoe box and dumped it over Reggie's fence, where Narcissus tore it to pieces.

Suzanne clutches Haag's wrist. "It's The Club," she whispers. "You warned me about them. Don't agree."

Haag is already rising to his feet. "What profile is counsel talking about? Danny Ricci has no serious offenses."

Peña raises his eyebrows questioningly at Vinson.

"We'll wait for probation's recommendation of course, but there are strong indications that Mrs. Ricci is an unfit parent." Vinson smooths his tie with fleshy fingers.

Danny's mouth hangs open in shock.

Haag squeezes Suzanne's shoulder to keep her from leaping at the prosecutor. "Your Honor, there's not a scrap of evidence supporting such a finding. We reject that contention in the strongest possible terms."

"This young man stole money for nearly a year," Vinson says. "He's been associating with another youth cited repeatedly for prostitution. His school record is spotty, and now he's using drugs. Every indication is, Mr. Ricci is out of control, and there's been no attempt at counseling, or other intervention."

Danny half-rises, but the bailiff presses him down with a heavy hand. It wasn't her fault, he wants to shout. She's good; it's just that he's felt so lonely this last year. He's wanted to be with Reno and Reggie because they don't see him as a freak.

Haag argues for rehab. This is Danny's first drug offense, and he's a good candidate for treatment. The look on the judge's face says he doesn't buy the idea.

A week later, Sarah Gardiner's probation report recommends the community mentoring program. Vinson is appointed guardian.

PART THREE

35

OCTOBER 1978

Autumn used to be Suzanne's favorite season in Bakersfield. Around Halloween, the heat eases, and a couple of early rains scrub the air of dust and oil. Suzanne opens the kitchen door and sniffs the odor of dry, crumbling leaves. She wants to squeeze this short reprieve like a miser with gold in his fist.

On the table, a wooden salad bowl is heaped with lollipops and bite-sized candy bars, ready for the first ring of the doorbell. Children's voices drift in, perhaps from Maude's. She's famous throughout the neighborhood for dropping dimes and quarters in the trick-or-treat bags.

Years ago, Suzanne and Carlo unfolded aluminum lawn chairs in the driveway and sipped beer while they tossed candy into the bags. Danny loved Halloween, one year creating a fabulous horse's head and torso from a cardboard box, and another, painting his face green and dressing as the Wicked Witch of the West.

Oh, Danny. He's so far removed from these innocent children that he could belong to another race. Tonight there's no boy in face paint. Danny has been at Vinson's luxury home in west Bakersfield for weeks.

The high-pitched voices seem tinged with menace now.

"What do you think?" Pete carves a leering mouth and pointed teeth onto the face of a ten-pound pumpkin. Seeds litter the table and floor, and his shirt's smeared with pulp.

"Not ugly enough," she says.

He twists the paring knife to gouge an irregular eye. When the pumpkin is finished, he puts it on the porch and lights the stubby candle.

They're together much of the time, either here or at his place. Pete looks different from when Grace was alive, skin stretched more tightly over his cheekbones. He moves carefully, as if to minimize an invisible pain.

Still, his presence is a welcome distraction from frustration and anger. They exchange everyday talk about wind and leaves and car crashes and the coffeepot at the station house. Sometimes they laugh at a television show. They have strange, intense sex, as if this will be the last time they ever do it. On the mornings after his twenty-four hour shift, he showers and climbs into bed, ready to go.

They push the boundary between normalcy and deviance until they fall into exhausted sleep. Afterward, they're awkward for a few hours; conversation is as constrained as a Victorian corset.

The doorbell rings. "Trick or treat!" Three kids dance onto the porch, two tiara-clad princesses and one Indian sporting a headdress and turquoise necklace. A handful of bite-sized bars go into each sack. The trio races next door to Reggie's house, but the porch is dark.

In the dining room, the telephone rings. She hands the candy to Pete and goes inside. Dutch is on the line.

"Is it Peña? So soon? What did he say?" she asks.

"Turned us down."

Her stomach cramps. With her palm over the receiver, she draws several shallow breaths. Their petition to Judge Peña to terminate Vinson's guardianship and send Danny to a rehab facility has been denied.

Haag sighs. "He says a community-based guardianship is preferable to institutional rehabilitation."

"Can we appeal?" she asks.

"Everything is stacked against us: DA, probation, the court."

"And the grand jury that never got back to me." The doorbell rings insistently, but she ignores it. Her voice breaks. "What's next?"

"I think we should let it ride. I could lay more legal fees on you, but realistically, I don't think we have a chance."

She drops abruptly into a chair. The smell of raw pumpkin flesh sickens her.

Pete reaches over and plucks the phone from her hand. "We'll get back to you soon, Dutch." The handset clicks as he replaces it.

During the weeks since Danny was made Vinson's ward, she's been tortured by what's happening. The assistant DA has decreed she may only see Danny alternate Saturdays for three hours, claiming she's an unfit parent.

They've gotten together twice; Danny stared at his BLT but didn't take a bite.

"What's wrong?" she'd asked the first Saturday. "Are you sick?"

He shook his head.

"I can order something else. A Reuben sandwich?"

"Nothing, Mom." His eyelids lifted, and his dark glance was disconnected, as though he were looking not at her but at a blank television screen, in which he saw only her distorted reflection.

She grabbed his wrist. "Danny, what is it?"

He'd taken a bite, chewing and chewing, until the food formed a ball in his cheek.

At the next visit, he fell asleep in the car after she picked him up. No longer in school: he's being home-taught. Liza found out that the so-called teacher Vinson hired is a former jail employee fired for smuggling drugs to inmates. Vinson's protégée somehow finagled a temporary teaching credential.

During that second visit, Danny's shirt sleeve slid up, and Suzanne spotted two small puncture marks in his arm. Her frantic call to Dutch resulted in their demand that juvenile court remove him from Vinson's to drug treatment.

Pete hands her a glass of water. "What now, Suzie?"

"Danny always liked Halloween." From a box of decorations, she absently picks up a paper skeleton and watches the arms and legs revolve around its metal joints.

"You make it sound like he's dead."

She tears the arms off at the shoulders and places them carefully on the table. "Where do I go? Who's on my side?"

"I am."

She crosses her arms over her chest, unaware she's crying until tears drip off her chin.

A crowd of kids on the porch rattles the screen, asking for treats.

She sighs. It's been weeks since she's slept through the night. Her joints ache, from the most delicate ones in her fingers to the weighty ones in her thighs.

Pete closes the front door. "You've got a child that's alive. There's still a chance."

"So, what, we snatch him and move to Costa Rica?"

"Not such a bad idea."

"We'd be in violation of a court order." Tears flow again, and she mops her cheeks with the tail of her shirt.

"What does a court order mean, in a corrupt justice system that didn't lift a finger for Grace? You've got to get him away."

Outside the back door, leaves rustle. Narcissus trots in and jumps up into Suzanne's lap, claws digging into her thighs to keep from falling. "And we'd eat what, mangoes and bananas? My business is here. I'd have no way to make a living."

"I've got enough years in; I could retire."

"What are you saying?"

"The three of us. We could go to Mexico. Or Canada. Vietnam War draft protesters have lived there for years and never been extradited. He could go to college. We could live well. A dollar goes a long way in Mexico. I don't know about Canada."

His ideas flow too quickly, a rockslide gaining momentum. Why would he give up house, job, friends, for her son? If it were Grace, maybe, but she's gone. He hardly knows Danny. And it's not love between Pete and her—they've never talked love.

"So they win. We give up everything and flee like refugees or criminals, as if it was our fault my son is being exploited, held prisoner by a twisted man who uses him for sex. A man entrusted by the state to keep us safe and protect us."

She snatches a handful of tissues and wipes her eyes and nose. Odd, that no blood appears, because it seems as though it should be leaking out. "There has to be someone who can help."

"And who would that be?" Pete says. In the dark, they listen to the doorbell ring.

———

Two nights later, Pete and Suzanne are clearing the dinner dishes when she sees a dark shape through the open kitchen door. Danny is crouched on the back steps, his face clutched in his hands. He's crying silently.

"Baby, oh Baby, what's happened?" She kneels beside him on the concrete porch. At her touch, he pulls away, fists clenched.

He's thin—much thinner than last time she last saw him. He wears a pair of cutoff jeans and a light blue tank top smeared with dark stains. Dried blood is crusted under his fingernails.

At the bottom of the steps, Pete hunkers down in front of him. "Hey, bud, you in trouble?"

Danny drops his hands from his face. It's covered with bloody scratches as if a cat's clawed him. "They're crawling under my skin. Hundreds of them."

His mouth trembles, and his breath is ragged as if he's been running. He rakes a broken fingernail down his cheek, opening a tear in his skin. "They're eating me, please, please, get them out!"

When Pete grasps Danny's hands, one slips free, and a fist connects with Pete's chin. Pete tumbles backward. Danny screams, louder than she's ever heard anyone scream, even in the hospital labor room.

Pete wrestles with him until he can pin an arm behind his back. Danny sags as if he's about to fall, but Pete drags him to his feet, panting. Her ears ring. She's stunned by the ways in which her life is being snatched from her.

"Suzanne! Go to the garage and start the van. We'll take him to emergency. He's having drug withdrawls."

"No! They'll call the cops."

"Do it! You don't, he could die!"

Suzanne starts the van and leaves the engine running while she opens the rear passenger door. Pete, his arm around Danny, guides him into the back seat, then climbs in beside him. She eases the van out slowly, afraid she might hit a child. In the street she's shifting out of reverse when she hears the growl of a V-8 engine. A patrol car blocking their way. Liza emerges, leaving the emergency flashers on. Red light slithers over the houses and shrubbery.

Suzanne's eyes narrow as her friend approaches.

"Hello, everyone." Liza scrutinizes Danny and Pete in the back seat. "We had a call about someone screaming. Person in distress."

Probably Maude that called. "It's Danny. He's not feeling well," Suzanne says.

Danny slides off the seat onto the van's floor; she can feel him at her back as he bumps against the driver's seat. It is a strange feeling, his pressing against her unseen, as if she were pregnant.

"Danny, hello," she calls through the window glass. "It's me, Liza. I need to talk to you."

"He came to see me," Suzanne says. "While he was here, he got very sick."

Liza shakes her head. "This isn't an authorized visit. He's a juvenile out of control. Ran from his guardian's jurisdiction in violation of his probation."

Liza's single plait is braided so tightly her eyes slant at an unfamiliar angle. Could this be the same officer who showed her such kindness the night Carlo died? The one who drove her around Bakersfield looking for Danny after Reggie's murder?

"Unlock the rear door, please," Liza tells Pete.

Pete leans across Danny and cracks the door open. "Officer, it's Pete Stannard. Remember me?"

"I remember you, Captain."

"This young man needs medical attention for drug withdrawls. Without treatment, he could die. I'm familiar with it from my paramedic training."

Danny's teeth are chattering.

Liza stalks back to her car, pulls out the car radio's mic and talks urgently. In a few minutes, she's back. "My sergeant's 10-47."

How long is a police dinner break? Suzanne listens to Danny scratching his face and arms. She recalls the morning of Reggie's murder, how she wheeled the van across the Hedges' lawn to avoid Liza's car. She puts the keys in the ignition.

A murmur from Pete whistles in her ear. "Where will we go?"

Danny groans and twists. A strong smell of men's cologne rises from his skin, and she opens the window. Minutes crawl on all fours until a Cadillac glides to a stop alongside Liza's car and double parks. The door opens, and Dennis Vinson strides over to the van. She rolls down the window.

Gray stubble dots his face and chin, and eyes are bloodshot. Rage twists his mouth. His mask of respectability—that of a carefully shaven and tailored prosecutor—has been ripped away.

"He's coming with me, Mrs. Ricci."

His bulk looms in the window opening filling the car with the smell of unwashed flesh and damp crevices.

Her hands tremble on the wheel. Pulse throbs in her throat and behind her eyes. The faces of the crowd are tinged with red from the blinking lights. She feels the pressure of Danny's suffering: the slights and hurts, the manipulation and injustice and cruelty. Her own helplessness twists through her until she can barely breathe.

"It's okay, Mom." Through the seat back, she feels Danny struggling to open the sliding door. "I need to be going."

His voice is strange, dignified, as if he's leaving a dinner party.

"No." Tears run into her mouth.

"Wait, Buddy," Pete says. "Let's see if we can work this out. Get you some medical help."

"I don't need any help, thank you." Danny rattles the handle.

She revs the engine and shifts into gear. Danny suddenly moves to leave, but catches his foot on the door frame and tumbles out.

"Stop, stop for God's sake!" Pete screams. "Danny's underneath."

The van rocks on its tires. The rear door rolls forward again, hitting Pete in the ribs. He clutches his side, but manages to grasp Danny with one hand and haul him from beneath the undercarriage. Danny is crying again, quietly, as if he had done it so often it had become a routine, like brushing his teeth.

Liza draws a pair of handcuffs from her belt. "Okay, Danny."

"Wait a minute." Pete inserts himself between the two.

"Get out of the way, Captain."

"He's in a near-psychotic state. He needs treatment."

"I'll determine the best course of action in consultation with his guardian. Now step back." Her baton slides from her belt.

"Listen to me!" When Pete steps toward her, she slams the baton into his injured ribs. Screaming in pain, he sinks to his knees.

Suzanne lunges out. Pete struggles to get to his feet. Vinson has moved to the black-and-white and leans over the microphone. Suzanne shoehorns herself between Danny and Liza, toe to toe with her friend. She smells coffee on Liza's breath and feels the weighty solidity of Liza's body, while at her back she senses Danny's fragility.

"When?" Hurt and anger stir a painful swell of acid in her throat. "Why did you stop being my friend?"

"It's not personal, Suzanne."

Leaning into Liza's space, she notices coarse hairs sprinkled on her friend's upper lip. "It must be ESP. Little bells ring in your head every time Danny is vulnerable."

"Get the hell out of my way, or I'll arrest you," Liza says.

"Vinson called you, didn't he? There was no complaint from a neighbor."

"Last warning." Liza's eyes dart toward something over Suzanne's shoulder.

Two more black-and-whites barrel up the street. Their PA systems emit short blips rather than full siren. Vinson's slacks flap around his legs as he hurries to meet them. He gestures toward the van, then the trio moves toward them in a full-court press. Suzanne can't take her eyes off Vinson. His smile gleams, white and hard.

He circles his fingers around Danny's bare upper arm.

Danny's hand trembles, and his cheek twitches, but in a moment of quiet dignity that Suzanne will remember the rest of her life, he straightens his back. He turns his back and offers his hands, knobby with veins and bones, to be cuffed. The revolving emergency lights catch the moist surface of his beautiful dark eyes.

36

At two AM, the restaurant at the Olive Drive truck stop hums with conversation. Suzanne and Pete grab the last empty booth and order coffee and toast. When the waitress is gone, they slump against the sticky plastic banquette. The restaurant's dangling canister lights turn Pete's face a jaundiced yellow.

Suzanne's nose is stuffed up and her lids scrape her eyeballs like sandpaper. Exhaustion floods her.

The waitress slides the plates on the table and fills their cups. Looking out the window, Suzanne watches a trucker chat with a police officer under the bright lights at the pumps. Behind their backs, a girl about sixteen in a miniskirt and knee-high boots climbs down from a sleeper cab and runs into the weeds at the edge of the lot.

The coffee burns her tongue. "I'm going to the FBI. Get them to investigate."

"Investigate drug charges and rape? Good luck. Those are state offenses. The county DA's office prosecutes those."

Suzanne rips a corner off her sourdough toast and chews as if she's gnawing bones. "How about this? Government corruption on the part of Vinson."

"He isn't politically corrupt, just a sodomist and drug pusher."

"Then it's political corruption on the part of Smithson, Osterman, Judge Simic, and the cops." Desperation creeps into her voice. "Either they're in The Club, or they're aiding and abetting."

He rubs the stubble on his cheeks. "Worth a try."

"You just dumped on the idea."

"It might work," he says.

She doesn't blink, hoping to catch up. "It's a lousy idea."

"It's worth a try, now that I think about it."

"Tell me," she says.

"There have been two deaths—Grace's and Reggie's—whose circumstances involve sexual exploitation of young people. Those, plus Danny's false arrest, illegal detention, and forced drug addiction. We don't know how many men are members of the sex ring, but certainly more than Vinson and Franzen."

"Criminal conspiracy." A current flows through her, creating an itch in her fingers.

"In Reggie's case, boys were used for sex at the party the night he was murdered. In Grace's death, sexual exploitation of kids is the central issue. We add Danny's case to those."

The waitress scoots by and raises the coffee carafe inquiringly, but Pete waves her off.

"The same people are involved."

Pete's lips curve in a savage smile. "If we can't get them on state charges like murder, rape, or false imprisonment, then backdoor them with federal conspiracy charges."

Suzanne breathes quickly. "The Feds can pick up where Strong left off. Identify all the conspirators, maybe ones we're not aware of. Put their asses in federal prison."

———

The next morning, she cruises the rows of one-story stucco buildings in an industrial park before she spots a small sign in black letters identifying the FBI's satellite office. Closed vertical blinds block a view of the interior. In the front window's reflection, she runs her tongue over her teeth and smooths her suit jacket.

The reception area is lit with a strip of fluorescent lights and furnished with a single chair. No one sits at the desk in the small office beyond the bulletproof glass. She taps the bell on the counter. The door in the rear of the office opens, and a woman crosses to the window.

"Can I help you?" She is short, with close-cropped hair and a straight back.

"I'd like to speak to an agent."

"They're both busy."

Suzanne looks at the tiny waiting room, receptionist's sparse office, and shiny white paint, relieved only by framed photographs of President Jimmy Carter and FBI Director William Webster. "Both? There are only two?"

"This is a resident office, Ma'am. The regional headquarters is in Sacramento. It would be best if you'd make an appointment."

"No, I need to see someone *now*." Suzanne leans closer to the metal grille in the glass. "My son's life depends on it."

The woman studies Suzanne, then turns her back and speaks quietly into a telephone on her desk. Almost immediately, a man opens the rear door and strides to the counter.

"I'm Special Agent Darryl Woods. How can I help you?" His smooth-shaven cheeks, clipped sideburns, and steady brown eyes make her want to trust him.

He rests an elbow on the counter, and she catches a glimpse of the shoulder holster under his suit jacket. When she repeats her plea about Danny, he buzzes her through a locked door. Inside, he stands at the end of a hall, silhouetted against spotless white walls and relentless ceiling lights.

The inner office is furnished with two gray metal desks, one occupied by a second agent pounding a two-fingered tattoo on an IBM typewriter while listening to someone through a telephone headset.

"Back here," Woods says, leading the way to a cramped, hot room, furnished only with a table and two chairs. He drapes his suit jacket over the back of his chair.

They sit down. Suzanne shifts uneasily on the hard, wooden seat. "Isn't this where you interview suspects?"

"Sorry. We don't have much of a facility here." He sounds as though he's had his fill of working in Bakersburg, out of the loop in cases like the nationwide search for the Unibomber.

"What can I do for you . . ." he reads a slip of paper the receptionist gave him, "Mrs. Ricci?"

She lays it out for him, the broken bones of Danny's life. She begins with Reggie's death and advances through Danny's abduction, laying bare the collusion among police, prosecutors, and courts. When she's finished, she studies Woods, trying to discern whether he believes her, but his brown eyes are unreadable. She concentrates instead on his hands, which clasped and unclasped as she talked.

"That's quite a story."

"It's not a story!" Her voice booms in the small space.

"I apologize—allegations. These allegations are very, very serious."

When he utters these words, her eyes sting. Strange, that relief would bring tears.

"If this proves to be true, it will break this county wide open," he says.

"It's true, I swear."

"I've got a four-year-old son, Mrs. Ricci. I can imagine this is very difficult for you," Woods says.

She blows her nose. "I'm shut down and blocked at every turn. That's why I've come to the FBI."

He nods.

"What's the next step?" she says.

"I'm afraid we won't be doing anything."

"What? You just said . . ."

"The FBI doesn't have jurisdiction in this type of case."

"But what about the RICO law?" Suzanne spent two hours this morning at the county law library researching the federal Racketeer-Influenced and Corrupt Organizations Act. "The Club is an organization maintained by criminal activity."

He shakes his head. "It's too big a stretch to argue this group, assuming what you say is true, is a criminal organization. I'd say it's more of a loose group of acquaintances. Sort of like a college alumni club."

Her fists clench in her lap, and she digs her nails into her palms. "They don't just party together and sing the fight song." Her voice is shaking. "There's planning. Coordinated criminal activity like my son's abduction and the suborning of Thurston's trial."

"That's possible, but the fact is, state law covers those crimes."

"The county prosecutor is intimately involved. Only an outside agency can do it," she says.

He leans toward her, and the odor of starch drifts from his white shirt. "Listen, Mrs. Ricci. We're a satellite office. The two of us handle local aspects of large cases. Violations of interstate commerce, interstate and international drug conspiracies, violations by federal officers, and terrorism."

When she doesn't say anything, he continues, like a father consoling a child, "You can go to the state attorney general. He has a unit that investigates corruption in public office."

"Smithson helped raise over a million dollars to pass Proposition 13 in June. You think the elected state attorney general would dare lay a finger on him?"

The whiteness presses on her—the bright overhead lights, blinds that block out shadows, spotless walls, everything scoured like the hard porcelain of a kitchen sink, and in the midst of the whiteness she finds nothing to hold onto, nothing dark and solid, no reassurance.

His hands are stacked on the table. He bends over them, seeming to examine the freckles and hairs. "I tell you what. I have a case winding up in the next week or so. I'll spend a couple of days on it and speak to my supervisor in Sacramento."

Hope is made of such small things.

37

"You're out of chocolate ship cookies," Chuey Venegas tells Vinson. She smoked weed all afternoon and is having a hard time enunciating. "And by the way, your son's doing good on his lessons."

Danny laughs. *Son.* Chuey knows he's not Vinson's son, but she keeps up the fiction, just like they pretend she's a home-schooling teacher and not a pothead former correctional officer carrying a weapon.

He might have seized the opportunity to run away while she was stoned, but he needs a fix, and Chuey's brother, Sixto, is late. Danny paces in front of the TV, collapses on the couch for a minute or two, sits on the coffee table. His nose runs, and he wipes it on his sleeve. Sixto does night guard duty at Vinson's house and sells him heroin.

Vinson, who changed from his suit to chinos and a pullover sweater after work, goes to his study. Danny imagines him transferring the gun from his briefcase to the safe. Danny first saw the weapon after he ran away to his mother's, and Vinson hauled him back with help from the cops.

Vinson returns with a stack of cash and counts out a week's wages on the dining room table for Chuey. In a low voice he says, "Get high again and you're fired."

"Last time, absolutely." She folds the bills and stuffs them in her boot.

Vinson switches on the television news. Danny, in the midst of his nervous pacing, catches the somber face of NBC anchorman David Brinkley announcing that San Francisco Mayor George Moscone and Supervisor Harvey Milk were murdered this morning.

The three of them gather in a semicircle around the screen staring at the image of Milk, the country's first openly gay elected official, being wheeled away. A white sheet is draped over his body. The camera moves to a single bouquet of yellow chrysanthemums on the steps of San Francisco's City Hall.

"He was a really, really great man." Tears fill Danny's eyes. When he and his mother visited the city, it was the first time he felt truly free. There was the physical part; he could bend his wrists, move his legs and hips with such abandon, without being watchful of every moment to ensure not a single of his gestures or steps, not the slightest turn of the head revealed his secret. But it was more than a matter of muscle and bone. His thoughts could roam, run headlong to places that in Bakersfield could get him killed. On the San Francisco streets last summer, he could look at men and think about kisses, about sex, about love.

Now in that city, where the wind from the ocean had carried the cold breath of a new life, fear and hatred had won. What will the world be like without Milk, his face soft and vulnerable, almost breaking his heart? Danny mops his cheeks with his sleeve.

"If he'd kept quiet, hadn't stirred people up with his rhetoric, he'd be alive," Vinson says. The television flickers on his white hair and thick glasses.

"You don't know anything, you stupid prick." Danny sweats, his skin itching. Every inch of flesh is begging for a fix.

Vinson calls Sixto to find out why he's late. Danny switches the channel. On the screen is footage of former supervisor Dan White being led away in handcuffs. How strange, the murderer and victim linked by color, white, the color of milk, Milk-White, the names of the two men merging and spinning until he can't remember which is which. He curls up on the sofa and cries.

Sixto opens the front door without knocking and brushes the sleeve of his coat. "Sandstorm's worse." He studies Danny, nods to his sister, and exchanges a look with Vinson. "Can I put my car in the garage? I don't want to lose the paint overnight."

"As soon as you deliver," Vinson says, and leads the way into his office. Once the heroin buy is completed, Sixto and Chuey walk outside to chat. Danny sees the bulge of Sixto's weapon stuffed in his waistband at the small of his back.

"Let's take a nap." Vinson tilts his head toward the bedroom, flipping one of Sixto's packets in his palm.

"Just give it to me!"

"I could report you to probation. Say you aren't complying with terms and conditions, and recommend you go to the Youth Authority."

"I'm terrified." Danny's loathing is so intense, he almost chokes on it.

"YA can be very unpleasant for someone like you," Vinson says.

"Oh, and this place is so fucking wonderful."

Vinson steps closer, the packet hanging enticingly from his fingers. "Nice kids up there. Shooters, cutters, baby Mafiosos. People you'd have lots in common with. They do art—tattoo themselves with gang signs and draw graffiti on the walls."

"Then I'd do as much art there as I do here, which is none." He hasn't held a pencil or pen in his fingers in months.

"Maybe we can do something about that, if you're cooperative," Vinson says.

In the bedroom Danny's hands are icy against his bare skin as he pulls his shirt over his head and sheds his pants and briefs. Vinson takes his time, matching the cuffs of his chinos before placing them over the hanger. As he shakes out the folds in his socks, his cock and the smooth melon of his belly grow flushed.

He places the lump of brown heroin on a tinfoil square and lights his lighter beneath it; Danny leans over. He breathes smoke up the cardboard tube as if it were clear water or blue sky or God.

"Kneel on the bed," Vinson says.

———

The next morning, Danny and Vinson enter Sampson Brothers a few minutes before teen class begins. Danny hurts from last night. He greets Will with his face turned aside, feeling like a pretender. He didn't fix on heroin again this morning because he didn't want to nod off, but the creative space in his head that used to be so juicy is dry.

"Danny!" Will flushes with delight. When he notices Vinson, his cheeks pale. In a low, stilted voice he says, "Missed you"

"Been out of town," Danny mumbles.

"Class begins in forty-five minutes. Are you in?"

"I dunno. Maybe I should think about it." Danny holds his breath, waiting for Vinson to pull out his wallet. Without money for fees and supplies, he can't enroll. How simple it was, when his mother gave him a check and bus fare and told him to have fun.

"The class has a couple of really talented kids. You'll like them." Will rings up the customer's purchase and counts the change. "How's your mother?"

"Good. She's good." Danny nods, more vigorously than necessary. Sometimes he can't remember her face, but only one feature at a time.

"Here's the supply list for the class." After a second's hesitation, Will hands the list to Vinson. "Get everything you need and bring it to the counter. Cindy will help you. I've got to set things up in back."

Danny selects pens, inks, watercolors, and paper while Vinson hovers behind him. Once Vinson has paid, he says he's leaving for a meeting at the office, but sits in the car watching the storefront. Danny thinks he's having second thoughts, like a jealous husband.

The other kids are already there—four girls, one boy about thirteen, and Danny. When he walks into the studio, he blinks to banish the prickle of tears. A trick of light brings Grace almost into view at the corner easel where she loved to work.

Will has set up a still life, not the usual fruit, vase and bowl, but a worn army combat boot, a framed photo with glass broken, two Fourth of July rockets, and a basketball. They're using ink and a Japanese brush to do studies from different angles.

"Work fast and don't watch the paper. Let your hand do the thinking."

The kids complain for a few minutes before they wet their brushes, dip them in ink and roll the tips to a fine point. Danny's work sucks. Trying to resurrect his skill hurts like jogging after a year of sitting on your butt. His brain cells scrape against one another. His shoulder joint is swollen and his fingers throb. The discomfort is mostly frustration, but it feels like the onset of the flu. A pile of wadded paper collects at his feet.

Will appears beside him. "Shake your arm and hand as if they're wet. Throw off all the muck."

"I'm drowning in muck," Danny says, and for the first time in months, he smiles.

Nothing he draws in the next two hours is worth saving, but as he stuffs his lame attempts in the trash sack and washes his brushes, he's surprisingly cheerful.

Cindy pokes her head into the studio. "Danny, your father called. His meeting is going longer than expected, but he'll be here in fifteen minutes."

Danny helps Will fold up the easels and stack them at the rear of the studio. The sun has moved to the south, and shadows gather in the corners of the north-facing studio among the frames, canvases, and feathery dust.

A bell dings as a customer comes in. Will closes the studio door behind them, and they stroll down the aisle between the shelves. "Someone you know came in a couple of weeks ago."

Danny thinks, Grace.

"A kid named Diego Luhan. Wanted to connect."

His roommate from High Endeavor. The surge of disappointment at missing him is overwhelming.

———

The next week, Danny wrestles a large tablet of drawing paper and a fishing tackle box filled with supplies from the car. Inside the store, Cindy wiggles her fingers at him while she talks on the phone. Danny doesn't see the boy at first. He's partially hidden between two rows of art books out of sight of the windows.

Will tips his head toward the kid, whose face is averted. Danny recognizes Diego right away. The boy gestures him to a secluded alcove between the books.

Danny sets down his supplies. "Surprised to see you."

"You good?" Diego asks.

"Not so much."

Diego seems different from last spring. His cheeks have lost their baby fat and his feet are too big for his body, which Suzanne always told him was an indicator a kid was going to be tall. At High Endeavor, Danny knew Diego was gay, although he was only twelve.

"What you doin'?" Danny asks. "Back with your uncle?"

Diego shakes his head. "He got out of prison, but him and my *tia* got deported."

"Sorry. How are you making it?"

"You know. Living the life."

Danny grimaces.

"Yeah, not so great. Thing is, I've got a problem."

"Go to the county clinic. They'll treat you for free," Danny says.

Will calls from the studio that class is about to start. Danny raises his index finger to signal he'll be there in a minute.

Diego crouches low, invisible over the top of the bank of shelves. "It's not VD," he whispers. "It's a guy."

With Diego's head bent forward, Danny sees a bruise on his back where his collar slackens. It begins greenish yellow on his neck and darkens to purple as it travels downward.

"You got somebody mad at you?" Danny asks.

"He's a..." Diego stumbles, then tries again. "I been living with a guy, you know."

Danny's mouth twists.

"I was living on the street, and this guy, driving a tricked-out truck, all gold, he say, stay with me, I'll give you three a day. You can go to school. I say, okay." Diego lowers his head. Danny hunkers close to catch the breathy whisper. He smells an expensive aftershave on Diego's smooth cheeks. The transfer of the scent from man to boy reminds Danny of a contagious disease.

"But next morning when I try to go outside his house, I can't open the door. Whole place is like juvie but worse. No door handles, only deadbolt locks. Bars on the windows. And he got the keys on a big ring on his belt." Diego's breath is uneven.

Years ago, Danny would have told him to call the cops, but not now. "*Amigo*, I can't do anything."

"I don't have nobody, and then I remembered from the group home, before we went to sleep at night, you'd say the places you liked. Like your mom's kitchen with the cat dish under the sink, and the tablecloth, and the nail on the wall where she hangs the keys. And you talked about this place. How you came every Saturday and squeezed out the colors and made pictures."

Danny doesn't remember telling him all this, but he must have because the details are accurate. "I can't help," he says.

"You got people. If I get money, I can go to San Fran. There's a place for kids like me."

"I've been to the Bay Area. Never heard of a place for queer kids."

"There is, I know it. Come on, you got a place. Help me out."

"I'm not at home." Danny struggles to describe his situation. "I'm. . . pretty much like you."

"But you get free. Someone drives you here. I come today because he plays golf Saturday mornings. I climbed out through the bathroom window; cut myself a little." Diego turns his palm up. A cut seeping blood extends along his lifeline. He wipes it on the leg of his bell-bottom jeans, leaving a dark smear.

"I don't have any money," Danny says.

"He buy you horse?"

"Yeah, but money's locked up."

Diego scoots closer. Danny notices the way his hair grows in a funny little whorl at the crown of his head.

"I don't need much. Forty or fifty, for food and a bus ticket."

"This would mess me up bad, Diego."

"I can't steal nothing because he locks his wallet in a drawer."

Two customers enter the store, a woman and a little girl about five. The kid runs straight to where they are standing and begins pulling books off the shelves. The mother, measuring picture frames, warns her to stop.

"He'll kill me. Please." Diego tugs Danny's shirt.

When they shared the room at High Endeavor, Diego used to cry in his sleep for his mother, who died of heat and thirst on their way to the United States from Mexico. Diego sucked his knuckles, filling the silence with soft, wet sounds. Danny never teased him about it.

Diego studies the cut on his palm and licks the blood away.

"I'll see what I can do," Danny says. "Come next Saturday."

————

Danny waits for a chance to search Vinson's house for money. Days pass before Chuey, who usually spends weekdays watching TV or playing solitaire, falls asleep on the sofa after lunch. Danny moves softly from room to room, fingering Vinson's shirts and underwear in his dresser, case files on his desk, dozens of manila folders in his filing cabinet, but doesn't find the combination to the safe.

He absently rolls Vinson's wheeled desk chair back and forth with his foot. The desktop is neatly arranged, with a pencil tray, letter holder, wire In and Out baskets, a photo of Vinson shaking Ronald Reagan's hand, and two dictionaries anchored by green jade bookends. Danny removes the back of the picture frame and finds the combination on the cardboard insert. He smiles with contempt at Vinson's lack of imagination and remembers his own use of that strategy years ago.

The gun is gone from the safe; Vinson carries it in his briefcase all the time now, but the $10,000 he keeps for drugs is here. The smallest denomination is hundreds, and all the bills are banded in neat packets. To extract a bill, Danny would have to tear a band, so he eases the door shut, spins the dial, and tiptoes into Vinson's bedroom. A search of the closet yields five $20 bills in the pocket of a suede jacket. He takes four.

"What the heck are you doing?" Chuey stands in the doorway, hands on hips.

The bills slide into his back pocket. "Trying on clothes." Heart beating fast, Danny takes the jacket, which reminds him of a smelly grandpa, and slides his arms into the terrible old thing.

"Get out of here." When they're in the hall, she closes the door. "And stay out."

During the week after Danny slips the money to Diego, Vinson follows him from room to room in the evening. "Did you steal it?" he finally asks one night, tinkling the ice in his martini. He interrogates Danny with the tenacity of a seasoned prosecutor until he extracts the full story.

Vinson's eyes bulge behind his glasses. "You ungrateful little turd." With a movement shocking in its quickness, he punches Danny in the face. Danny staggers, but Vinson crowds him and backhands him across the mouth. Danny sways for a second, the room swimming, before pain fills him. Blood drips from his nose onto his shirt. His hands rise, palms up, as if he has no way of fathoming what has happened; then he bends over and slowly collapses on the carpet.

There are no more art lessons.

He doesn't know what's happened to Diego. That Saturday when Danny gave him the money, Diego snatched it without saying thanks, but pressed his lips together as if he were going to cry. The last Danny saw of him, he was jogging across the parking lot, and the fog had swallowed him up. He wonders when Diego will be back. There's no refuge for homeless gay kids in the Bay Area.

38

Suzanne is still in bed when Pete, dressed for work, leans over to kiss her goodbye. He tastes of toast and jelly, and she licks his lips. Her hand slides over the front of his uniform pants.

He presses himself against her palm. "You're a devil woman." Breathing quickly, he straightens and shoves his wallet into his back pocket.

She wiggles her fingers at him. "Tomorrow, same time, same place." After he leaves, she showers and heads for Taft to meet Lucky for breakfast. The wind kicks up as she drives along Highway 33, stirring the sand into piss-yellow clouds that obscure the view of McPherson Peak to the west.

At Tito's, Lucky sips a cup of coffee at the bar before he starts his shift in the kitchen. The bar/restaurant doesn't open until 11:30, and it's gloomy inside, the floor still littered with spilled food and torn decorations from the New Year's Day football party.

Lucky's eyes are red and watery. "Mom had a snootful and fell off Red's front steps. Emergency said she was okay, but this morning she couldn't get out of bed. It's not a good job for a guy, getting an old lady up in the morning. The nightgown thing."

Suzanne pours sugar from the dispenser into her coffee. "I'll stop by before I leave." Mother will spin her usual story: she wasn't drinking; she's weak and needs to move in with Suzanne.

Not in a million years.

Tami, the bartender, flirts with Lucky while she refills his cup and slides a plate of eggs and pancakes in front of Suzanne. "Sure I can't get you some food, Lucky?" Her red fingernails fluff her hair.

Suzanne whispers in his ear. "She liiiikes you."

"That one's left the station. Got married last year." He doesn't look sorry. "How about Mr. Hot? Any developments?"

Tami hauls a wire tray from the dishwasher, and glasses tinkle as she stacks them behind the bar. When she goes to the kitchen, Suzanne leans close to Lucky. "We're waiting. The FBI guy promised to talk to his boss in Sacramento. I told him it's a good case for federal RICO charges."

He scrubs a hand over his day-old beard. "Not what I meant. Are we talking an item, you and this guy?"

She grimaces. "We're like two colonies of army ants trying to merge."

"Not injuring each other, I hope?"

"No, but Danny's buzzing in my brain all the time. I can't sit still, I can't read, I can barely work. Pete's the same way about Grace."

Last night in bed, her body refused to climax. Her nerves were too busy, flashing first here, then there. And Pete, when he came, looked not at her but at something over her shoulder.

She pushes the plate away. "I feel so alone." Other than Pete and Special Agent Darryl Woods, Lucky is the only person she's confided in. Her friend Liza is lost to her, and despite all the people she knows in Bakersfield, there's no one. Sometimes at night when Pete's on duty and the house groans in the wind, she even suspects him. Is he leaking information? She hasn't known him that long, after all.

Lucky waves off Tina with the coffee carafe. "How long since you've seen Danny?"

"Not since Halloween. Probation has cut off my visits."

"Grab Danny and run away somewhere." Lucky glances briefly at a bottle of Johnnie Walker behind the bar, then leans on his elbows. "Canada, maybe. He's still a kid. You could start over."

"That's what Pete says."

"He's even smarter than I thought." His mouth turns down at the corners, and she knows he's thinking about Carlo. Lucky always had thought Carlo was too insecure to be her husband—a short man trying to compensate.

Tami nudges open the kitchen door and arrives with a tub of ice that she dumps into the stainless steel sink beneath the bar. "You heard about the murder?"

Lucky pats his shirt pocket for a pack of cigarettes. "Somebody lose a parking lot fight?"

"Nope. This here's big and juicy. The guy who owns Star Petroleum Equipment got beat to death last night."

Suzanne chokes on her coffee. "Connie Fitzgerald?"

"That's him. Heard about it from my husband, who works there. Employees got told this morning."

"I know that guy. The one with the gold-plated pickup truck," Lucky says.

"Was it a robbery-murder?" Suzanne remembers the clink of the heavy key ring on his belt.

"Don't know. It didn't happen at headquarters, but his place in Bakersfield."

Suzanne feeds two quarters into the pay telephone next to the restrooms. While she's on hold for Hedges, she thinks about the Star Petroleum building, with its opaque windows that hid what was happening inside.

"Yeah, we've got it," Hedges says. "Henry's on police this week, and BPD called him. You thinking about a column?"

An extra assignment means money in the bank. "He's a local guy who does business all over the world. Dines with Arab princes."

"Okay. Talk to Henry about the murder details. We'll run it tomorrow as a sidebar."

She stops at the *News-Daily* on her way home and finds Henry Monson in the lunchroom unwrapping a peanut butter and banana sandwich. He's a pale-skinned man in his fifties who glances at her nervously.

She buys a bag of potato chips from the vending machine. "Can you give me info on the murder?"

His eyes narrow. "Why? You're a freelancer. Is Garrity dicking me around?" He clutches his sandwich to his chest the way she did when she was a kid, to protect her breakfast bacon from the Stooges.

"Relax. I'm doing a career retrospective on his stature in the oil industry." She smiles in what she hopes is a reassuring way. The newsroom is up in arms over Managing Editor Garrity's strategy of pitting reporters against each other on the same story.

"Just after midnight, the highway patrol stops a kid on 99 at Mettler for speeding," Monson says. "He's got no license, and he's driving Fitzgerald's fancy truck. They hold him on suspicion of auto theft, and when they go to Fitzgerald's house, they discover the guy in his rec room. His head has been bashed in with a pool cue."

The smell of his banana sandwich eddies around the table, strong and offensive.

Monson sighs. "It's going to be another of those nightmare deals with Garrity all over it. Like the Franzen case."

Chips crumble in Suzanne's fist.

"Seems Fitzgerald was a pederast," Monson says. "The boy lived with him and got a roof and three meals in exchange for sex."

"Who was he?" The third murder. This could blow the thing wide open.

"A throwaway. Police aren't giving out names, since he's thirteen, but a source told me his name's Diego Luhan. Claimed it was self-defense, that he'd been held prisoner. Could be true. It was a strange house, windows under lock and key, no knobs on the doors."

"He confessed?" Her heartbeats drown out Henry's voice. If the kid's confessed, Whitman can't squelch the story this time.

"According to the police flack." Monson pours coffee from a thermos. "What a mess. Not just Garrity giving me trouble, but also interference from the His Eminence."

"Don't tell me…"

"Whitman wants to review the story before it runs."

She thanks Monson and drives home. Instead of rounding up quotes for the column, she dials Pete to tell him about the murder. The fire station's private line rings a dozen times but no one answers; he and the crew must be out on a call. Her house is cold and stuffy. She opens the back door. The air is saturated with refinery emissions. Narcissus slinks inside, home after a week of prowling who-knows-where, and sniffs at her empty dish.

Suzanne dials another number.

"Federal Bureau of Investigation, Bakersfield Resident Office." The recording tells her to leave a message. An agent will return the call as soon as possible.

"This is urgent," she says. "I have new information concerning an ongoing investigation."

Three calls come in, none from the FBI. As she interviews her oil industry sources about Fitzgerald, details come back from her visit to his office: the hair on his hands and fingers and the heavy-handled pool cue displayed in a velvet-lined case. A thirteen-year-old picked up a cue and crushed Fitzgerald's skull with its weighted grip. She imagines what the boy endured under those broad, hairy hands before he was cornered, driven to smash his tormentor's eye socket, sloping forehead, and crown. Danny couldn't— no, no. She squeezes her eyes shut to banish images of Danny with a cue in his hand.

———

The column's last page and carbon copy roll out of the typewriter. On the way to the office, Suzanne gooses the accelerator, afraid Special Agent Woods will call while she's gone. She leaves the van in a No Parking zone directly in front of the *News-Daily's* brass-handled front doors and runs the pages upstairs to Hedges. When she returns to the VW, a parking ticket is clipped under the windshield wiper. At home, the light on her message machine is blinking. Woods has left a number with a San Francisco area code.

On Hold, she paces the dining room, snapping the phone's long black cord like a whip.

"Hello, Mrs. Ricci," Woods says. "Sorry I took so long to get back to you. I'm really busy." In the background, telephones ring, and she hears a clamor of voices.

"Have you heard about yesterday's murder?" she asks.

"In Bakersfield? Afraid not. I'm up here in the City."

"A big-time oil industry exec was beaten to death last night. Police have arrested a thirteen-year-old boy that he abused and held prisoner." Words tumble out so quickly she stutters. "It's another case involving The Club, and the kid has confessed. With his information, we can expose the whole thing."

"Yes, yes, I remember now, city and county law enforcement possibly involved." The last words are muffled and he puts her on Hold. While she waits, she watches the Elston kids across the street fight over who will climb the ladder to take down strings of colored Christmas lights from the leafless trees.

After a minute, Woods is back. "Sorry, Ma'am, you were saying . . ."

"The murder. More deaths surrounding the sickos who've snatched my boy."

"Right, right."

"This latest murder will give you plenty of evidence—more than enough to take a conspiracy case to the US attorney."

"There's no one in the Bakersfield office right now. My partner and I are on assignment."

"You *are* going to investigate? You told me you would." He didn't really say that, but a knot of desperation is forming in her chest.

"I'm very sorry to tell you this Ma'am, but the FBI won't be able to pursue this matter, at least for the foreseeable future."

"That's crazy. There's new evidence." Her legs wobble, and she sinks into a chair.

"We're in San Francisco. Virtually every agent in the state is working on the mass suicides and murders in Jonestown, Guyana. That's our top priority."

"But Guyana is thousands of miles away. This is right in your backyard."

"When a US congressman is murdered overseas, it's most certainly the FBI's jurisdiction. And in crimes this egregious, the investigation must be extremely thorough. We've got a hundred agents working on it."

"The congressman is dead. Beyond help." She hunches over the phone as if to push her words down the wire more forcefully. "There are kids here who are being exploited and ruined."

"Listen, Mrs. Ricci, your best avenue now is to contact the state attorney general's office."

"Nobody in Sacramento gives a rat's ass about Bakersfield. Especially when Vinson and Smithson are tight with the Reagan bunch."

"I'm sympathetic. I have a son of my own, but we're a resident office. Not in a position to do anything. It's a matter for the state."

The Elston kids are dismantling a Styrofoam Santa Claus that decorated the porch. She hadn't put up a tree or even hung a wreath this year. The house is gray and dusty like the residence of an old woman whose family is dead and friends are gone.

When Danny was with her, he would wake up early on Christmas morning and make two cups of hot chocolate sprinkled with small marshmallows. They sipped them in front of the pine-scented tree before opening gifts, steam from the drinks warming their faces and melted marshmallow creamy on their tongues. When they'd opened gifts, the day was spent stuffing and roasting a store-bought duck, their version of the holiday dinner Carlo used to cook with ducks he'd shot in the valley marshes.

This Christmas, Pete had barbecued a steak for the two of them at his place, but they drank too much JD. He'd seemed a stranger, as if they'd been accidently marooned together in a lonely place.

The creeping January darkness frightens her. A year ago tonight, Reggie was murdered. Everything she counted on was swept away. She hears the high-pitched hum of the telephone wires on the pole beside the house. The smell of dampness and rotting leaves is strong. It rained that night—she remembers now. With rain and darkness and failure all around her, she hates Reggie, for all he has caused—betrayal, lies, and demolition of their lives. At this moment, she could kill him herself.

————

She's pouring JD over ice when Pete calls, back with his crew after extinguishing a truck fire.

"I've got news," he says.

"Me too."

"Is yours bad or good?"

"Bad and really bad," she says.

"Come by the station."

It's dinner time when she parks in the fenced area for employee vehicles. The van door squeaks as he slides into the passenger seat. Two large sacks containing cheeseburgers, fries and chocolate shakes are waiting in the space between the seats, filling the van with odors of beef and grease.

"You're an angel." He digs into one of the bags, and takes a big bite from his cheeseburger. He chews, then stops to study her. "You smell of booze."

"There's been another Boys Club murder."

"Jesus Christ, who?"

"Conrad Fitzgerald, president of Star Petroleum."

"Victim or suspect?"

"I guess you could say he's the victim. He's dead, anyway." Anger seeps from her pores, turning her skin dry and hot.

"And . . ."

"The suspect is a thirteen-year-old boy he'd been abusing."

The grinding of his teeth sounds like bones breaking. "Is that the bad news, or the worse news?"

"You pick." She takes a long breath to help her deliver the next bulletin. "The FBI isn't going to take on a criminal conspiracy case despite the new murder. In fact, it's dropping the whole thing. The bureau in California is tied up with the Jonestown investigation. At least that's what he told me."

Spoken aloud, the hopelessness of their situation seems complete—the words are like hard, flying insects swarming in the air.

Deep laughter and the clatter of plates come from inside the station. Someone turns on the television. Pete's mouth tightens, like men do when they want to cry, but don't want anyone to see it.

"I'd like to blow this whole town to kingdom come," he says.

"Wouldn't do any good." She takes a drink of the shake. "The only survivors would be cockroaches and members of The Club."

They stare out the windshield at the openings in the gray chain-link fence surrounding the station's parking lot. The stores in the shopping center next door are indistinct in the fog.

"What's *your* news?" she asks finally.

"Oh, yeah." He rouses himself. "I've found Kevin Jance. He got arrested for burglary in Redlands day before yesterday. He's being held in juvenile hall in Riverside County."

Suzanne feels like a fighter who's taken too many punches, battered and aching from these latest blows. What difference will it make if Pete has finally tracked down Galen Franzen's teenage sex toy? No one in power will touch The Club.

"I think I heard you say, 'Great news, Pete.'"

"Right."

"No, really, it's good," Pete insists. "I called Harry Strong this morning to kick his ass yet again, and he told me about the kid. He's going down at the end of the week to question him."

"About what?"

"To begin with, illegal disposal of a body."

"That should really shake things up." She stuffs the uneaten food in the bag and tosses it over her shoulder into the back seat.

"Listen, Suzie, at least we're in a position where Strong can ask him what really happened the night of the party. Kevin's the only one left. Jade's disappeared, and Franzen and Grace are dead."

"Why should he say anything? He might actually be the murderer."

"No way. He had no quarrel with Grace. She was just a sideshow." His voice quivers, but he plunges on. "Strong says Kevin's facing time in the Youth Authority. He might be willing to snitch in exchange for less time."

"Harry Strong isn't going to investigate anywhere close to the actual murder. I bet the charges concerning the body are a misdemeanor. He just wants to get you off his back," she says.

"Well, fuck, I'll go down tomorrow and talk to Kevin myself."

Suzanne feels a blip of energy. "Not without me, you're not."

39

As it whips past the big rigs, the Cutlass's engine hums like a man with a broad chest. Cottony Bakersfield fog thins as they climb, until, at the Tehachapi crest, winter sun burns the last wisps away.

Although they're still three hours from Riverside, Pete is tense, his hair full of electricity and his fingers drumming the wheel. Suzanne slept badly last night. Dreams had been infested with images of Reggie and Danny at Jonestown. She twists the radio knobs, but the only stations that come in clearly offer wailing Mexican ballads or revivalist preachers. She chooses the ballads. Once I-5 snakes down into the LA Basin, she tunes in to a rock station playing Springsteen and beats a rhythm on Pete's thigh to *Hungry Heart*.

"Feeling horny?" He throws her a distracted look.

"Maybe."

"Nothing I can do about it now."

Her hand moves to his crotch. "Ever had a highway blow job?"

"Not personally, but I rescued a guy and his girlfriend once from a smashed-up Mustang. He'd run off the road and hit a tree."

"When you got to him, was he hanging out?"

"Like a sausage at a Polish picnic."

Suzanne laughs, unbuttons his jeans, slips her hand inside.

The Cutlass veers across white lane markings. "I don't know if I can . . ." His breath is loud and unsteady.

"Shhh." She bends over, feeling the car's vibration in her thighs, catching the smell of his damp, hidden places. She's done this only once before, when she was young, with a boyfriend on a narrow road in the Coast Range. Pete's heat touches her face and she draws closer, leaning into this dark, constricted space where she can forget everything, the failures and lapses and disappointments. His scent surrounds her, she hears the low sounds in his throat. She is all feeling, motion, and taste. She is consuming and consumed.

Afterward, she rests her cheek on the rough denim of his thigh. He combs his fingers through her hair. Her burden of guilt dissipates, and for a few moments she feels content.

A big rig driver looking down at them from his cab blasts his air horn.

————

Since Suzanne had seen Kevin the night of Franzen's suicide, his shoulders have broadened, and his Adam's apple is more prominent. His red hair is clipped close.

Coins jingle in the soft drink and snack machines as parents buy treats for the evening visit. Suzanne searches for a way to begin. When she'd visited Danny at juvie, she'd been simmering with fury and alarm, demanding that he tell her everything. Most of it spilled out, because Danny loved her, but it's fantasy to think Kevin is warm and fuzzy.

What should she say? Sorry you're in trouble again? Tell us immediately everything we want to know?

"How's the food?" Pete says.

"Just like Mom's." Kevin's brown eyes roam over the gouged walls and stained ceiling tile. The visitors' room has four structural pillars, and each one has a guard stationed next to it, scanning for signs of fights, drug exchanges, or sexual activity.

"Another member of The Club has been killed," Pete says. "A businessman named Connie Fitzgerald."

Kevin flicks him a glance. "The guy with the fancy truck."

Though she's not touching him, Suzanne feels Pete's buzz of excitement.

"You know him?" Pete asks.

"Not really. Seen him around."

Suzanne itches to slap him. "You know him. The night Grace died, you were at Romano's with Fitzgerald." She's not sure of this, but feels a surge of triumph when he stirs restlessly in his chair.

"A thirteen-year-old's been arrested," she says. "His name hasn't been released, but I hear it's Diego Luhan. Fitzgerald apparently met him at the Bakersfield Greyhound Station and took him home."

Kevin swallows and his Adam's apple jumps.

"Luhan's probably going to CYA, and then to prison when he's old enough," Suzanne says. "You're here. Danny is trapped in a court-ordered detention with Vinson. The Club is playing while you guys are paying."

Kevin drums his fingers on the table. "You're really after Dennis, aren't you?"

Pete flashes a sidelong glance at Suzanne. "What makes you say that?"

"You yap-yap about how sad it is for us, but Dennis is the one. He holds the whole shitty club together. Without him, all those big shots would be facing charges." He spits his words, an angry flush creeping up his white, freckled cheeks.

Pete's intervention in the discussion has somehow stirred the boy's anger. Suzanne intercedes to ease the tension. "You can help us, Kevin. Tell us what happened at the party."

"Nothing happened. We played some music, drank some Cokes, smoked some…" He mimes smoking a joint.

"Don't." Pete gets in Kevin's face. "Her blood was found in the bathroom. The floor and fixtures were torn out to hide it."

"So you say."

"Listen, if you tell what you know, then others, like Jade, will open up, too. The attorney general would have enough to take the case," Pete says.

"No attorney general is going to listen to you. You're nobody."

"That's right," Suzanne says. "Us and you, the nobodies."

A toddler teeters away from his family and squats beneath their table, plucking at the plastic on Kevin's jail-issue flip-flops. Kevin wiggles his toes, making the little boy laugh. The guard looms over the mother and shakes her by the shoulder. Eyes wide, she dashes over to retrieve him.

Kevin chews the inside of his cheek. "Okay. After we ate pizza, Galen dropped me at his place and went to buy stuff."

When he returned, the old man had set up a drug buffet, Kevin says: weed, reds, and crystal. After a couple of hours sampling the weed, Kevin realized the dogs were barking furiously at the front door.

"It was Stone, with the cameras and lights. They took all the equipment to the garage, where I fixed things up like the other times. Dragged out mattresses from the bedrooms. Put up some screens to hide the clippers, knives, and flower pots—crap that belonged to the old lady."

Pete adjusts his chair, legs screeching on the tile floor, a sound that makes Suzanne cringe.

"Galen says, 'You're gonna do it, right?' He meant the video, and I said, yeah. Didn't want to get beat up."

Suzanne flinches at his casual tone.

"When did Grace arrive?" Pete asks.

"After eleven, her and Jade."

"Other kids?"

"Luhan and Reno. Bunch of boy stoners from Highland High. Jesus and other guys from the group home."

"And the men?"

The noise level in the room has increased. After the initial awkwardness between visitors and prisoners, conversation is more animated. The boys were probably complaining about food, cellmates, lawyers, and lack of television selection, same as Danny did at juvie. The nearest guard is a few feet away, but his eyes are focused on something across the room. Suzanne follows his gaze, but sees nothing out of the ordinary.

Kevin is distracted. He wrinkles his face at the toddler and evokes a grin. His nails scratch at a patch of acne on his neck. He glances at the clock.

"What adults?" Suzanne reminds him.

Kevin's attention flips back. "The dead guy, Connie." His fingers tick off the other guests. "Tasman, a dude who works for the county doing something. Sully, a political guy. And Dennis. He kept hassling me about your kid."

Her hand reaches for Pete, who grips it hard. "What did he want to know about Danny?"

"Whether Dan-o was coming, what time, do I know his number. Like that." Kevin's lip curls. "Oh, yeah," he says, "and Harris was there. You know him, right?"

"Whitman? The owner of the *News-Daily*?" Suzanne feels like a drooling idiot.

"The newspaper guy, yeah. You're surprised?"

A bell clangs, signaling visiting hours are over. "Wait a minute." Pete grasps Kevin's arm.

The guard claps a hand on his gun belt. "Hands off."

"Hang loose, Mr. Stannard. Saturday's the next visiting day; I'll see you then," Kevin says.

40

The officer on Saturday afternoon duty at visitors' sign-in consults his list. "No inmate named Kevin Jance."

"What?" Pete's bellow sends a ripple through the long line of juvie visitors waiting to be processed. Hoping for excitement, a few crane their necks.

"You heard me—kid's not here." The officer grasps the handle of his baton.

Pete softens his voice. "I saw him two days ago. He was scheduled for a hearing next week."

"I'll check, but it'll be awhile." The officer signs in each visitor, locking up purses, wallets, and pocket knives. The line plods one by one through a metal detector. Meanwhile, Pete and Suzanne pace the lobby, too agitated to sit in one of the molded plastic chairs.

When he's finished, the officer makes a call to the watch commander. "Jance was released yesterday to his mother's custody," he says, hanging up the phone.

"He's got no mother, not since he was five," Pete argues.

The officer signals an incoming visitor to come to the checkpoint.

Back in the car, Pete's fingers clench the wheel as if he's got Kevin by the throat. He'd taken no chances this morning, leaving Bakersfield at eight to guarantee they arrived in plenty of time for one o'clock visiting hours. He skids out of the parking lot and roars onto the 215, cutting across to the fast lane.

"You're over the speed limit," Suzanne says.

"Leave me alone."

She snatches his wallet from the center console and dangles it out her open window. "You're not driving. Pull off at this exit."

They glare at each other as they exchange places in a McDonald's parking lot. He slams the passenger door, and her eardrums hurt with the surge of pressure. On the freeway again, the powerful engine accelerates easily.

"Ease off," she whispers to herself.

"How'd he do it?" Pete slides down in the seat and braces a knee against the dash.

Could've called Vinson, Suzanne thinks, but juvie wards need money to call long distance on the pay phones. He might have gotten his lawyer to do it. She remembers the visiting room guard, who stood close but seemed so disinterested in their whispered conversation. He might have seen something in it for him and contacted Kern County, where Vinson arranged Kevin's release.

"However he did it, the dance steps were perfect," Suzanne says.

During the climb north over the Tehachapis, Pete falls asleep. With his neck twisted at an odd angle against the passenger window, he looks like a hanged man.

The Cutlass tops the crest, where the sun hovers over the mountain tops, painting the clouds with pink and gold streaks. They drop toward the San Joaquin Valley on the Grapevine, a stretch of I-5 so steep that gravity alone shoots the car downward. On one side, mountains tumble to rock at the bottom of a canyon, and on the other, a granite cliff looms. Fog slithers around them.

Big rigs roar past, drowning out the sporadic crackle of the radio. Trucks sniff the car's rear bumper. As they roar past, eighty thousand pounds of steel inches her toward the granite cliff wall. Her wrists and biceps ache with her struggle to steady the wheel.

No more, she thinks, and cranks the car into the fast lane, refusing to let her eyes drift to the canyon, only a few feet from the door. Instead, she lets the Cutlass rip. It flies as the downgrade steepens. Wind squeals through gaps in the air vents.

With every mile they descend, the fog thickens. Tail lights gleam, red and dangerous. Her thoughts boil with events—Danny's abuse, Reggie and Connie's murders, the casual perversion at Franzen's party, Grace's death and Pete's anguish, the long line of unknown but abused young people.

The car clings precariously to the curves. Sweat from her hands makes the wheel slick and greasy. Traffic thins for a few seconds, leaving only the hum of the engine. Pete snores gently. She blinks to forestall tears.

Before her vision fully clears, a truck pulling a set of doubles veers in front of her. She hammers the brake, jerks the Cutlass back into the slow lane. The interior fills with the smell of burnt rubber. She's alongside the truck now, its running lights small and concentrated like yellow acid, the black trailers looming above her, the huge engine roaring.

Her cheeks are hot. Her shirt is thick and hot against her ribs, and her feet burn inside her shoes. She cuts in front of the truck, surging ahead.

In less than a mile, the steep stretch is past. The road is flat and straight to Bakersfield. She's going fast, and fog is thick, but she ignores the danger. She knows what she's going to do.

41

It's still dark, but residents of Lucky's trailer park already are heading out for the day shift in the oil fields. From the window over his kitchen sink, Suzanne watches the twin arcs of headlights. An engine in need of a valve job knocks as it passes.

Two heaping scoops of coffee go into the percolator. She plugs it in, then folds up the sofa bed, storing blankets in a trunk that doubles as a coffee table. The last two nights, she's slept here and lived out of a suitcase. The makeshift arrangement reminds her of her girlhood when she slept on an even saggier couch and stored her clothes in a cardboard box.

On the counter, the pot huffs. Her drive with Pete to Riverside three days ago seems distant. Even after their long trip, they argued all night over Suzanne's scheme to snatch Danny from Vinson and leave the country.

"I should go north with you" Pete said. "It's too dangerous for the two of you to go alone. There will be snow storms. The roads are icy."

"It's not that hard. I believe there *are* women who've driven to Canada in winter."

His fingers were tight on her wrist bone. "You'll have the law on your heels."

"I don't think so. Danny and I aren't on people's radar, but having you along would be a whole different deal. There'd be missing persons reports distributed everywhere for a decorated fire captain who mysteriously disappears."

"Vinson's got Danny on his radar, you can be sure of that," Pete argued, but he hadn't been able to dissuade her from going without him.

Toward dawn, they'd made love, holding each other tightly enough to bruise, as if excessive pressure could convey what they meant to each other.

The house on Filbert Street is locked now, shades drawn. She left everything: sofas and chairs, canned goods in the cupboard, high heels, flower pots, photo albums. With money she borrowed from Pete, she bought a used white Pinto, as near as she could come to a nondescript government car. Luggage, camping gear, and her typewriter are hidden under a tarp in the hatchback. She's an oil field roughneck's daughter again, living on the edge.

Lucky pads barefooted into the kitchen and leans over to scratch Narcissus behind the ears. Since he agreed to adopt her, the cat has made herself a permanent nest on a kitchen chair. He pours himself a cup of coffee. His eyelids are swollen and his jowls droop, looking so much like their father that Suzanne takes a sharp breath. She misses her father, his conviction that she was always right.

"Today?" Lucky asks.

"Yep." The coffee goes down wrong, and she coughs.

"Where will you be?"

"Canada."

He shoots her a disgusted look. "I know that. How will I be able to get ahold of you?"

"I'm telling you the same thing I told Pete. Once we're settled, I'll set up a way to communicate."

"How long, do you think?" Lucky asks.

"A few weeks. Tell Mom I'm really, really, sorry. I'll write her."

"Anything new I need to know about today?"

Suzanne wipes away thoughts of her mother and focuses on her watch. "It's just after six. Vinson should leave early, about 6:40, because Dutch has set up a 7:00 meeting at the DA's office."

She's developed her plan based on what she knows about the luxury enclave where Vinson lives, and information she'd gleaned from Haag yesterday over the phone.

They drive to Bakersfield, she in the Pinto and Lucky ahead of her in his pickup. She misses the familiar rattling of the van's muffler. Winter sun hasn't quite risen over the Sierra, and the oil pump jacks are black against a yellow sky. Wind comes from behind, giving the car a boost. *This is going to work*, she tells herself.

As they near Bakersfield, the wild, low-growing chaparral and buck brush yield to Modesto ash and sycamore trees, then lawns and tightly-pruned, dormant roses. It's 6:30 when she passes through the enclave's wrought iron gates. Rows of palms line the streets, their trunks still lit with tiny white Christmas lights. Suzanne glides to a stop across from Vinson's home. Lucky is parked at the curb a few doors down, his truck newly washed, with a ladder and tools in the bed, suggesting he's a plumber or carpenter.

Suzanne slides down in the seat as Vinson's Cadillac backs out of the garage and rolls past.

Once he turns the corner, streets are empty again. She wonders what other secrets are hidden in the houses on this street, behind the camellia bushes, the oleanders and tree roses, the manicured topiary trees. Corrosive images of Vinson and Danny eat at her. She sends Danny a mental telegram that she's close. Her stomach cramps on the chocolate bar she ate while she waited for Lucky to dress.

Beginning a little after seven, residents drive past on their way to work. She chews a fingernail. The drug-dealing ex-felon on night duty ends his twelve-hour shift at 7:30 when Chuey takes over.

Cars thin out. The Pinto is cold, and she blows on her stiff fingers. She doesn't turn on the engine to warm the interior for fear of attracting attention. Her brain swarms with scenarios: she is captured trying to free Danny; the two of them are nabbed as they enter Canada; one of them is shot during the escape.

Lucky lifts the ladder and toolbox from the truck and disappears behind the house, which opens on the golf course. A stun gun is tucked in his waistband, hidden under his windbreaker.

Somewhere nearby, a mower starts up. Her teeth worry her lip. If this is going to work, it's got to be now. Pete agreed to sacrifice his pristine Cutlass to a minor fender bender with Chuey, delaying her arrival.

Suzanne crosses the street, moves purposefully up the brick sidewalk, and punches the bell. A visitor at the front door may provide enough distraction to allow Lucky to enter from the patio and snatch Danny. Otherwise, Lucky will stun the sleepy guard, who's been up all night.

No one answers, so she rings again. Leaning close to the door, she catches no sound from inside. The mower buzzes on the green belt and more faintly, trucks hum along the parkway in front of the complex. She knocks sharply, imagining Danny, arms covered with needle marks, nodding from a heroin injection.

A three-wheeled motorcart rolls to a stop at the end of the sidewalk. "Security" is printed on the door in gold letters. An overweight man with acne-scarred cheeks lumbers toward her.

"We don't allow solicitors here."

"I'm not a solicitor." To keep her voice from trembling, Suzanne concentrates on her story. "My name is Martha Neiman. I'm from the school district. We received a report of a high school boy living here who's not enrolled in a state-approved education program."

"I don't know nothin' about any school." His jaws work, and she fears he's about to ask her for identification.

She straightens the lapel of her blazer, the only dressy thing she's brought along, and throws her shoulders back. He's barely five-six, and she has three or four inches on him. "Do you have a roster of the legal residents of this complex? Names and ages?"

After a quick glance up at her, he looks away.

"As the school district's truancy officer," she says, narrowing her eyes, "I must be assured the adult at this address isn't harboring a truant."

"There ain't no high school kid here playing hooky."

"The caller was very fearful the youth might commit a burglary or act of vandalism while she's at the office."

"You know who lives in this unit? The DA. No crimes are happening at this place while I'm on duty."

She ignores his mistaken assumption that Vinson is the elected district attorney. "The caller may have been wrong about the address, but she was very insistent. Before I report to my supervisor, I need facts on the residents."

The guard purses his lips. "The kid's gone."

"You're saying there was indeed a truant on these premises?" She flexes her fingers to keep from shaking him until his brains scramble.

"Moved him out yesterday. I saw Mr. Vinson pile suitcases, a skateboard, stuff like that, in the trunk of his Caddy. He and the kid took off while I was making my AM rounds."

42

Suzanne calls Haag from a Dunkin' Donuts shop. Obscenities and phone numbers are scratched on the wall around the pay phone. The receiver feels sticky. "Dutch, he's hiding Danny somewhere. Security at the condo complex saw them drive away yesterday." Lucky's sodden handkerchief is balled in her fist.

Lucky leans close, trying to hear. His chin juts like it did in his drinking days when he'd made a habit of getting in bar fights. Grease pops and spatters as the cook lowers another basket of doughnuts into the hot fat.

"I know," Haag says.

"How? I just found out twenty minutes ago myself."

"In the meeting. I arranged it claiming I had issues with Osterman—which I do. After we hashed that out, I asked him about my client, Danny Ricci, and he told me."

"Where the hell is he?"

"Drug rehab, but Vinson refuses to say where."

"Vinson can't just take him away. It's kidnapping."

Haag sighs. "I know, Suzanne. It's all wrong, this whole screwed-up chain of events. I've fought him every step of the way and haven't won a single round."

"Just when I was about to take Danny away." She's saturated with weariness, as if years without sleep.

Lucky leans close to the mouthpiece. "You think Vinson knew, somehow?"

Suzanne tips the handset so he can hear Haag's response.

"I think what precipitated this was Fitzgerald's murder," Haag says. "His death could cause a lot of blowback: a rich, powerful man in the habit of imprisoning vulnerable boys. Vinson needed to move Danny before word spread about another perv abusing a kid."

"Maybe Peña will order visitation, now that Danny's in treatment," she says.

"I asked Vinson about it. According to him, the rehab program mandates thirty days with no contact to establish new patterns of behavior."

"Vinson's a goddamn liar." She kicks the wall, adding a scuff mark to those left by other frustrated callers.

"Probably true, but the judge has consistently ruled against us on visitation."

"I'm going to find him, and when I do, we'll leave this country in the dust."

"Not a bad idea, considering everything," Haag says. "Gotta go. My case is up in twenty minutes."

A fresh tray of chocolate doughnuts covered with sprinkles attracts a crowd of retirees around the counter. She and Lucky walk outside, where the pallid yellow sun struggles to break through the clouds. She turns up the collar of her blazer. Rather than stand outside in the cold, they slide into Lucky's truck, where they sit in silence for a minute.

"Bastard. I could kill him," he says.

Her eyebrow cocks at him. "That's what I need, two of you in the clutches of the justice system."

"Okay, a severe beating with missing teeth and crushed balls."

"I appreciate the thought." She surveys his lived-in face, with its scar and crow's feet, as comforting as warm soup on a cold day. They've always been like this, out of tune with the world, but in harmony with each other. She kisses him on the cheek, feeling his skin wrinkle self-consciously.

"What can I do to help?" he asks.

"Be on call. And loan me some money."

"The Bank of Lucky Marlowe is open."

After he leaves, Suzanne drives aimlessly, past the courthouse, around the block where Reggie had his shop, up to Panorama Drive. Sun is shining here on the heights. Mexican yard men have parked their trucks while they prune the rose bushes and crepe myrtle trees. Below her, fog has settled over the river, hiding the banks and drifting up the other side where pump jacks in the Kern River Field nod slowly.

The intensity of the last few days dissipates; she feels suspended. The car slides past Franzen's house. Windows are boarded up with plywood; advertisements and soggy newspapers disintegrate on the wet sidewalk.

At Pete's, he doesn't answer the bell. She uses her key to let herself in. Grace's painting is no longer perched on the mantel. Suzanne stashes her suitcases and gear in the spare bedroom. The telephone book yields the names of two teen rehab centers.

"I'd like to speak to Danny Ricci," she tells the man who answers the first number.

"Can't say one way or another whether such person is a client here," he says.

"It's extremely important that I speak with him. He's my son."

"If that were true, Ma'am, you would be aware of our policy regarding calls. Clients in the appropriate stage of treatment may call out between 8 and 9 p.m. Goodbye."

The second facility gave her a similar message, less politely worded.

The library opens at noon. She thumbs through dozens of publications and receives an unwelcome introduction to the thriving industry of teen addiction treatment. One brochure features color pictures of a sun-drenched Malibu beach, where kids carry their surfboards to the creamy waves of the Pacific. In a Christian alternative program, handsome faces are bathed in light from the church's stained glass windows. Programs boast of pools and spas, gourmet meals, wilderness therapy, Zen meditation, and vision quests. Parents can choose from campuses in the redwoods, South Carolina barrier islands, "pristine forest of the Rocky Mountains," and a 50-acre gated estate at Deer Creek, location undisclosed.

More research reveals that Deer Creek is on the shore of Lake Isabella near Kernville, just over an hour's drive from Bakersfield. Outside, it's dark, and the fog stops her breath like a hand over her face. She's unlocking the Pinto when she sees Liza drive by in a patrol car. Suzanne doesn't wave or acknowledge her, but Liza makes a U-turn and pulls alongside, rolling down the passenger window. Traffic edges into the middle lane to avoid her.

"Long time, no see," Liza says.

"Your fault." It seems to Suzanne that Liza is from a different life, one she might have dreamed about and just now remembered.

"I did the wrong thing last fall. I'm sorry."

"That's nice." The Pinto's door sticks. Suzanne rattles the handle.

"The oral interview for the sergeant's exam was coming up. I thought it would give me an edge, if the brass knew how committed I was."

Suzanne recalls the way Danny looked as the black-and-white whisked him away that night, as if he were taking a dignified trip to the firing squad. "How did that work out for you?"

"I didn't make the list." Liza's lips twist in bitter amusement.

"Well, that's good to know." Suzanne has one foot in the Pinto when Liza leans over the black-and-white's window sill.

"I need to tell you something." The smell of liquor drifts from the patrol car. "You remember the kid, Reno, the one that was Danny's pal?"

A drift of cold air touches Suzanne's neck. "What about him?"

"He and another twisted kid were arrested this afternoon. They killed Tasman, the county finance guy, and burned down his house."

Suzanne struggles to breathe. The Club's influence is spreading as if it were Valley Fever, corrupting and infecting the young while the cadre of degenerate adults remains untouched. She feels ashamed at the scorn she heaped on Reno in the past. Could it have made a difference if some good-hearted person—if *she*—had befriended him? Her teeth gnaw at the inside of her lip. She's been unable to save her own son.

It was clearly too late now for Reno. To locate Danny and take him out of the country, she's got to use her repentant friend.

"I can't do anything about the man or that poor, mixed-up boy, Liza. Danny's my priority now. Remember when Carlo died and you helped me? I need you again. Vinson has taken Danny to some rehab facility, but he won't say where, or let me see him. Find out where my son is, Liza. You owe me."

43

The next morning Suzanne wakes up in Pete's rec room still in her clothes. Her dress shoes lie on the floor beside her armchair. The bottle of JB sits on the coffee table, and a glass half full of melted ice has made a white ring on the surface. Her mouth is dry, and it hurts to move her head.

The television, which was broadcasting the *Tonight Show* when she fell asleep, is airing news. Anchorman Troy Knox announces the arrest of two male juveniles on suspicion of murder and arson in the death of County Finance Director Bruce Tasman.

It's still half-dark outside. The German shepherd next door begins to bark, and in a minute she hears Pete, home from his shift.

"Why are you still here? What happened?" He looms over her, the shifting light from the TV playing over his face.

"Vinson has taken him somewhere. Supposedly to drug treatment." She touches her forehead and winces at the pain.

"How did you find out?"

"From Haag. Lucky and I went to Vinson's, but Danny was already gone."

"You think Vinson's telling the truth?"

"Who knows?" She turns away, unable to say anything more.

He gets a glass from the kitchen and returns to pour himself a generous splash of JB. Slouching on the sofa, he drinks as he watches the weather girl predict early morning and late evening fog.

"There's no end to it, is there?" he says.

She feels the same immense burden of resignation, but she doesn't dare answer his question for fear it will overtake her. Leaving him in front of the TV, Suzanne showers and unpacks jeans, a flannel shirt, and sneakers from her suitcase. She remembers the closets and drawers in the house on Filbert Street. The scarves, belts, and dresses she's worn, the handkerchiefs, purses, and pantyhose, all of it seems part of a stranger's life.

She dresses and calls Hedges.

"Where's your column? Mother said the house was dark, and she thought maybe you were on vacation," Hedges says.

"I'm gone, Carl. I quit."

"Oh, shit. Any chance I can talk you out of it?"

"No chance."

"Sorry to hear it. You're a damn good journalist, far better than a lot of the deadwood around here." His regret sounds genuine.

"Thanks, but there's a hellava lot more wrong at the *News-Daily* than deadwood. Whitman is one of them."

"One of whom?" he says slowly.

"You know, Carl. The pederasts. The Club. My God, everyone at the paper has heard the rumors."

"But never about him. He's married and has three step-children."

"Whitman was at the party where Roman was killed, and again at the death of the girl."

". . . and you know this, how?"

She knows his question comes from long years in the news business, but Jesus, his skepticism irritates her. "From two kids that were there."

"Not exactly solid gold sources," Hedges says.

"They may actually be more honest than adults, but now both of them have disappeared."

"If only I were still at the *Times*. We'd be all over this, but here, the big boys tell us what to print." He sighs. "Good luck, Suzanne."

She asks him to send her final check to Pete's address. When she looks in on Pete, he's pouring another drink.

"I need a pair of binoculars," she says.

He doesn't look up. "On the closet shelf in my bedroom."

The highway to Lake Isabella winds upward through the Kern River Canyon. As she drives, Suzanne tosses two aspirin into her mouth and washes them down with coffee from 7-Eleven. The narrow two-lane road has virtually no shoulder, hugging a vertical basalt wall of steely gray rock on one side and a sharp drop to the fast-moving, boulder-strewn river on the other. Her head throbs, and a rattle in the Pinto's passenger door plucks at her nerves.

The road is busy with weekday traffic—liquid propane trucks and grocery supply vans. The mountains are bare, rising out of the ocean of leaden fog below. Once she's in the small town of Lake Isabella, she turns south along the shore. Despite miles of blue water, the pines and oaks are stunted and twisted. Twice, she stops to consult her map, then spots the black wrought iron gate and a sign alongside: Deer Creek School.

With the car screened by trees and red-barked manzanita, Suzanne hangs the binoculars around her neck and climbs through strands of a barbed wire fence. She hikes to a hilltop above the facility. Six cars are lined up in front of what's maybe an admin building. Other structures that look like a dormitory and a school overlook the lake. She perches on a rock and waits, the resinous smell of mountain misery plant sharp in her nose. A Stellar's jay with a menacing black head and crest berates her.

Half an hour passes. Boys emerge in twos and threes from the school until there are about forty gathered on the paved basketball court. A couple of kids trade punches, others kick imaginary stones, cluster in loose groups, or stand with shoulders hunched. It's been many months since she's heard the uneven rise and fall of adolescent voices spiking from low to high, and she feels the deep ache of loss.

A counselor wearing Bermuda shorts and athletic shoes blows a whistle, and the boys line up on the basketball court for calisthenics.

She tenses, twisting the knob on the binoculars to sharpen the view. While the boys listlessly perform situps, pushups, and jumping jacks, she squints at the faces, returning momentarily to four or five, but none of them is Danny. She'll have to widen her search.

44

In another life, the name Golden Sierra Ranch would've made Danny laugh. Gold is what the company rakes in from rich parents who pay to have somebody else straighten out their messed up kids. Danny figures Vinson is coughing up plenty for his stay at this place, five hours northeast of Bakersfield in the Mother Lode country.

It's strange to be around kids his age again. He attends classes, eats meals with other teens, and swims in the pool. After months alone, their voices, sometimes shrill, often staccato and angry, seem to Danny as exotic as tropical bird calls.

"We put our clients on methadone," says his psychiatrist during their first meeting. A paper cup containing a pill rests on his desk. "It's a safe drug, one that reduces the physical effects of the abstinence syndrome and blocks narcotic craving."

He tells Danny to call him Lee, rather than Dr. Shapiro. Lee rubs his upper lip, as if he's trying to stimulate growth in his sparse mustache.

Danny washes down the pill, grateful he's being spared the nausea, tremors, sweats, chills, and hallucinations. Darren, his roommate, endured several cycles of addiction and withdrawal before arriving at Golden Sierra.

But a couple of weeks in, Danny confides to Lee he's suffering from depression and nightmares. "You're just hooking me on some other drug."

"Don't worry." Lee crochets a potholder as they talk, and his hook dips and twists. "Over a period of months, we detox our clients, reducing the methadone dose one to two milligrams a week, until you're drug free."

The clients. That's what they're called, as if the big bucks paid to Golden Sierra are buying estate planning or legal advice. There's no question, however, that kids here are damaged. There's darkness, a black well of suffering in the boys, either from being punished or punishing themselves. Darren has a jagged wound on his temple from a self-inflicted pellet gun shot. Down the hall, a boy has bare patches of scalp where he jerked out his hair. And Danny has the ridged scars on his wrists from his suicide attempt.

After lights out, he huddles in bed. Some nights he dreams the room is filled with Dennis' cigarette smoke. His arms and legs become too heavy to lift; Danny hears him coming, feels the bed sink under his weight so he's unable to struggle out.

Despite group and individual therapy, he keeps the secret of what's happened to him. He's not worried about what people here might think; everyone has unpleasant stories. His mouth stays shut because he's sure Dennis has laid the groundwork to make himself look like Mr. Clean.

Danny can almost hear the voice Dennis used when he talked to staff, that reasonable courtroom voice: here's a boy who lies, who thinks the police and legal system are out to get him. Who had hallucinations under the influence of heroin. Who might have a relapse at any time, and continues to be very unstable. Lee, crocheting his potholder, probably only half-believed Vinson, but has fallen under the influence of the fat checkbook.

The power of the unsaid is draining. Nothing connects him to the person he used to be. He knows there's color in leaves, berries, and cloudless mountain sky, but all he can see is gray. Dennis' cigarette smoke was gray; so was the dirty half-light of his bedroom.

Worst of all, Danny can't get his art back. The ranch offers art therapy twice a week, taught by a woman named Luisa. Students mostly talk and goof off—grind crayons under their shoes or splash their arms with paint. When Danny grasps a pen, it might as well be a twig. His brain and hand seem unconnected. What was it like, when he drew and painted? His head is clearer now and vision sharper, but ideas have evaporated. He feels as though he's walking, day after day, on a surface the color and texture of cardboard.

Nights are endless. He longs for Grace, Will, and especially his mother, the warm scent of her shirt and cadence of her voice. If anyone can lift him out of this miserable time, it's her.

"Can I see my mother?" he asks Lee during the next session.

"Sorry Danny." Lee is crocheting with orange and green yarn today. "It would interfere with the therapeutic process."

Danny wakes that night to the sound of his teeth grinding. Without waking Darren, he slips out of bed and pulls on jeans and shoes. Lee opened his office window this afternoon to let out a couple of flies, and if it's still ajar, he can climb inside and call her from there. The night resident is in his cubicle, chair tipped back. His voice rises and falls as he murmurs into the telephone. Danny tiptoes past and tests the door from the connecting dorm wing to the courtyard, but it's barred. At the other end of the hall, the communal dining room is open, but connections with the girls' wing and the kitchen are both locked.

For awhile, he squats in the bathroom's tiled shower. One of the toilets drips sporadically. It was so easy at home: three phones, his mother's business phone, wall phone in the kitchen, and extension in his bedroom. The memory of the kitchen phone niggles at him. He dodges past the resident's open door again. Next to the kitchen is the food service manager's office. The lock is flimsy, and after manipulating the knob, the door opens. On her desk, a phone.

When he dials home, a recorded message clicks on. The number has been disconnected. He tries three more times, getting the same response. The office clock casts a bluish light on his hands. On the hill above the ranch, a coyote howls.

His mother knows more shit about Vinson than anybody but him. With Fitzgerald's murder, The Club is in danger of exposure. Who knows what might come out at Diego's court hearing? That's why Danny's been moved hundreds of miles from Bakersfield. He's a free radical that needs to be neutralized. But his mother is still in town, and she's gone missing. Chilly air in the unheated office touches the sweat on his face. He stumbles back to bed and tries to sleep, the memory of Reggie's stabbed and beaten body returning to him in waves.

The next morning he pretends he's sick. Once the dorm empties and kids are in class, he creeps outside. The cold air stings his cheeks, but the sky is a clear, deep blue. Carl, the groundskeeper, is sawing a dead branch into yard-long lengths.

Propping the saw against his battered truck, Carl strolls down the path to the kitchen. Luisa, the art teacher, emerges with two Styrofoam cups. Under a twisted oak tree, they sip and smoke. Laughter, light as a spider web, drifts toward Danny.

He scurries to the truck. Carl, who apparently expects to come right back, has left his keys in the ignition.

Classes will break in a few minutes. Danny's ribs hurt with the tightness in his chest. The truck door squeaks as he inches it open. He slides into the driver's seat.

With his hands on the wheel, Danny takes a deep breath. He hasn't driven a stick shift since last summer in the Cutlass, and he was a klutzoid then. When he twists the key, the rumble of the engine reverberates between the buildings like thunder. He lets out the clutch, fumbling with the stick shift. The pickup lurches forward and dies. He swipes his damp hands on his jeans and tries again. Gears grind into first.

His heart thumps as he guides the truck down the small rise. It speeds along the service road, past the admin building, between the soccer field and pool. The rear view mirror flashes an image of Carl running from the patio toward admin.

45

<hr/>

Suzanne has been gone for a couple of days, trolling for Danny's whereabouts at rehab facilities near San Diego and Palm Springs. Pete stands in the shower with his back to the nozzle. He drank too much again last night, listening to the neighbor kids laugh as they bounced a tennis ball against the fence. The stall feels small, and he's too depressed to masturbate or even soap himself. It's eight-thirty, maybe, when the phone rings. He trots down the hall, leaving wet footprints.

"Mr. Stannard?" the caller whispers.

Drops run from his hair down the back of his neck. Outside, metal cans clatter, and gears grind as the garbage truck makes its pickup.

"It's me, Jade."

He can't breathe for a second. "Are you okay?"

"No." Six months ago, her whisper would have sounded like something from a B movie, but now he absorbs the thinness of the sound and tries not to think of knife blades.

"Where are you?"

"Hiding, but I think they've found out where I am."

"I'll come get you," he says.

"Don't bring your Cutlass. Everybody knows it."

Within the hour, Pete's rolling north on 99 to Delano in an F-150 borrowed from the guy across the street. His eyes dart from the road to the rear view mirror, watching for the highway patrol. He's driving over the speed limit, afraid Jade will run before he gets there.

Fog is lifting off the fields, where an occasional lonesome farm worker, hunched over the grapevines, prunes last year's canes. Following Jade's instructions, he leaves the freeway and heads through Delano, past stores where Cesar Chavez began his grape boycott fifteen years ago. He continues west out of town. The bare fields are littered with cotton tufts left in the dirt after October's harvest.

The mud-splattered house and garage squat on a small rise surrounded by a few cottonwoods with broken branches. He shuts off the engine and waits. Other than a '49 Ford pickup on cinder blocks, there are no vehicles. No one peers from the house.

He steps down from the truck. The side door to the garage is open a few inches. He knocks on the cloudy glass.

"Anybody here?"

A metal roof vent clicks. Aware he's outlined in the doorway, he ducks quickly inside. The place is a pigsty, a squat for illegal farm workers charged outrageous rents during the summer months. Cold, compressed air smells of decaying food. A camp stove perches on an unpainted crate, and stained mattresses are stacked against one wall. In a corner, like a dog's bed, are one mattress and a sleeping bag.

"Jade, are you here? It's Pete."

Wind whines through a crack in the closed overhead door.

"Here." She peers from behind a ragged cloth strung over a corner as a makeshift dressing area. Her eyes dart past him to make sure he's alone.

"Were you followed?" She wipes dirty palms on her shirt.

He shakes his head. "I watched in the rear view. Got your stuff? Let's go."

"Where are we going?" She's hoarse, as if she hasn't spoken for awhile.

"Morro Bay. My sister lives there." The last of Leslie's five children took off for college last fall. He'll call from a pay phone on the way over, and promise her anything if Jade can stay awhile.

Jade curls her fingers inside the cuffs of her sweatshirt, as if getting the feel of this thought; then she nods. From a pile of clothes, she pulls two cotton laundry bags. He hefts one over his shoulder and reaches for the second, but she wraps her arms around it. His bag sails into the bed of the pickup, but she tucks hers between her feet as she settles into the passenger seat.

"It'll be a couple of hours, so get comfortable."

"I know. I've been there." Jade turns up the heater and moves her ragged tennis shoes closer to the vent. Her olive skin is gray from the cold.

His bones ache with longing for Grace. Despite his earlier excitement, despair strikes a sharp blow to his heart. He crouches over the wheel, the truck wobbling a little on the pavement. Light glitters on the pits in the windshield dug by flying sand.

He remembers his daughter's sweet, clean scent when he hugged her, and feels slightly sick at Jade's stale, unwashed odor. If Gracie never had met this deeply troubled girl, raised by a drug-addicted mother, how different their lives would have been.

They ride for thirty miles in silence, Jade throwing him fearful glances from the corners of her wide, black eyes.

"I'm hungry," she says.

They stop at a pancake house in Wasco. The breakfast crowd is gone, and the only other customers are a stooped old man seated across from a younger woman with long, straightened hair, perhaps his daughter. Jade disappears into the women's restroom. She's gone so long, Pete begins to think she's run away. When she finally slides into the booth, her hands and face are clean and her hair is fastened with a rubber band. Pete drinks coffee while Jade devours four waffles and two orders of sausage.

"How long were you hiding at that place?" he asks.

"I dunno. Since Danny got taken. How long is that?" She doesn't look at him, but mops up the last of the syrup.

"Who's after you?"

"The same ones," she says.

"The men in The Club? The ones you introduced to Grace?"

282 | ANNE DA VIGO

"It wasn't me. Grace was the one. *She* knew those guys."

He pushes his face inches from hers. "Stop lying."

"I'm not! It was Grace. She was the one who knew them—Kevin, Connie, Harris, and the DA guy. All that gang."

"It couldn't have been Gracie, you conniving little witch. I don't know why I'm doing this for you." Grace was basically a good kid, he tells himself, just going through a rough patch. When kids are that age, they defy their parents. The books all say so.

"You didn't come to get me because you're Santa Claus or Jesus or somebody; you want to know what I know." An angry red rash spreads over her cheeks. "Why would I screw this up, your big rescue, if it weren't true?"

Pete takes a deep breath. If he doesn't play it cool, she'll take off again. He wants her story. Later, he can navigate the falsehoods. "You've got a point. Are you finished eating?"

He pays the check and calls Leslie from the pay phone. "I've got a big favor to ask."

"Like?" Leslie asks.

"Could you take in a homeless girl, a friend of Grace's?"

"How messed up is she?"

He has the urge to lie, but resists. "Quite a bit. Her parents are both in prison, and she was there when Grace died."

"That's all?"

"I know, it's bad, but she's got nowhere to go."

"She's in trouble with the law, right?"

"She's in trouble like Grace was in trouble. Please, Les."

"I loved that girl, and think about her every day." She sighs. "Okay, bring the kid over, and we'll give it a try. Where are you, around the corner?"

"We're in Wasco. See you soon." Thank God for Leslie, her calm competence and roomy heart.

Back in the truck, Jade hugs the laundry bag against her chest like a child with a teddy bear. "She doesn't want me, does she?"

"She wants the two of you to get to know each other. That's fair, isn't it?"

Jade nods slowly. They ride in silence for several miles. The heater huffs, and occasionally a car whizzes past with a slap of wind against the driver's side window. He feels Grace's absence more keenly. Jade no more makes up for his daughter than a department store dummy takes the place of a real person.

"You know Stone, the creepy guy with the tattoos?" Jade bites a torn cuticle.

"I've seen him."

"He's connected to a big-time porn guy in LA who's worth millions and millions."

His fingers tingle, as if he's grabbed a hot wire.

"He paid us, and brought good stuff, especially crystal, to the old man's parties." Her face softens with a dreamy look. "Crystal is fabulous. Like you're at the north pole, only it's not cold, and everything is white and sparkling for a thousand miles, and the light, it gets in your brain, and your thoughts are so clear and beautiful."

She presses her cheek against the window. "It makes me sad to remember it."

"And Grace?"

"Yeah, Grace, too."

Pete's face aches. He's always liked life to be certain. The smell of fish on his father's hands. The rhythm of his job, twenty-four on, forty-eight off. The ornate furniture Janis bought that he couldn't bring himself to get rid of. He'd been so confident of Grace: her goodness, her purity, her intelligence. Her love.

"Sometime last summer, Grace and I went to the mall to get a present for her mom. She was shitfaced mad because you wouldn't let her go to Nashville for Janis' birthday."

Why did he say no? He can't remember.

"The Strangers were going to Canada on tour, and she decided to run away and join them. To get the money, she said yes to Stone about the porno."

Questions that have gnawed at him for months seem clearer. Why had she agreed to attend Franzen's parties when she hadn't been involved with drugs before? Why had she returned after she'd been raped?

He glances at Jade. As soon as he accepts the possibility she was telling the truth, his mind veers away again. Jade is night to Grace's day, her skin the deep brown of Mexico's Indians, her black eyes wary, guarding too many secrets. Grace was the child of sunny-day eyes. He'd been proud that she was a billboard, and he was a father who knew his daughter.

Ahead of them on the road, a pickup saddled with an oversized camper labors on the long upgrade. Pete's foot twitches, and he stomps on the accelerator to power past.

"How many times?" he asks.

"A few. The last couple was when things went bad."

"You could've stopped."

"Grace wanted to tell you after she got beat up, but chickened out."

He enunciates carefully along a cliff of words. "And that night . . ."

"It takes hours to film even a minute or two they can use, because the director keeps moving the camera and lights. After we were done, we stank of each other's sweat."

She pulls her knees up to her chest and wraps her arms around them. "We took a shower in Galen's bathroom. When Grace's makeup was off, I could see circles around her eyes, like she was super tired. All of a sudden, Dennis opened the door. He wanted to know where Danny was."

He looked terrible, Jade says, his hair sticking out in clumps, and the tail of his wrinkled shirt hanging half out of his waistband.

"I said, 'Go away, Dennis, I want to pee.' I wrapped a towel around myself, but Grace stood there, starkers. I could tell she was mad. She says to him, 'Danny didn't come. He hates these parties.' I thought, oh, no, no. Tell him Danny has a stomach ache, or his ride fell through.

"Dennis' face got red, as though he were going to stroke out. 'I want him here,' he says."

"Grace needles him. She says, 'You sound like a baby. A baaabeee. Danny doesn't want to see you.' She tried to push him out and shut the door, but he went for her."

"Gracie went bonkers. She says, 'Danny thinks your belly is gross, and you smell like an old man.'"

Pete can't swallow.

"Danny never said any of those things, but the guy went crazy. He was shaking Grace and screaming, and her head was flopping, and she scratched his face."

Jade's icy hand touches his.

"Dennis picked up Galen's barber scissors from the counter. I can still see them, they kind of sparkled in the light."

Jade is crying. Pete brings her fingers to his mouth and breathes on them.

46

Danny's got the hang of the gears. Wind from the pickup's open window cools his neck and cheek as he rolls down Golden Sierra's long driveway. The air smells of earth and dry grass. The truck is in high gear as he approaches the junction with the county road.

He's unsure which direction to turn. The ranch is somewhere between Placerville and Auburn, he's pretty sure. It was dark when they arrived in Dennis' Cadillac, and it seemed as though they traveled for eons over unlit country roads before they turned onto the gravel drive. Across the road is an apple orchard, and off to his right, a pasture with cattle clustered around a muddy pond.

The truck's tires squeal as he makes a skidding, last-second left turn. A cow looks up. He downshifts, then up to third. Side roads branch to the left and right, but the signs—Mount Alice Road, Sheep Valley Road—offer him no clues.

Pursuit will be only a minute or two behind. Danny veers onto Horsefly Ridge Road, driving fast, getting used to the truck's cranky steering. Sweat drips into his eyes, and he swipes at his forehead with the back of his hand. Quick glances in the rear view mirror reveal no cars behind him, and after a few miles he loosens his grip. With the maze of country lanes winding through the hills, searchers can't check them all.

The road climbs, then levels out on a ridge. He stops the truck to still the trembling in his hands. From here, he can see a drop of two thousand feet to a shiny green ribbon at the bottom. The American River, he's pretty sure. He'll follow it west until it intersects with I-5. Then, it's about five hours from there to Bakersfield.

The shadow of a hawk drifts across the truck's hood, as if it's spying. Out the side window he sees a red car, a Matchbox toy from this distance, winding up the grade behind him. When he shifts clumsily, the truck lurches onto the shoulder. He restarts the engine and inches away from the edge, his hand damp on the gearshirt.

The downslope is steep, narrow, and curvy. He pumps the brake pedal often, rather than risk shifting to low. A hot, metallic odor fills the cab. His bowels feel empty, as if he's shit himself, but he hasn't. Afraid to take his eyes off the road, he can't tell if the red car is getting close.

On the hairpin turns, the lurch and sway make him dizzy. He recalls going to the playground in Taft with his father, who seated him on the swing, twisted the chains like a windup toy, and released him into a spin. He didn't like Carlo much, but now he wishes his dad were here, solid and confident. His father could drive this road with a little finger on the wheel.

A horn blast from behind shatters his nerves like glass. The red car is riding his bumper. He speeds up, so rattled he passes a turnout without stopping. Sun reflects off the car's windshield; he can't tell who from the ranch is driving. His truck and the red car round a curve a few feet apart.

On the straightaway, the driver pulls alongside, flips him the finger, and passes. In few seconds, the car rounds another turn and disappears.

Danny pounds the wheel in victory. This dry hillside is gold, strip of river is jade, gouged pavement is onyx. The world is more beautiful than he could ever paint it. Even the hamburger wrappers and cigarette butts on the floor of the cab have a seedy charm. Two Harleys sweep past, going uphill, and Danny waves out the window at the helmeted drivers. He'll buy a motorcycle in a couple of years, drawing and painting as he crosses the country.

He switches on the radio and fiddles with the knob. He wants rock music—Seger or Springsteen. No Haggard, no country music ever again. When he looks up, his truck has drifted to the left.

In its path is a third motorcycle.

He twists the wheel, feels the slide, the spin. Images roll past in a blur of form and color before he sees only black.

47

Every hour on the trip to Sacramento, Suzanne stops to use a pay telephone while Pete stays in the Cutlass with the engine running. Danny is in critical condition, the nurses say. When they pull up to the hospital's covered walkway, it's 4 a.m. Reflected light trembles in the rain puddles.

"I'll park and meet you inside," Pete says.

Suzanne jumps out and runs to the information desk in the hospital lobby. The security guard consults his printout.

"Ricci is in 4230, surgical intensive care, fourth floor."

She leans against the elevator wall. A polka is playing on the intercom. She and Pete had been in bed when Liza knocked on his front door. She'd heard from a highway patrol buddy that Danny was in a Sacramento hospital after wrecking a stolen truck.

The elevator dings. In the dusky corridor, her footsteps are silent on the industrial carpet. She presses a bell, speaks into the intercom to identify herself, then hauls the ICU's door open when it buzzes. Inside, three nurses work under fluorescent lights, their circular desk the hub in a cluster of glass-walled cubicles. In her frantic rush, she doesn't stop to ask questions, just plunges into 4230. Two monitors beep in an irregular rhythm, and beneath those sounds, a ventilator whispers.

At first, she fantasizes the highway patrolman has made a mistake. The patient is tall, his big feet tenting the bedclothes, but this young man's hair is shaved; white sterile pads are taped over his eyes. The bridge of his nose is flat. His forehead and cheekbones are sunken, like the ground over a sinkhole. The small patches of unbandaged skin are the color of raw ground meat.

Someone filched Danny's wallet, she thinks, dizzy with relief. The thief stole a car and crashed it. This lanky youth with the mangled face is some broken boy who went wrong.

A jungle of tubes loops from his body. A ventilator tube is affixed to his half-open mouth, a drain from his head, catheter, blood pressure and heart monitors on the left and right, plastic tubes from his hand and the crook of his elbow.

The shrill tweet of a monitor draws her closer. The back of his right hand is pierced by a needle attached to a plastic tube. She stares at the curved knuckles, the fingers, these telling arrangements of undamaged bone and flesh. They move her like nothing ever has, not her father's death, not her marriage, not Danny's birth.

She very simply falls to the floor.

Next, she's aware that Pete holds her on one side and a nurse is taking her blood pressure on the other.

The nurse, a Filipina with gray, wire-like strands running through her black hair, says, "There now, take some deep breaths."

The air is hard as polished metal and hurts her lungs.

Suzanne is hoisted up by the armpits. "I'm Angelina," the nurse says. "Sit in the chair and put your head between your knees."

"I'll keep an eye on her; I'm a firefighter with EMT training." Pete kneels by the chair and touches the pulse in her wrist.

Suzanne's head pounds with a rush of blood. From her upside-down angle, she can see the dust on the chair legs. When she sits up, Angelina is checking Danny's tubes and resetting the heart monitor.

"What happened to his head?" Suzanne asks.

Angelina jots a note in a thick binder. "He apparently was thrown from the vehicle and landed on his forehead. The surgery last night involved some preliminary repair work and insertion of a tube to relieve pressure on his brain."

Pete's eyes narrow. "Intracranial bleeding?"

"That's what this line is for." Angelina tweaks one of the tubes, which snakes down to a container of bloody fluid.

"And the repair work?" he asks.

Angelina closes the binder. "Dr. Chan did the surgery. He was here until late, but he'll arrive for rounds in an hour or so. He can answer all your questions."

"Yeah, good," he says.

Suzanne struggles to take it all in. The room is a health factory with the tools of recovery arranged around her: blinking wall lights, restless blips, slow drips, glowing green monitors on wheeled carts, oxygen canisters, tripods hung with bulbous fluid bags.

Her scenarios of how she and Danny would be reunited seem like fairy tales. Months ago, she dreamed he would return to the house on Filbert Street, they would open a map and pick a new home, somewhere with clear air, green trees, and fine schools. She would help him with his homework and trim his hair. He would cook Southern fried chicken once a week. When he graduated, he would enroll in a good art school.

Despair is mixed in a strange, confused way with joy at his life, his nearness. Shaky on her feet, she stands. The room tips a little. She rests her forearms on the bed rail. Her hand hovers over the curve of his head, his torso, the small, visible patches of his face.

"Honey, it's Mom. I'm right here beside you. You're in the hospital, but don't be scared. They're taking good care of you. Pete's here too." Meaningless words, but she's unable to keep silent. "Lucky will be up to see you in a day or two, and Grandma says hello."

She'll call as soon as she can collect herself to tell them he's hurt.

Angelina returns with two Styrofoam cups. "Here's some coffee. It's from the nurse's station, and probably not too bad. Feel free to come to the break room for doughnuts."

Dr. Chan arrives, smelling of soap and clean clothes. He wears a suit and tie; his cheeks glow from a fresh shave, even though he was in the operating room half the night.

"Aaah, Danny's mother?" He leans toward her in an odd, formal gesture, as if bowing to an elderly woman.

"Tell me," she says.

"Yes, yes. Your son took the impact of the crash between his eyes. It crushed the bones in his forehead and nose." His long-fingered hand arcs over Danny's face. "X-rays show bits of bone floating under the skin."

She recalls Danny as a newborn. The space between his eyes was flat, and she watched it anxiously as she nursed him, rubbing the fine baby hairs. Would he grow up with a simian face? Within a month or two, his features took on shape and angle, and she forgot about it in the excitement of watching him grow. Bandages cover that place now. She's glad she can't see it.

"Last night, we drained blood from his head to relieve pressure," Chan says. "We determined at that time that his right eye is dead."

Pete slides an arm around her back. "And the left?" His voice is hoarse.

"We won't know for a while. We're going to keep him in a medically induced coma for a week or so to reduce the possibility of brain damage; then we'll assemble surgical teams, one to remove the right eye and repair the socket, and another to reconstruct his face."

Chan speaks more softly now. "It may be months, even a year, before the left eye stabilizes."

Tears roll down her cheeks and onto her shirt, spots dotting the fabric. Pete hugs her, but she barely feels his touch.

Chan murmurs softly, poring over Angelina's charts. He scribbles notes with his pen; then moves on to the next room. A burst of chatter in the hall announces the arrival of the day shift.

A pale dawn seeps up from the east. Mourning doves coo in the eaves. In the opposite hospital wing, a few lights are on, yellow squares that gleam and disappear as tree branches shift in the wind.

Dishes clatter as food is delivered to the room next door. Gilbert, the day nurse, introduces himself. He's a bearlike man, with friendly lines bracketing his mouth and creasing the corners of his eyes.

His pager buzzes and he leaves, but in a few minutes he's back. "Mrs. Ricci? There's an officer here about Danny."

A highway patrolman wearing a tan uniform with a holster on his black leather belt steps past the nurse into the room. "Good morning, Ma'am. I'm Officer Blaney, following up on a reported auto theft and crash of a stolen truck."

She blinks her swollen eyes.

"Involving your son," he says.

"Haven't you done enough?" She takes a step toward him. "Haven't you fucking done enough?"

Officer Blaney touches the metal nightstick on his belt.

Pete grabs her elbow. "Come on, Suzie. Let's take a break."

She twists to get away, but his fingers tighten, and he drags her, struggling, into the hall. His hand remains clamped on her bicep as he hauls her into the elevator.

"I hate you," she says on the way down.

"You were on your way to getting arrested."

"It would've been worth it, to feel my thumbs in his eyes."

In the lobby, a nun in a white dress and black headscarf passes them on the way to the chapel.

"How about it?" Pete says.

"I'm not a God girl. Never have been."

"Let's give it a try. For the kid."

A spotlight illuminates the small chapel's bare wooden cross, and a carved statue of the Virgin Mary reigns over a side altar. They slide into a pew.

Pete closes his eyes and folds his arms across his chest. His sleeve brushes hers; she feels the rhythm of his breathing. Other than funerals, she hasn't been to church since she was a girl. Nevertheless, she prays. *Forgive me for what I did to my father. Do whatever you want to me, kill me or maim me, infect me with a terrible disease, anything, but let my son be alive and whole.*

The nun is kneeling in front of the Virgin. She whispers softly, strikes a match, and lights a votive candle. Soft footsteps mark her departure.

The candle releases oily smoke that stings Suzanne's eyes. Her face is still sticky from crying. "If I pray he dies, do you think God will grant my request?"

"Vinson? Doubtful."

"Is there no way to stop him?"

"I don't think so, short of murder," Pete says.

She studies his face. "You're serious?"

"I dream about it sometimes, but—no." His eyelids sag. "I went on a call once. A man was having chest pains. While I was taking his vitals, his breath and pulse stopped right under my hands. It was like I'd died myself. I couldn't do that, stop someone's life. Not even for Grace."

Back at the fourth-floor nurses' station, Gilbert is scribbling on charts. "The cop's gone. We're to notify him when Danny begins to wake up."

———

Late in the afternoon, Pete looks up from the magazine he's reading. "I'm going to find us a motel and buy some take-out. Want to come?"

She turns away from the window and shakes her head. "I can't. Could you find a phone while you're out? Call everyone?"

After he's left, the equipment's mechanized wheezes and beeps make her sleepy. She's nodding in the chair when Gilbert comes with an extra pillow.

"Good medicine for neck pain." Gilbert smiles and tucks the pillow gently behind her head. The unexpected kindness makes her want to clutch his waist, put her cheek against his heavy chest.

When she awakens, Pete is there with cartons of Chinese food. "Come on, Suzie, eat something."

Her stomach is tight, leaving no room for food. Danny's feet twitch restlessly. Tired of inaction, she loosens the sheet and blanket at the end of the bed and touches his cold, graceful arch.

The tendon is tight as a guitar string. She kneads it, following along to the dense ball of his foot, his long toes.

"Pete's brought moo shu pork, Danny. Your favorite." She babbles and works his feet, unable to see his features but feeling his muscles relax. "You've always liked those thin little rice pancakes. Remember once we went to LA, got lost in Koreatown, and ate Asian?"

Gilbert arrives with another unit of glucose and a syringe of medication. "Oh, good, you brought dinner."

"Feel free. There's plenty." Pete pushes the cartons toward him, but the nurse shakes his head.

"We had some calls inquiring about Danny this afternoon," Gilbert says. "You were asleep, Missy, and your man was out." He hands Suzanne a list.

She scans it quickly. Lucky, Maude, and Carl; Leslie, her mother, and Carlo's sister. Liza must have put out the word. Tonight, she'll call them back from the hospital lobby.

"There was another call," Gilbert says. "A man, but he didn't leave his name."

48

One evening in September, Dutch calls. "How are things going?" he says.

"Not bad." Suzanne rolls her chair away from the typewriter. Hearing his voice is like a chance meeting with someone you knew long ago.

She hasn't talked to him since he was in Northern California last spring, negotiating a plea bargain in Danny's auto theft case. Dutch finagled the charge down to a misdemeanor with informal probation. Once the deal was struck, Dutch quit his law practice, moved to LA, and started a business brokering high-end vintage cars for wealthy collectors.

"Danny's back from his course at the blind school in Berkeley, and I've rented a place for us here in Sacramento."

"Ah," he says.

"He's got some sight in his left eye, enough for him to see some forms and colors."

It's late afternoon, and dredging up a cheerful voice is an effort.

"That's good. Sort of." He clears his throat. "Actually, I don't know what to say."

"I understand, Dutch. We get that a lot."

"Well, I've got news from the bad old days. A former colleague called me. Reno Goulet was sentenced today in San Bernardino. As an adult. Thirty to life for Tasman's murder."

At dinner, she tells Danny.

He fingers the black patch covering his empty eye socket. "Reno isn't such a bad person. He just got pushed, you know. People wanted him to do stuff, and they kept at him, wouldn't let him say no."

Danny's face is still misshapen with swelling, and thin red scars trace his hairline where surgeons, in a horrific operation, peeled back the skin to rebuild his face. Sympathy gets the better of her, and she touches his cheekbone. He pushes her arm away. "Leave it alone. I don't need you to go all weepy."

He retreats to his room, able to walk without his white cane in this familiar space. The rock band *Queen* begins on his eight-track player, and the lyrics, "Spread your wings and fly away," drift down the hallway.

Suzanne cleans the tabletop and scours the sink, reciting her mantra, *Be patient,* with each swipe. She mops the kitchen floor, using her shoulder to dry her cheek when tears fall. After dark, she sits in the backyard under the sycamore tree. Brown autumn leaves click in the evening wind from the Sacramento River Delta. Narcissus hops up, nestles into her lap, and begins to purr. The vibration warms the sensitive flesh between Suzanne's legs.

On nights like these, she closes her eyes and tries to remember Pete's tall solidity. The perfect match of their bodies. She hasn't seen him since the days immediately after Danny's accident. Once he used up his vacation time and returned to Bakersfield, she had no time. All her energy is focused on Danny's tests, operations, appointments with multiple specialists, psychiatric counseling, and occupational therapy. Squeezed between all this is her struggle to assemble a new set of freelance clients so she has enough money to buy hamburger and rent a place to throw down a couple of mattresses. Days go by when she drops into sleep without thinking of Pete; then suddenly she burns with longing—for the feel of him inside her, working his slow rhythm that made her forget everything else, but also for his gentle hands on her skin, and fingers massaging the sore places in her scalp.

She lifts her pajama top, letting the wind cool her breasts. Last time Pete called, he told her he'd gone on a date with a friend of Leslie's.

The music drifting from Danny's window stops. It's been twenty months since Reggie died, just over a year from when Grace was found along the road. Back then, Danny was struggling with his sexuality, Grace was lonely for recognition from her mother.

The one glimpse she'd had of Reno was in juvenile court after Reggie died. The boy was hard-faced and sullen, his ash-blond hair growing out black. She imagines Reno's mother wrapping a towel around her son's shoulders to cover his shirt, dipping a cotton ball into a bowl of hydrogen peroxide, bending his head forward, exposing his bare neck.

———

The Plexiglas barrier between her and Reno at San Bernardino County Juvenile Hall is cloudy with hundreds of fingernail scratches.

"Thanks for coming," Reno says through the handset. Tomorrow, he'll be transferred the Youth Authority prison, where he'll stay until he's old enough for the adult system.

His bleached hair has grown out to dark brown, and starchy jail food has settled in his jowls and neck. He looks older than sixteen.

"I read Danny your letter," she says. Reno had written weeks earlier, before the Tasman trial opened.

"I was thinking about the old days. We had some great times back then."

Was his nostalgia for the time when he and Danny were arrested driving Reggie's Mercedes?

"I came because I thought you'd want an update on how he's doing." She wonders if Reno is curious about her flimsy excuse.

"That'd be good." He tips back slightly in his chair, restrained by the phone cord.

"He lost his right eye, you knew that?"

"I heard." A grin creases his face. "Too bad he can't get a mechanical eye, like the Six Million Dollar Man."

"Actually, there could be a show just about Danny," she says. "The doctors used titanium strips to replace his nose, forehead, and cheekbones."

"That stuff's valuable. Hope nobody kills him for his head . . ." When he sees her face, he rocks forward and puts his palm to the window. "Sorry, sorry."

His hand is surprisingly unchanged, still slender, with small, boyish fingers. "What's Danny gonna do now?"

Despite the grim setting, she feels a spurt of joy. "He's started to paint again."

He screws up his face to take this in. "Huh. A blind artist. I guess that's not so weird. Some paintings look like a blind guy did 'em."

"There's a very successful blind artist in Sacramento, and they're painting together, working in acrylics."

Reno looks wistful. "Guess you're glad about that."

"I'm happy he can do something he loves." Danny's life, no matter how filled with pain and disappointment, is rich compared to this young man's.

The first time she'd driven Danny to artist Joe Belmont's studio, Danny was frightened. "I can't do anything, I never was any good, I'm a freak," he said.

A fleck of jam lurked in the corner of his mouth, but she didn't wipe it away. This wasn't the time to hover. The Pinto idled, and after a couple of minutes Belmont's assistant hurried down the walk. He offered his arm, and Danny touched it lightly, as he was taught at the school for the blind: don't cling to the sighted person, let him guide you. The two men had moved like a strolling couple to Belmont's studio at the rear of the house.

After that visit, Danny hadn't been transformed, as she hoped, yet now he stands with his shoulders back instead of slumping. When they speak, he looks directly at her to catch her shadowy outline or the color of her T-shirt. For the first time this weekend, he'll be taking a bus to the studio, where he and Belmont are working together on a large canvas.

Reno is watching her, the handset resting on the shelf in front of him. He puts the phone back to his ear. "You've forgotten about him, I guess."

"Who?"

His lip curls. "Dennis."

Sometimes hours pass, while she taps out her latest freelance assignment, when she doesn't think about Vinson.

"At my sentencing," Reno says, "I told the court all about Dennis and the other guys, how they said they wanted to be friends, but really wanted to fuck us." He sighs. "I named names and everything. Didn't do any good. Nobody wrote about it."

"I'm sorry no one's paying attention. I tried my best." She wonders if it's true, if she did enough after Reggie died.

How sophisticated Reggie seemed when they first moved next door: his styled hair, linen slacks, and fastidiously decorated house. Back then, she was an awkward woman with an unruly mop of hair who was never taught good manners or fine living. He was her standard of excellence.

"Did you . . ." She tilts the handset away from her mouth. There is danger in knowing. Once facts creep close enough, they sink their claws in. "Forget it."

Laughter rocks him back in his chair. "Go ahead, ask. My case is done, and I'm going away 'til they carry me out."

Something pushes her. ". . . that night at Reggie's?"

His eyelashes flutter. "You want to know, did I kill him, or was it the pussy college boy?"

"Yes."

"It could've been me. It would've been righteous." He leans close to the glass, as if they are two girls comparing notes on last night's date. "I mean, I could've, but I didn't."

Voices from other visitors ricochet off the high ceiling, flying toward her. She presses a hand tightly over one ear to block them out.

"I'd sucked off Dennis, the college boy, and Reggie, but he wouldn't pay me. He was still pissed over a few dollars I'd taken from petty cash at the shop. I had to go back and tell my old lady I didn't have no money, and she beat me up. Reggie was a thief—a guy with a house, pool, store, and Mercedes—and he tries to stiff me."

He takes a deep breath. "I don't have nice parents who go to PTA meetings and save for college." His face softens with a boyish wistfulness. She glimpses how he might have looked if there'd been someone—a grandmother or aunt or teacher—who cared about him.

"I'm not much, but I'm somebody, and I should get what's due me, don't you think?"

"Yes." Her voice is hoarse and uneven. "He owed you."

In the newspaper account of Tasman's murder trial, the victim had been angry at Reno and Jesus because they'd stolen a television set and sack of antique marbles. Reno denied the theft, but Tasman threatened to call police if the pair didn't give him free sex.

It wasn't the degradation, she thought, but the unfairness. The injustice was more devastating to Reno than all his sordid acts.

"Now it's my turn, right? I get to ask you a question," he says.

She slides her chair back, putting some space between her and the window.

"You love your kid, and he's had shit done to him. Don't you want it too?" he asks.

Dread fills her chest. "Want what?"

"You know." His dark eyes pin her like a butterfly.

She feels naked, as though this sixteen-year-old can see all her faults, private desires, secret motives, and raging anger, which is threatening to erupt.

Reno smiles. "I think we're a lot alike. Otherwise, why would you come all those miles, just to tell me about Danny?"

49

Suzanne speeds toward Sacramento, glad she rented a car for the trip to visit Reno. Her Pinto always has been a beater. By late afternoon, she's over the Tehachapis and down into the valley. Familiar Bakersfield off-ramps flash by. Her chest aches and her skin is hot, as though she's contracted valley fever, the fungus-borne disease in the Bakersfield soil.

The next exit is the thoroughfare that runs past Vinson's ritzy neighborhood. Her legs stick to the seat cover. At the last moment, she veers from the fast lane onto the ramp.

She cruises twice past Vinson's house. There's no sign of the security guard's motorized cart. Vinson's windows are dark, confirming that he's not home from work yet, so she parks across the street. Her nape touches the back of the seat as she settles down to wait.

Wind flings dirt against the windows. A vehicle approaches. It rolls past and turns right. Another draws near, and this time Vinson's automatic garage door rolls up. The Cadillac pulls into the driveway, brake lights pulsing, and glides inside. Taking a deep breath, she climbs out and races across the street. The heavy door's going down; when it's just a few feet from the concrete, she ducks under.

Inside the two-car garage, dust swirls in the beam of the overhead light. The Cadillac is parked near the connecting door to the house. The garage's vacant side is cluttered with a barbecue, spare propane canisters, a dusty rowing machine, hoses, shovels, saws, power drills, and an axe.

The car door opens and keys jingle. Briefcase in hand and suit jacket over his arm, Vinson steps out. His eyes brush past her, then fly back. He drops everything, staggering against the open car door with a high-pitched, almost childlike cry.

"Get out, get the hell out!" Feet tangling in the suit jacket, he falls to his knees and scrabbles frantically for his briefcase.

She lunges, snatching it from under his searching fingers. "You got a gun in there?"

Vinson props his hands on his thighs and hauls himself to his feet. She blocks him inside the vee between the car and the open door. Sweat shines on his forehead and dribbles down his cheek.

"Police will be here in thirty seconds," he says.

"Not unless you hit the alarm, but you can't. It's inside, isn't it?" Surreal to see him, after her lurid, demonic dreams of him. She realizes she's the taller one. He's diminished, stooped.

"I'll charge you with trespassing and assault on a public official." His shoulders straighten, but his voice trembles.

She takes a step closer. "Are you sorry at all?"

"About what?" He feints in an attempt to slip past her.

"Don't mess with me, Dennis." She jabs at him with the briefcase's metal-tipped corners.

His hands go up, placating her. "It's sad about your son. Drugs led him to make some very poor decisions."

"You abused and addicted him, you and your underworld posse."

He thrusts his chin out. "I tried to save him, but he was out of control. Dealing drugs, committing auto theft. He was on a downward path, and you did nothing."

The smell of stale cigarettes and sweat pour off him. Danny must have felt this same disgust, but he had to endure it—Vinson's touching. Entering.

"You've got to end it," she says. "Make it right."

His lip curls. "End it? You're fantasizing I'll commit suicide?"

"I'm not a fool. Resign. Leave the state."

"My God, the sheriff's got a wire on you!" His hands contract into fists. "I'll make that fucker pay."

"Nobody's trying to trap you." She lifts her shirt, displaying her bra and bare torso. "From the very beginning, you wanted Danny, didn't you?"

"Don't be ridiculous."

"You saw him at Reggie's party, but Reggie was grooming him, and you didn't have a chance. Who would want you, overweight, gray-haired, and in the closet? Danny could hang out openly with Reggie and drive his Mercedes."

"No!" he cries.

In the house the telephone rings, ten, twenty times.

"You were at Reggie's party. I saw a pack of Virginia Slims on the coffee table the morning Reggie died. You're the one who smokes a woman's cigarette."

For hours she thought about it while she sat beside Danny's hospital bed, sorting the pieces, arranging them first in one pattern, then another.

"After Reggie died, you went to Franzen's, counting on seeing Danny—the boy you'd desired for months—but he didn't show. Instead, beautiful Grace was there, the one he shared everything with."

Vinson's throat works, trying to swallow.

"A woman, a girl really, yet she took him away from you. They could even have been sexual with each other. Maybe Danny liked both men and women."

"It was Franzen who stabbed her!" His eyes bulge behind his glasses, and face is purple, as if he's about to have a stroke. "That's why . . . why Franzen shot himself. He couldn't face the shame of what he'd done."

"But, as the ranking member of the DA's charging panel, you recommended not to file charges against him. Why, if you believed he killed her?"

"It was a weak case. We couldn't have gotten a conviction." He recovers a little. His voice is stronger.

"You couldn't have convicted Franzen because there was a witness who saw *you* murder Grace. You got rid of Grace because you wanted Danny to yourself."

"You lying cunt."

His slur slides past; she's focused, as if sighting through a rifle scope. "I'll tell you what Franzen *was* guilty of: cleaning up after you. When he discovered you'd stabbed her in his house, training told him to sanitize the crime scene. He washed Grace, he dried her, and in a final attack of decency—maybe because he once loved his wife—he got Kevin to dress her in bra and panties before he dumped her."

The telephone rings again. He shakes his head as if to dislodge a mosquito on his forehead. "I'll drag you into court for defamation. When I'm done, you'll be nothing but a used-up piece of trash."

She unleashes her anger, feeling its delicious flow in her veins. "You lied. You dealt drugs, kidnapped, murdered, and you did it all for nothing. Danny hates you."

His chest rises and falls. He's so near his ragged breathing touches her face. "I would've had a chance, if it hadn't been for you and that girl."

"He's always hated you, from the first second at Reggie's. Every second, every minute, all the days since that first time, he's despised you." These words, small contractions of her throat, are a forlorn response to the magnitude of wrongs, a monstrous insufficiency.

"You *should* kill yourself. Pay for it," she says.

His hand shoots out and grabs her wrist.

"You're going to get rid of me, too?" she screams "Where are your scissors?"

He twists. Pain paralyzes her fingers and shoots up her arm. She drops the briefcase.

The phone begins again, and he turns for an instant.

With every ounce of her strength, she slams her knee into his balls.

Vinson inhales a huge gulp of air. His knees wobble, and his spine bends like a folding chair. Glasses slip off his face. Hobbling sideways, he enters the house and slams the door. A spark flies from the loose metal weather stripping.

She slumps against the Cadillac's fender, sucking gulps of air. Her wrist throbs. Through the wall, she hears the rise and fall of his voice on the telephone.

The Cadillac's suspension groans as it cools. The spark from the weather stripping lingers in the corner of her eye.

Footsteps from inside approach the door, but before it opens, the phone rings again.

She closes the car door and skirts the briefcase lying on the floor. Beside the barbeque sits a spare propane canister. Kneeling on the dirty floor, she brushes dust off the canister's fuel gauge with her shirt cuff. Full. She imagines Vinson grilling steaks on his patio while Danny was in the hospital having his forehead rebuilt.

She twists the valve. Escaping gas hisses softly, its smell cloaked by residual car exhaust. She presses the garage's toggle switch and waits while the overhead door hums upward. Has he heard? There are no sounds he's coming. A second jab at the switch. She ducks outside as the door descends.

50

Keeping her speed at twenty-five, Suzanne drives away from Vinson's. Her heart is thumping erratically. She crosses Marston Avenue and glides into a shopping center directly south of his gated community.

Passing the Sav-Mor grocery, she parks near a gas station facing the main entrance to Vinson's enclave. A waterfall sparkles in the beams of the artful landscape lighting. She slides the seat back, careful not to jostle her painful wrist.

Sounds flip from the radio as she twists the dial: the Bee Gees, news of a $1 billion Chrysler Motors bailout, Vin Scully announcing a Dodgers' game. The radio light glints like a half-closed eye. She rolls down the car window. Scent of the parking strip's junipers drifts inside.

Ten minutes pass. Her wrist throbs. She twists right and left in the seat, unable to escape the memory, lingering at the edge of her hearing, of gas hissing through the valve. She's digging the heels of her hands into her scratchy eyes when a punch of sound rattles the car.

A flaming column shoots into the air, boiling and shifting, opening like a poisonous flower.

A woman in cutoff jeans and a man in a billed cap run from the gas pump to the street. "Holy shit," he says, with a high, girlish laugh. "Damn, I bet somebody is cooked meat."

His companion punches his arm. "Shut up, you sicko."

Suzanne presses her knuckles against her lips, torn between horror and satisfaction. Her mouth tastes of blood.

The fireball hovers, then drops behind a line of trees.

She climbs out of the car to join onlookers on the sidewalk. Sirens scream as a fire truck and ambulance roar through the Marston Avenue intersection. From farther away come the sounds of a ladder truck's claxon, which clears motorists from the intersection before the immense vehicle thunders through.

A second explosion shoots above the trees. Blast impact whips her face and sets the utility wires swaying along Marston. She's unsteady on her feet, like a weaving drunk outside a bar. Her ears ring.

The cloud expands, climbing a hundred feet in the air. This time, debris sails gracefully upward and floats back to earth. Black, irregular shapes flash in the last rays of the sun—large pieces that might have been the garage door.

Cackles of laughter come from the crowd. "That's fucking righteous!"

Suzanne imagines investigators picking through hunks of stucco, broken sheets of wallboard, splintered wooden spears torn from doors and ceilings. Shards from the white propane canister, the Cadillac's distorted steel. Scraps of clothing.

Body parts. All this she knows, from long ago.

There will be more, things searchers will never discover, tiny bits too small to pluck with a rubber glove or lift with a shovel. Tufts of gray hair will find their way into birds' nests. Scurrying lines of ants will carry off scraps of flesh. Blood and fluid will sink into the dry earth.

On the sidewalk, a pajama-clad baby held by a sweet-faced young mother begins to cry. The child's screams loosen a barrier within her, and Suzanne cries too, releasing decades of pain and loss, unable to tell if she's grieving for Vinson, Danny, her father, or herself. She stumbles to the car.

When her tears run dry, she mops her face with a tissue and starts the engine. Cops have set up roadblocks in both directions on Marston, so she zigzags through a neighborhood until she reaches 99.

She swoops north, the oil refinery stink diminishing as miles click by. Big rigs rush past on their way to Sacramento and Seattle. Her headlights catch shredded truck tires and scraps of fender flung onto the shoulder in some forgotten crash. A hundred miles later, a radio news update announces remains of a man believed to be Kern County Assistant District Attorney Dennis Vinson were found in the aftermath of an explosion at his Bakersfield residence.

"Investigators say it's still too soon to comment on the cause of the explosion," the broadcaster says, "but preliminary findings indicate the possibility of a defective propane canister in the victim's garage. Before his death, Vinson was believed to be a top contender for election to the State Assembly."

As she drives, she waits for the heaviness to come, the weight that had nearly crushed her during her girlhood. Her father's death was an accident, but she'd carried the guilt. When someone praised her, she struggled to stand upright, knowing she didn't deserve it. Any moment of stolen happiness had nearly sent her to her knees.

Years had lightened that burden, but she knows the millstone of this new crime is coming.

Was Reno right? Are they alike? She thinks of his slim fingers with thin, translucent fingernails, boyish hands seemingly so unfit for murder. Yet he lashed out to reclaim his life from men who had stripped him of his humanity like dogs gnawing a bone.

For the past months, revenge has seemed beyond her. Even after Jade revealed that Vinson killed Grace, even when the crash cost Danny his sight, she didn't fantasize about some vigilante-style retaliation. Her days had been filled with Danny's doctors and medications and surgeries and rehabilitation. Nights, she wrote articles in her struggle to buy groceries and pay the rent.

It had taken a meeting with Reno, who would spend a generation in prison, to reawaken her outrage. He'd brought home to her that there were other kids besides Danny whose lives had been shattered—Reno, Diego, Kevin, Jesus, and others whose names she will never know.

As the miles pass, cotton fields give way to peach and plum orchards, marching away from the highway in crisp rows. This attempt at order seems valiant, as if straight lines are the farmers' way of shaking a fist at the depredations of insects and drought.

She turns off the freeway into a rest stop. Beyond the parking lot, orchards stretch in a thick, dark mass. Trees hold the day's heat, and the air smells of earth, irrigation water, and late peaches.

She sips sun-warmed water from the fountain near the rest rooms. Back in the car, a coating of dust has settled on the dashboard. She traces a pattern with her forefinger.

Reno is correct. They are alike. The boy had seen a sign of their connection, like a family resemblance. Guilt has marked them both. Her tragedy from long ago, and the guilt she'd accepted as her part in it, had changed her indelibly.

And now, Vinson's death. Her culpability has increased a thousandfold. She feels no sorrow for this new transgression, but she braces herself for the new weight of crushing guilt. Maybe the years have made her stronger, more able to endure. She survived her childhood and Carlo's death. She'd fought for Danny in every way she knew how.

What does the future hold for Reno? There will be long periods—years, perhaps—when no one will visit him other than his court-appointed appellate attorney. If he's fortunate, he may fall under the protection of a stronger inmate in exchange for sex.

Suzanne starts the engine. Danny's more independent now, taking the first steps in creating a new script for his life. With his care consuming less of her time she could visit Reno once a week. Maybe they'd talk. Find something to laugh about. Work on his reading. Danny told her once that Reno stopped going to school after the third grade.

The rental's headlights sweep the orchard. Leaves gleam like polished jade. Orange globes of fallen peaches lie between the rich brown furrows. She sees them differently now, letting the nodes of color soak in, trying to see them as Danny might see—hue and tint, luminous light and deep shadow

She sits up straighter, one hand firm on the wheel, and allows herself to smile. A story is emerging, one embracing her and Danny and Reno. She wonders how she will see the colors of this new life.

———